FIGHTING FOR YOU

A SMALL TOWN ROMANCE

VETERANS OF SILVER RIDGE SERIES

CLAIRE CAIN

CONTENT WARNING

Dear reader,

Fighting For You is a closed-door romance featuring some themes that may be difficult for some readers. Please take a moment to consider whether reading this book is the right choice for you.

The characters' pasts include a broken engagement after infidelity and death of loved ones. Secondary characters are involved in assault, kidnapping, and underage substance abuse.

I've added this so that readers who might find this content to be particularly sensitive can make the best decision for their health and happiness when choosing to read this book. I want you to walk away with all the swoony, lovely feelings I know you'll experience with Jess and Jude, and I hope you'll feel safe proceeding with this information in mind. If you have questions or need more information, don't hesitate to contact me at claire@clairecainwriter.com.

My very best to you,
Claire

For the readers who've been waiting for Beast and Jess's story. This one's for you. I hope you love it.

CHAPTER ONE

Jess

An ember of rage smoldered in my belly. I gritted my teeth against the rising fury and maintained my neutral face because I could see where this was heading and any attempt to change it would be an attempt to stop a runaway train with a high five.

The meeting had started normally enough—a recap of all assignments each Saint Security employee had been tasked with and looking ahead at the rest of the final quarter of the year in broad strokes. But quickly enough, we'd arrived here... to the doom.

And the only other person in the room who should be as infuriated as I was stood coolly in the corner like an inert Goliath with a case of resting jerk face.

"There's not much wiggle room here while Eddie's travel starts Thursday. Cookie's down for at least another seventy-two hours with the flu, Tristan's out of town, and we've got just about everyone else tasked. So Pop and Beast, you two will head to Snowberry Resort and run the op for Ms. Halter."

The buzzing in my mind went quiet when Bruce's words hit the room. Or maybe that was the pin-drop silence shrouding the conference table. Could've been the feeling of every person in attendance shifting their attention not-so-subtly to me.

Adam cleared his throat lightly and spoke up. "Are we sure there's no—"

"No. It's the plan we've got. Beast has agreed to the out-of-town assignment." Bruce's gaze flicked up to meet Beast's, who grunted with arms crossed. "And that's what we're going with so we can get this place vetted."

He set his hands on his hips and exhaled, waiting a beat before taking us all in. Eight of us sat around the conference table in the Saint Security main office, and he stood at the far end in front of the screen where he'd been clicking through his all-hands brief.

We did this every Monday morning, and mostly, it served to get us all on the same page. They kept it short since we all had work to do. Today felt like a particularly quick one compared to last week's when they'd doled out assignments not only for the next few weeks, but who we'd be tasked with guarding during the upcoming Silver Ridge film fest.

Typically, these meetings didn't elicit the feeling of acid burning my trachea. Generally, I didn't experience much in the way of emotions here beyond interest or light satisfaction with an assignment.

Unless *he* was here, hulking and grunting in a corner.

He always stood. He was six foot six-but-might've-been-a-thousand inches of disgruntled man-child who refused to behave like a normal human and speak in complete sentences. And yes, some people did have legitimate reasons for limited speech. But I'd met Jude Rawlins aka Beast a decade ago and he hadn't had a problem stringing together a few phrases to say what he needed then.

Somehow, while the rest of us were growing and changing and rolling with the punches of life, Jude had devolved into a literal brute of a human being... at least when it came to me.

Actually, no. He made sounds of agreement or refusal rather than speak words in meetings or with his friends... it wasn't just me.

Bruce had moved on to review assignments for the film fest, checking in with those who'd teleconferenced in from Europe and Asia, but my mind circled the situation he'd just shoved me into.

"If anyone needs anything, I've got a half hour in my office before I have another meeting. Otherwise, have a great week and see anyone who can make it for drinks on Friday."

He double-tapped the conference table between where Kenny and Eddie sat at the far end, then gathered his notebook and coffee mug and exited the room as everyone else slowly stood and stretched.

Wilder left right after him, and I didn't bother pretending I wasn't crawling out of my skin to speak with them.

"Can I talk with you?" I asked, jogging to catch up with the two men—my fellow former EMU soldiers and now my bosses.

Wilder sent me an inspecting glance, then notched his head toward Bruce's office. I followed them in and shut the door. Bruce took a seat behind his desk, and Wilder leaned against the file cabinet to the left. I stood behind the seat I should've taken but didn't, given how I didn't want to feel like the smallest or shortest person in the room about now.

Eddie and I were, by far, the shortest people in the office. A few others fell under six feet, but somehow, every man here had ended up drinking from the tall guy well.

"Go ahead, Pop," Bruce urged, his voice pleasant and measured as always.

I hadn't thought about what I would say, but I wouldn't let the fury that'd built a little pyre in my chest explode. I had self-control, and I would use it.

"I think you both know why I'm here."

Bruce nodded immediately, and Wilder dipped his chin.

Dang it, I'd hoped they'd give me a little more... something. A hint about alternatives, something.

Since I'd signed on with them a little over a year ago, I'd made clear I couldn't work with Beast. We had too much ugliness in our past, and though I hated to admit it, I genuinely couldn't stand to be around him. He'd also made clear he felt the same way, never backing down, dropping snide comments, and generally acting like the beast he was named after whenever we were near each other.

But he'd signed with them first. So when I got my contract, they'd made sure I understood he was already employed, and he didn't plan to travel. I hadn't fully absorbed this until last spring when I got sent on a five-month assignment overseas after telling them I couldn't be near Beast.

Problem was, I didn't want to keep getting sent away. I'd discovered a love for this town, and I had friends here—real, actual female friends who loved me. *Me.*

They weren't brothers and sisters in arms who cared about me the way these men did—out of a shared history of duty and honor. No, these women were my friends because we had interests in common and by now, we'd been through a few things together. We'd *chosen* each other instead of being assigned, and I didn't want to leave that again—at least not for months at a time.

So I'd decided to play ball—to suck it up and *not* complain about Beast.

We'd avoided each other quite effectively the last while. But now?

"I don't understand how this happened," I tried, wishing they'd clarify how they'd assigned me and the one person I couldn't work with on a TDY trip together.

Wilder simply waited while Bruce explained.

"We've been over the scheduling issue. You were supposed to take this one with Cookie, but he's sick, and he's *really* sick, so we're not going to task him with a weekend trip when he's barely recovered."

"Sure, that's fine. But him?" They knew who I meant. "I thought he didn't travel."

Wilder's eyes flicked to Bruce, then back to me. "His circumstances have changed, and he was available this weekend."

I ground my teeth together, my jaw aching. "And he can't switch with... anyone? Adam? Kenny? No one has flexibility?"

Bruce took a beat, assessing me in that way he did when he meant business. Bruce was all charm and charisma and nice guy boss, but when you got down to it, he was a trained killer with excellent managerial skills. This expression—the origin of his nickname, Jaws, and the dead-eyed shark look—meant I was unlikely to love what came next.

"Gotta tell you, we need you to roll with us on this. We've done everything we can to respect your boundaries, but we've arrived at a point where we need you to both handle your issues and function as a part of the team."

Something sharp jabbed at me, but I stayed quiet as he continued.

"You have history—we know this. Don't know all the details and frankly, we don't need to. What we do want is for Saint Security to do what we are contracted to do—and in this case, it means sending a couple undercover to vet this resort before we take our A-list client, who has been severely harassed at similar locations recently, and expose her to a bad situation. After reviewing the schedule, this is the way we can make it work. If you're telling us you can't or won't do this, we will take that under consideration. But we are asking you, as a professional, to please keep in mind we are trying to run a business *and* take care of our people, and this is what we came up with."

My heart sank low, low, low. Bruce and Wilder weren't all that much older than me, but they'd felt like older brothers for a long time now. Their disappointment stitched into me, a needle puncturing in and reemerging, the thread pulling through the small wound at the hint of pleading in his words.

Was this an ultimatum? Were they really saying that if I didn't go pretend to be Beast's wife on this mission, I wasn't a team player? They deeply valued the quality. Were they hinting at the end of my time here if this caused more trouble than it was worth?

Every strong, independent part of me shriveled up at the thought. All my justifications and anger fled, and I caved in seconds. "No. I'm not saying I can't. Or won't. I'm just... I just wanted to make sure there were no alternatives."

The clocks on Bruce's walls showing different cities around the world tick-tick-ticked.

"Not this time."

I nodded, accepting it. "Okay, then. I'm in. And I'll... we'll handle it."

"Good."

I nodded again and slipped out, hating the crush of embarrassment coating my insides, instantly replacing the anger I'd felt so righteously earlier.

Maybe they weren't giving me an ultimatum, but they needed me to step up. And wasn't it time I got my crap together and stopped acting like Jude Rawlins had any say in my life? Was I going to let his grunting bad attitude jeopardize my place at a job I loved with a group of people who'd become like family to me?

Absolutely not.

I pushed down the hallway, encountering the thorn in my side in question as I went. He towered in my path—an actual beast of a man looking like he should be flipping giant tires for a living—and stared at me through his dark eyes. His hair had grown out lately and he looked, well, now that I'd actually taken in his face, he looked remarkably disheveled.

Typically, I avoided looking in his direction because his massive form only sent me into a rage spiral, but when I'd glanced at him, he typically had buzzed hair, or at least cut very short. Now, it'd grown unruly over his ears and flopped into his eyes. His usual close-trimmed stubble had become a full-on beard.

Still, it didn't hide the cruel twitch of his lips. Never a smile or anything civil like it. Just a little speck of movement holding back criticism or judgement or plans to eat babies—whatever to-dos misanthropic giants made in their spare time.

The fury that'd bloomed during the meeting and withered in the face of my bosses jumped right back to the front lines, burning a literal path from my chest right up my throat. "Are you seriously going to block me right now?"

Inevitably, he grunted—in response? In greeting? In protest of my existence?

Something sizzled in my gut, the low smolder turning to a flame of anger. *He* was the problem. All the bad feelings between us? They came from his choices and his way of handling things in the past.

But that's where they'd stay. I wasn't going to open up our history and let those memories suck me in, even if they did try nightly these days. I huffed audibly, out of words or the ability to express myself.

Maybe I should try grunting.

He dropped one of his gigantic hands and gestured like I was welcome to move past him, but there was sarcasm in the movement, impossible though it might sound.

I'd never know what he meant by it, and such was the problem with grunting as a first line of communication. Not that I actually wanted to know what he thought or would say when he deigned to open his mouth. Though there'd been a time...

No.

Today, now, I didn't want anything from him.

I slipped past him without touching, breathing through the overwhelming urge to scream into a pillow.

Back in my office, I shut the door and leaned against it, closing my eyes against the world. The smooth wood panel met my shoulder blades. My grapefruit candle I never burned still gave off the fresh scent. The beat of my heart pulsed in my ears.

I can handle Jude Rawlins, grunts and all.

I would prove it to myself and everyone here.

Beast though he may be, at his heart, he was just another man.

CHAPTER TWO

Jude

The afternoon lull at Diner mirrored my thoughts—largely empty.

Catherine bussed a table that'd just emptied out. She'd already brought my coffee and pie. I hadn't taken a bite yet.

I shouldn't have come today, maybe, but I always came here on Mondays and had afternoon coffee. I brought Omi —my grandma—when she was up for it. They had a sugar-free banana cream she loved. She'd smile and act like it was the best part of her week sitting here with me. She always made me feel like I was right where I should be when I sat with her. The sense maybe I didn't belong never once crept in when I sat across from her.

I nudged the sugar-filled version of the same pie in front of me. I loved pie, but my appetite had flagged so much lately, I only ever managed to eat what would literally sustain me. Taking pleasure in food felt like a memory.

Pleasure in almost anything felt distant lately, but memory had provided some sanctuary. And showing up here, reliving the time I spent in this place with someone who simply loved me... it ached, but like a bruise I couldn't stop pressing on.

Catherine sank into the booth across from me and heaved a sigh before gazing at me through her long, dark lashes. She had fair, freckled skin and a kind face. She was hardworking and endlessly helpful. And she'd never been scared of me, so that was something.

The first time we'd ever spoken to each other outside of a morning breakfast order was at Tristan's wedding, when we were paired together to walk down the aisle as part of the bridal party and later for pictures. An oddly intimate thing I'd never thought much about since I'd never been in a wedding until that day. Despite my reputation for being a jerk, she hadn't shied away, only greeted me with a softness and gentle grace I hadn't expected or deserved.

Certainly a treatment I'd never received from... some people. But maybe I'd brought their way of dealing with me on myself. Either way, Catherine's gentleness had, on occasion, made me wish for more of the same from... people.

"How are you, my friend?" she asked, glancing at the uneaten pie.

That it'd sat there for five full minutes and hadn't diminished, let alone vanished in seconds, was sign enough of my state.

"Fine."

She raised a brow. "I can see."

I shrugged a shoulder—or, if I didn't, I thought about it. Sometimes, I felt like I expressed myself overtly when really, things stayed internal. Locked up in this head and heart with no outlet. More lately.

"Anything interesting going on at work?" she asked, knowing full well there was only so much I could tell her about any given assignment anyway.

I grunted. More was simply too much.

"Whoa, whoa. Give me a minute to breathe here, friend. That's far too much at one time." She winked.

"Ha."

She chuckled and gave me the soft, empathetic smile that'd cut through my sharp edges months ago. How someone hadn't snatched this woman up was beyond me. In another life, maybe a different version of myself would've been that person.

"Tell me about you," I said, not wanting to dwell on me. I wouldn't tell her about the assignment with Pop, and anything else was... too exhausting.

She huffed but the reluctant smile told me she'd give. If Catherine was anything, she was humble and the least self-focused person I'd ever met. She gave endlessly, worked tirelessly, and it could get maddening to witness when she exhausted herself. She would never hint at needing help, nor would she tout her accomplishments unless I pushed her. We'd been back and forth about it enough that she finally gave in without my browbeating her to share her victories.

"The business is coming together. I'm picking up more work and my Instagram is growing well."

She read my scowl right and laughed. "I know what you think of social media, but it's making me money, so can we agree it's a good thing?"

"You get money from Instagram?"

Her grin widened. "I can recommend products I use and like and then when people use my links, it gives me a tiny percentage of the sale. It's not much yet, but the last check I got was enough to buy a full load of the cleaning products I used on a deep clean in the Ridge." She raised her eyebrows a few times.

I dipped my head. "Nice. Good work."

She beamed. "Thanks. It's small and kind of silly, but it's making me happy."

She glanced to the counter of the diner and just past it, presumably toward her boss, the chef.

"I'm glad."

She nodded, accepting my comment, then sobered enough that I braced for her compassion.

"Anything I can do?"

I instantly shook my head. If only this situation I'd found myself in could be helped, but the only thing I'd figured out was to dive head-first into taking an out-of-town assignment with Pop. Beyond that, there was no helping some things.

She reached out and squeezed my wrist lightly, then released. Just a quick contact, a gesture of care, and she stood. "Keep me posted. I'll see you Friday?"

She meant at Craic. Sometimes, I went for happy hour, but if I did, Pop left. Fair enough since we couldn't manage to stand in the same room, let alone at the same table very well. But not this week, regardless.

"I've got work."

"Ah. Okay then. Next Monday? Rick said he's going to do apple cinnamon."

She meant pie. "Sure."

She greeted a couple who stepped inside right as she left the booth, and I tossed a twenty on the table, wishing I had any desire for a few more bites of the nearly untouched pie, and snuck out. She'd be mad at me for not waiting for change.

Go ahead and get mad.

A gust of brisk mountain air swept by me. The sun was setting, and the late afternoon already felt like evening. Or maybe everything lately felt like the sun was just about to go down and stay there.

I'd embraced that for a while—I'd let life exist in the sneaking dusk. But now, through the dark of the night, I could imagine seeing a glimmer of dawn. And as best I knew how, I was walking toward it.

"Hey, man."

Kenny jogged toward me as I reached the parking lot, his boots crunching fallen brown and burnt orange leaves. Since Diner and Saint Security were practically next-door neighbors, I hadn't had to come far.

I notched my chin up at him.

"You okay? You going to handle things with Pop?"

He'd been in the meeting, so he knew as well as I did what I'd signed up for. He'd also seen us butt heads over the years enough to know just how antagonistic things could get between us. For a peacemaker like Kenny, a man whose sunshine personality had literally garnered him the nickname *Barbie* back in the EMU, I was fairly certain it killed him to know we didn't get along and there was nothing he could do about it.

There was nothing I could do either. It wasn't my problem she'd decided to make me the worst person in the world—that all her ruined plans piled on top of me instead of the reality she refused to acknowledge.

I'd never thought of myself as a particularly hateful person, but when she made it clear she genuinely blamed me for everything she'd lost, and actively, truly hated me?

I embraced it.

Why fight? Why beg someone bound and determined to dislike you to do anything else?

So I'd spent the last few years of active duty avoiding her—easy enough since we were on different teams after things blew up with her ex. And here at Saint, for the most part, we'd stayed apart.

Until this assignment.

Yes, it'd be a test of sorts. Yes, a small red flag was waving in the back of my mind, suggesting this was a bad idea. But I had nothing to prove to anyone, and I needed the change of scene. And in some way, this was me, walking toward the horizon in the east, trusting that sometime soon, the sky would lighten and the sun would rise.

I'd never see it if I stayed buried in darkness by choice. So I was summoning all the will I possessed to move and make a different one.

So...

"Yep."

He crossed his arms. "I know you're particularly tight-lipped right now, and I can respect that." His expression darkened, and he swallowed. "But I gotta have more from you. 'Yep' is not gonna cut it, and we *are* going to discuss how you're not only going on your first out-of-town mission since arriving here but also, you're going with she who shall not be named."

I scoffed at the moniker. He'd started acting like I thought of Pop as Voldemort. He had no idea all of this had started because she'd started thinking of *me* that way and I'd surrendered to it.

The other part of his little speech... I couldn't pretend I didn't understand. I'd fallen into monosyllabic responses at best these last few months and I'd never been what anyone would call loquacious. That wasn't me. The people who spent time with me, the people who were the family I'd chosen, they accepted me this way.

That said, for all his persistent cheeriness, he did love me. I knew that. And he had a point—if I wanted to climb out of this pit I'd been in, one small thing I could attempt would be upping my communication. It was facile and shouldn't matter, but in my gut I knew.

Making the effort might matter.

So, I tried for more than a grunt.

"It'll be good to get out. We may not get along personally but we'll handle this professionally."

His mouth stretched into a skeptical swoosh. "That easy?"

A grunt was all he'd get this time because I didn't need to explain myself, nor did I need him winding me up about something that wasn't going to change. Pop and me... we might've gotten along like sage brush and matches, but professionally, we were damn good operators. We could function the way we needed because I'd taken the job and she would never *ever* back down from doing her best, especially when faced with a challenge.

"You know she tried to change it, right? She asked Wilder and Bruce to—"

"Yeah. Tracking. And they said no. So here we are."

I'd seen the wide-eyed look of disgust and even the tremble of her lips, the fury that'd knit her brow, and no doubt a sense of betrayal had struck her. It was nothing new when it came to how she reacted to me—my nearness, my manners, my existence.

But what was new was this thing in me... the only thing that'd made me feel alive in a while. It was the offer I'd made to take the assignment. It was the low-key feeling like something was waiting—in the night, after dark, long after the sun went down. It was the closest to anticipation I'd had in what felt like years, and so I wouldn't worry about how much she didn't want to work with me.

She'd rise to the occasion because her grit and sense of duty and unending need to stand firm against *me* wouldn't let her back down.

So for now, I'd just keep walking toward dawn and see what happened.

CHAPTER THREE

Jess

We drove the mountain pass in silence.

Truly shocking.

And by that, I meant I fully anticipated his broody silence radiating at me from his place at the wheel. The quiet had an almost gelatinous quality, like the summer humidity in the South, but this was just *us* in a small, enclosed space.

So. Neat.

He filled every millimeter of the luxury sedan's driver's side, his head only a few inches from the roof while I stretched out rather comfortably in the passenger seat next to him.

For a split second before I got in, I'd considered sitting in the back and pretending he was my chauffeur. Would've been kind of fun, except we did have a little work to do, and it wouldn't be great for our cover once we arrived at the resort.

We'd e-mailed a handful of times with plans, less out of a desire for efficiency and more for the sake of avoiding any additional face-to-face time before we couldn't avoid it any longer.

I couldn't speak for him, but I assumed we were on the same page. That was likely folly, but what else could I do? Saunter into his office, thump out a cheery knock on his door, and say, "Hey, Beast, can I sit and chat with you about our fun weekend plans?"

Not likely.

The last time we'd had a congenial chat had been somewhere around ten years ago. Maybe closer to nine, because our friendship didn't shift until about the time I got engaged to my ex. It was like all of a sudden, I became this off-limits person and he wouldn't be seen talking with me unless we were in a group.

I couldn't think of a single time we'd spoken kindly to each other in the last five years. We'd cooperated on missions locally when needed, but there'd always been buffers with other Saint staff.

Locked in a small moving box with no music and certainly no friendly catch-up on the horizon, I questioned the sanity of the assignment on and off between songs streaming into my earbud. I kept one ear free just in case, but as a decently intelligent person, I'd planned ahead for the verbal drought of the ride.

The drive took an hour and a half one way, and we had less than twenty minutes left. Some of this we did have to actually speak about, and so, I mentally hyped myself into a place of noncombative assertiveness and began.

"We need to run down our plan. We both have the

checklists of things to review, and we can take care of some of those individually after check-in, but then we'll hit our dinner reservation at seven."

His hands didn't move or flex on the steering wheel. His chin didn't dip down like Tristan's would've, nor did he respond with words like Bruce or Adam or Kenny or literally anyone else. Even Stone likely would've given me a visual hint he was listening.

But I'd pep-talked myself into oblivion last night. If I'd been in a movie, it would've been a montage of an athlete psyching herself up through lifting heavy and running stairs and fist-pumping at the top of a mountain. Granted, I did none of that save a solid run before dusk, but *mentally* I'd "Eye of the Tiger'd" my way to bed knowing I could handle anything Jude The Beast Rawlins threw at me.

Even deafening silence.

There's no way he hadn't heard me. With nothing else *to* hear, he had to be tracking everything I was, too. I may not've liked the guy, but I had no issues with him professionally save the small failure to communicate. Still, I didn't doubt he'd come prepared, and that was the only thing saving my sanity at this point.

"I figure we check in together, make a show of things, then we'll be seen at dinner. We'll be able to look into the property under the guise of touring around together, but again, I think we can get away with the solo tasks we outlined earlier this week."

Aaaaaand nothing.

Despite his refusal to acknowledge anything so far, I continued. I was nothing if not persistent, and eventually, the fact that responding to one's coworker was the very least one could do when on assignment with them would penetrate his thick skull.

"Cookie said Jenna Halter's biggest concern is room access, so obviously staying in the same suite she'll have will give us that angle, but I'd like to expose floor access points. We'll do the usual security review tonight and double check at zero-two."

He might not need the refresher, but I preferred to verbally review the plan. It was how team leaders did it in the EMU and we'd both come from there, so this should be no surprise to him. It was how I ran ops when I did them, even still, and I figured it was a common language we spoke.

But silly me assuming he'd deign to speak.

I tapped through a few more pages of our op plan and did my best to ignore the frustration pumping through me. It buzzed in the pads of my fingers, making me feel electrified with irritation by the time he parked the car outside the sprawling, gorgeous mountain resort.

Back at home in Silverton, Silver Ridge Resort was truly beautiful, but it still had a cozy feeling thanks to the historic lodge located right next to the newer, fancier hotel. An hour and a half southeast from Silver Ridge sat Snowberry Mountain and Snowberry Resort. Silverton had become a destination for A-listers of all types—that's how we at Saint Security had so much business and were ever-growing—but Snowberry? Snowberry was similar to the fanciest resorts in Utah, like Sundance or Deer Valley. And now, we were about to recon this place to make sure it was safe for Jenna Halter.

"It's really pretty," I said, momentarily forgetting I spoke to a brick wall. The whole drive had been a parade of Utah's glorious fall colors, from gold to the pinky-oranges and deepening into burnished reds. But I'd appreciated none of it until right now with the wind rustling in the chilly autumn air in this tucked away place.

Astoundingly, this earned a grunt.

"Oh, so you're not ignoring me anymore?"

His dark head turned slowly—a little creepily, if we're being honest—and panned toward me until he stopped, his unsmiling face pinned to me.

"I was never ignoring you. I'm on board. You can calm down."

"I can calm—" I snapped my mouth shut and clenched every muscle in my body in search of the self-control I'd convinced myself I had last night and this morning.

Has anyone in the history of forever actually calmed down when someone says they should calm down?

"Thank you so much for the helpful commentary. I'm so glad you're on board with the job we were assigned to and are being paid to do." And with that, I got out before I started snarling.

Good grief, he made me want to literally scream. Nothing sent me into an unnecessary rage like his smug, rude responses.

But what would that do aside from eliciting yet another one of his non-responses and give him something else to judge me about? Not that I cared if he judged me, but I wanted him doing it out of my space, and there'd be no such distance between us for the next eighteen-ish hours.

The crisp mountain air hit my face, and I gulped in a calming breath. I'd never get over the dry air here. I'd lived in a lot of places growing up as my mom moved place to place chasing jobs to keep food on the table. I'd spent most of my military career in the South and finally the last eleven years in North Carolina. I hadn't ever lived west of the Mississippi, and now that I did? I had no plans to venture back to the swamp-like summers of the South and East.

Give me skin-splittingly dry winters and cooling-air-in-the-shade summers all day, every day. Add to that the glorious variation in fall colors as opposed to the last place I lived that was ninety percent pine trees, and I could hardly love it more.

A grumble alerted me to Beast's presence, and I turned in time to see him nudge the door of the trunk closed, the straps of both our bags looped in his giant left hand.

"I can carry my own bag," I said quietly, not wanting any chance of being overheard.

"I'm aware you're capable." He moved to my door and set a hand on it, everything about his expression impatient.

Taking the silent cue and choosing not to comment on the miracle of him using multiple complete sentences in the last few minutes, I grabbed my purse, shoving the tablet into it, then raised my brows at him. With zero change in his expression, he pushed the door closed, then strode past me to the sidewalk. I followed quickly, uninterested in trailing in his broody wake.

When his hand brushed against mine, I jumped and leaned away. He stopped, exhaled a gusty sigh so full of exasperation I could practically *see* it, then pinned me with his gaze. Without looking away, he grasped my wrist with his warm, rough fingers and waited. I didn't jerk away like I had earlier, stubborn to the end, and though he didn't move a muscle, I sensed his approval.

Which did *not* matter to me.

Then his hand slipped down and laced our fingers together. It should've been uncomfortable, his massive digits knitted with my comparatively delicate ones, but it actually felt pretty natural.

In an alternate universe where we hadn't lost everything but enmity between us, it might've even felt... good.

He straightened and began walking without a word,

and I didn't speak because... what would I say? He wasn't holding my hand because he wanted to, and I definitely didn't want it either. He did it because we were here to present a united front as a loving couple arriving to celebrate our anniversary. The contact had me inwardly squirming, squiggly lines looping around in my belly like they'd fallen off a page. Based on the way his jaw flexed under the longer than usual beard he was sporting, he wasn't loving this either.

But as he guided us inside and up to the reception desk, we were greeted by friendly hotel staff who beamed at us, evidently just delighted to see we'd arrived. They called us by our cover name—Mr. and Mrs. Hanson—and prepared our cards. They congratulated us on a happy five-year anniversary and told us our room was ready.

"Can we take your bags, Mr. Hanson?" Jerry the bellhop asked.

"Thank you, Jerry, but I'll get them. If I don't make myself useful, I might not get another five years." Beast winked at the man who chuckled and nodded good-naturedly, like the joke had landed and I, the shrewish woman at his left, would leave a man for not carrying our bags.

His voice speaking such congenial words should've sounded like a record scratch. It should've been discordant and odd, but the idea that this Mr. Hanson was the counterpart to mine, that I was acting as his wife, made the sharp lines in my head go fuzzy.

Of course they did, because everything with him was messy and muddled, and it was all his fault.

Plus, I hated little more than the sour stereotypes of the ball and chain or the nagging wife and of course that'd been his charming, *haha don't let the wife ruin our fun* joke. Cue eye roll my mother used to warn me about getting stuck like that.

Maybe my dislike of the drag-you-down wife joke came down to having had a relationship that crashed and burned through no fault of my own but that had, when I allowed myself to remember it honestly, contained a lot of that dynamic. Not to mention the fun of finally accepting the truth that my former fiancé had never wanted to get married and had only gone along with an engagement because I'd expected it... *cool.* Fun combo.

However, I pointedly did not allow myself to remember these things because I didn't hate myself. *Anymore.*

Either way, I shot *Mr. Hanson* a look.

His giant paw found my lower back—another thing that a different person in another life might've enjoyed—and he ushered me toward the elevator. That fictional person in a different universe might relish the warmth of his hand pressed to the curve of her spine or the sheer bliss of his large hand covering so much surface area. Said person might even imagine the absence of material between the rough pads of his fingers and the soft skin of her back, or anticipate the slide of his palms over her curves, hungry and wanting in a way that made her stomach drop.

Cheers to the multiverse—I'd pour one out for the poor sap stuck in that version of the story at dinner.

When the doors swung closed, he let it drop and straightened, almost like he couldn't find a comfortable way to stand still.

"Quite a performance, Mr. Hanson."

His eyes cut to mine, but he said nothing.

Fine. He didn't have to. We didn't want the staff touching our bags because A, we were only staying one night and B, they contained a few little gadgets that would help us gain access to locked doors and do other nifty things around their property we didn't want them aware of.

When the elevator opened, he placed a hand over the door as I walked through, then followed me down the hallway to our room.

Our room.

Because we were undercover as a married couple. And we'd need to stay in this suite because it was the same suite Jenna Halter would use when she came next month. We'd check every angle, every part of it, for security risks. We'd outline every possible place a hidden camera could be tucked away, then we'd move out from there—access points to the floor, the building, the property itself. After what she'd been through as her fame skyrocketed along with her security risks, we'd take nothing for granted in terms of her safety.

Tonight, I'd share this room with a man I'd loathed for years. I'd peacefully coexist in close proximity with him longer than I had in nearly a decade since we met, and I'd stomach it all because it was a part of the job.

Even if it made me want to scream into a pillow.

CHAPTER FOUR

Jude

Ten years ago

The moment after we were introduced and she said my name for the first time and I fell in that no stopping, no turning back *aaaas youuuuu wiiiiish* tumble down a mountainside like Cary Elwes in *The Princess Bride,* that's when *he* stepped up.

She'd walked into training, one of three women in a group of fifty people, and she'd had the attention of everyone there. Her counterparts had also been under inspection, but she'd had this fire I couldn't look away from.

Or maybe it'd been those dark brown eyes and her dark hair twisted into a tight bun at the back of her head. Full lips and delicate-looking ears and a voice that sounded like she hadn't gotten a full night's sleep in a while—a little husky and rough.

She hadn't exactly smiled at me, but she'd extended a hand. "Jess Korbel."

My hand had swallowed hers, though that wasn't unusual for me, being larger than the average bear. "Jude Rawlins."

And then it'd happened.

"Jude," she'd said, like my name—*my name*—had charmed her.

Cue the tumble.

She'd given me a half-smile and a little nod as she'd dropped my hand, then pivoted to my right. To Kurt, she'd said, "Hi. I'm Jess."

He'd grinned his charm-the-pants-off-a-girl smile he'd used countless times and replied, "I'm Kurt. It's a pleasure to meet you."

Emphasis on the pleasure, like he had plans to provide her some at his earliest convenience.

And as though she was meant for me, she'd laughed right in his face. "Are you serious with that? *Pleasure.*" She'd rolled her eyes and walked away like she'd never been less impressed.

I'd never liked anyone more. Not that Kurt didn't occasionally get shot down, but the man had little to no humility.

Was it wrong how I savored her response to his best effort? If so, then call me wrong.

"She can laugh now, but she'll see." He'd said this with a smirk on his face and the competitive gleam in his eye that made me want to take a nap.

Normally, I wouldn't respond at all to his big talk. That was just who he was. I'd looked up to him since joining the unit a few years ago because he was a damn good soldier, but we'd known each other since childhood. He'd been my best friend growing up, and though we butted heads, we were like brothers.

Or so he said. As an only child raised by my grandparents after my mom died having me, and my dad passing soon after due to what everyone said was heartbreak, I didn't know. But we'd looked out for each other and ended up in special operations together a few years apart, and most of the time, I was glad about it.

Until maybe right this moment.

Because I'd never cared when he talked about wanting to wear a woman down. I'd never minded if he bragged about his many "conquests" as long as he confirmed anyone involved was on the same page.

Until now.

"Might want to let that one go." I said it quietly so no one else heard. His eyes were glued to Jess's back—well, lower.

"Don't think I will, brother Beast. Don't think I will."

She was catnip to Kurt, and apparently, Jess didn't mind being chased—or if she minded, he eventually wore her down. Two years later, they were engaged. You'd think he'd want to lock her down, especially considering he knew how many of us were half in love with her, too. Funny how he'd been outspoken about his aversion to marriage, though I couldn't fault him for reconsidering the stance when it came to Jess. He had to have known how special she was.

Before she said yes to a ring from him, we were friends. We had coffee and sipped beers in the team room after missions. She met my grandparents, and I could see my Omi making plans for us.

"You know, Jude, I think she's special," Omi said the day after I brought her to lunch. Kurt was TDY, and I'd convinced myself taking her to lunch with my grandparents was for her, to distract her from her boyfriend being gone and make sure she had a good meal.

It had been for me. Only for me.

"She is," I agreed.

What more could I say? That she set my heart on fire with her dark eyes? That her calm under pressure, her ready energy on mission, her strategic mind... they fit together into a dream I had night after night?

"Might be a good idea to tell her you think so," Omi suggested, her knowing eyes seeing straight through me.

I nodded, but I also knew the truth.

She was dating Kurt, and this had crossed a line. Maybe not for her, but if I told her how I felt, she'd see the reality that I'd taken my best friend's girlfriend to meet my family because I wanted her for myself.

And damn, but I wanted her. Like I'd never wanted anyone or anything. It shredded me, this longing for any glance my way or tilt of the chin or brush with her.

It was pathetic.

So I vowed I wouldn't do that garbage again. I was better than that, and even if I'd felt the wedge between me and Kurt easing us farther and farther apart, I wasn't trying to make a move on Jess. God forgive me, I'd simply been drawn to her.

I'd discovered the definition of inexorable—my preoccupation with her and her footsteps away from me, into Kurt's arms.

It was three years before they set a date—three years I put space between us so she wouldn't know, so I couldn't tell her, and so I wouldn't betray my friend.

And then it blew up, and she never looked at me with that smile again.

CHAPTER FIVE

Jess

I had six minutes to get downstairs to the lobby and meet Mr. Hanson for dinner. If only he was my handsome date and not Beast waiting to silent treatment me through our fake anniversary meal.

Finished confirming the roof-access security, I slipped back inside. Though it'd be a feat for someone to actually enter the hotel from the roof, we weren't taking any chances. Jenna Halter's privacy had been invaded too many times, and after Jo's stalker had kidnapped her this summer, we simply wouldn't assume anything until we put eyes on it.

Beast had set out almost immediately after dropping our bags in the two-bedroom suite to work on his list. In the meantime, I got ready. Our dinner was supposed to be an anniversary celebration. Why a couple celebrating their anniversary would need a two-bedroom suite, one could only guess, but thankfully, rich people did weird stuff like that all the time, so the hotel hadn't seemed confused. I was not about to *only one bed* with a man who literally made my skin crawl with rage—sorry not sorry.

And that would've been too much to ask. Even in their need to see us cooperating, Bruce and Wilder wouldn't expect us to get *that* close.

I walked as quickly as I could toward the elevator, subtly hiking up my strapless bra as I went. I wore a strapless black dress that hugged my body, and I accessorized with a sparkly clutch. My dark hair was lightly curled and brushed my bare shoulders just like it had on the drive here, but I'd darkened my makeup, slicked on a red lip, and even put in some earrings. I should pass the woman-about-to-go-to-an-anniversary-dinner test should anyone be paying attention.

Part of training in special operations was funneling energy where you wanted it to go rather than letting it control you—nerves, anxiety, worry, adrenaline... all of these were normal parts of anticipating a mission, but they could either heighten performance or hinder it. I used the training now, feeling more anxious than I had in a long while just to walk into a restaurant and sit down at a table with a man who was hardly an acquaintance anymore, let alone a friend or lover.

He used to be a friend.

I shook my head against the thought, unwilling to venture down that sad sack of a rabbit trail. Yes, Jude Rawlins had been my friend once upon a time. I'd cared about him, and I thought he cared about me. But then he got my fiancé kicked out of the unit, lied to me about it, and had never once even acknowledged he did something wrong.

So yeah, not my friend anymore. And with hindsight, probably never was.

But as a badass professional woman? I could do this.

Stepping out of the elevator, I moved right to the hotel bar where Beast sat—more like hunched like a gargoyle on the barstool even though he had rather excellent posture—and rose on my toes to kiss the air near his cheek.

I didn't get near him often. We kept our distance. So it'd been a long time since I'd stepped close enough to catch the scent I remembered from when we were friends. An alarmingly appealing combination of woodsy and laundry and mint.

For another person, who didn't feel bile rising at the simple reality of his proximity, it might've been intoxicating.

"Ready for dinner, honeybear?"

His gaze swung to meet mine, a total lack of amusement the driving force of his expression. His movement stilled and his eyes dropped to take in my dress and the strappy heels on my feet, then slid back up to my face. He swallowed and a beat passed before he dipped his chin.

The whole perusal was a bit much, but the wonders never cease! He actually responded!

"Someone mark the time—Beast actually acknowledged my words when I said them," I said under my breath.

A man rose and brushed past me, knocking into me enough to make me wobble. Beast was out of his seat and grasping my upper arm to steady me in an instant, the grumble he made causing the man to look back.

Pure murder painted Beast's face, and the man who'd quite accidentally knocked me off balance literally ducked and ran. If the poor guy had had a tail, he would've tucked it under in submission for sure.

After another moment of glaring, Beast released my arm and extended an elbow for me to take.

My mind, expertly trained in compartmentalization, stoutly ignored the zip of sensation traveling up my arm at his firm grasp, and the cool relief now that he'd released me. Definitely relief and not some anxious sense that I was feeling a clashing mix of disappointment and something else I couldn't pin down when Beast let go. I tucked away the *something* that'd fluttered around at the dark, protective glare he'd sent the poor man. None of it mattered. It was all part of the cover. None of it had anything to do with anything.

I gripped his arm—or part of it, because his bicep was egregiously large—and nearly jogged to keep up with him as he walked toward the restaurant.

That's more like it—barreling toward the next thing without thought for anyone else.

Whatever had gotten knocked off-kilter a moment ago had been firmly righted. *Whew.*

"Can you slow down? Your legs are twelve feet long and I'm wearing heels." I spoke through my teeth with a plastered smile, as if anyone was paying attention. Likely, they weren't, but it defeated the purpose of all of this if we lost sight of our happy couple cover.

"I know for a fact you can run in heels."

I glared up at him right as he looked down at me with those somber eyes. The fact he knew anything about me still swiped at me with a weird clash of nostalgia and, if I didn't know better, longing. But that wasn't it because I didn't miss the mess of those days we'd worked together and been friends—or, if I did, I certainly didn't miss what it all eventually came down to.

We'd been on missions when I'd been in heels, but far

more of them when I'd worn the same combat-style boots he had.

Then there were the times we'd gone out in a big group, or the annual unit ball when the men wore tuxes and the women wore gowns, no uniforms in sight because it'd be too conspicuous. Sure, I'd maybe ended up jogging at one of those, depending on what ridiculousness Kurt had—

I cleared that thought before it finished. "Still short, though."

One of his brows rose ever so slightly, but his gait slowed, and soon we reached the maître D. We were seated quickly at an intimate table tucked away in the beautiful restaurant. Every corner was gleaming with crystal details and onyx surfaces and cream linens.

"Wow. Mr. Hanson knows how to treat his lady," I said, opening the menu and wondering if I should choose the most expensive thing just to annoy Bruce and Wilder. They wouldn't care, nor did I actually want to annoy them any more than I already had. So I tried to just... think like a normal human out at a fancy restaurant. Even though I didn't go to fancy restaurants, and my life was essentially work and my friends, and right now, work was feeling strained because I'd disappointed my bosses...

This thought sobered me right up, the glitz of the place wearing off and the reality of the moment—of sitting across from Jude—settling in my gut like fast-drying cement.

We perused in silence. Maybe we looked peaceful—comfortable after these years of marriage. Would we remain silent the entire time?

If so, I'd rehash the romance novel I was currently reading in my mind, and then I could finish it later when we went to bed.

Thank God for the two-bedroom suite.

"May I take your order?" A waiter bent with palms pressed together at our tableside. Beast nodded to me.

I placed my order. Beast spoke as many words as I'd ever heard at one time to order his. Then we were alone again.

I fiddled with the end of my fork before taking a stab at conversation. "So..."

His gaze fell heavily on me, but I couldn't actually think of how to proceed. What did I want to know about a person I actively avoided? A man who'd ruined my life, showed up in the one place I'd wanted to use as an escape once I retired from the Army, then made *me* be the one to leave when we couldn't work together?

Goodness, I felt like I was flipping back and forth between being able to tolerate him for the sake of this mission and being overwhelmed by how much he'd ruined... how much he'd hurt me.

The soft music from the live pianist filtered around us, as did the light clink of utensils on plates and the low hum of conversation. I drew nothing but blanks for what we could talk about, and blessedly, the waiter arrived with our appetizers.

Fortunately, my beet and goat cheese tart was truly marvelous, so I let myself become fully absorbed in the experience of the dish. It was a Michelin-starred restaurant, after all, so why not enjoy the food, even if the company was poison?

Problem was, I couldn't forget about the man. He was literally impossible to ignore because he was just so huge. With the dark suit and open collar of his button-down, he'd be almost handsome if he had somewhere to tuck away his perma-scowl.

I could vaguely recall a version of life where I *had*

thought he was handsome—incredibly so. Before... everything.

Before he'd turned into his nickname.

"So how's life these days? Are you liking Silverton?" That was neutral enough, wasn't it? Had nothing to do with anything between the two of us.

I glanced at him to see he was chewing—acceptable reason for not responding right away. I took a bite, then startled when he actually replied.

"Why would I tell you? You've never cared what I had to say before."

CHAPTER SIX

Jude

Five years ago

Fury boiled in my veins as I watched him do it... again.

Kurt's arm caged a woman sitting at the bar, clearly touching her. She'd already brushed him off once, but I hadn't registered it when it happened. I'd thought maybe he'd cracked a lame joke or... something. Anything other than hitting on a random woman at a bar when he'd given an engagement ring to Jess.

But then the scene shifted into slow motion, and he crowded closer, dipped his head, and whispered something in the woman's ear. She straightened, and I instantly knew.

"Hey, man. Food's here," I said, hand on his shoulder and not so gently pulling him away.

His head whipped to me with a scowl until he registered who it was—not a random guy encroaching on his conquest, but me. *Yeah.*

"Right. Yeah. I was just telling Ally here to have a good night." He winked at her with a sly smile and shoved off the bar with one hand, snatching his beer and moving toward the table we'd chosen twenty minutes ago when we'd walked in.

I parsed through what to say—what words to use instead of punching him directly in the face.

"Damn, that girl just said the nastiest—"

"Don't start." He spun stories like no one else. It was how he won people over—all that charm and ease with words. Skills I didn't possess, and after witnessing how they could poison things, never cared to develop.

"Come on, man. *You* don't start. We were just talking." He chuckled like it really was all fine. Like sliding your hand around someone else and whispering in their ear wasn't a betrayal.

I waited until he stopped avoiding my eyes, and then I held his gaze.

"Don't pull that BS, or I'll tell her."

The easygoing smile twitched, and his friendly mien hardened, his chin jutting out. "Not your business."

"It's my business if you're going to hurt her."

He swore. "She's mine, Beast. I know it kills you, but you can't go looking for reasons to break us up."

How had I ever cared about this guy? How had I ever loved him like a brother? I'd had so few people in my life as a kid—grandparents and a few neighbors. I'd never felt unloved, never felt the lack of parents who'd died when I was a baby because my grandparents had loved me so well.

But Kurt was a constant through grade school, then high school, joining the Army, and now EMU, and it'd mattered to me that we'd traveled so much road together. I'd spent a lot of years looking away from all the crappy things he did, but lately, I couldn't.

"This has nothing to do with that. If you don't want to be faithful, break it off."

He scoffed. "You'd love that." His slick smile returned. "Don't worry. I'll make Jessie happy, and you don't need to worry your tiny brain over how it happens."

I'd accepted he wasn't the man I'd grown up thinking he was a while back, but I'd still had hope for him. We were stuck on a temporary assignment together and had a whole week to work one-on-one, with literally no one else with us. So me storming out and leaving him here would only slow things down. I'd never wanted to screech out of a parking lot like I did tonight.

We watched the game. My team won and things were looking up, right until I said I was ready to go. He'd switched his attention to another game and blew me off. "Nah, I'll stay. I'll grab a cab home."

I should've insisted he come with me, but he was a grown man and obviously didn't want my opinion. I took off, promising myself I wouldn't worry about what he was doing. It wasn't my problem. He and Pop had a relationship, and I assumed she trusted him, and vice versa. Granted, I couldn't imagine her doing anything to break someone's trust because she had more integrity in her little finger than Kurt had in his entire body, but oh well.

When he texted an hour later saying he couldn't get a cab and asked if I'd come get him in twenty, I pulled on my jeans and drove the ten minutes back to the bar to get him.

He didn't come out right away after I found a spot in the busy lot near the back, so I stayed in the rental car waiting, tension knotting in my stomach, my foot tapping impatiently.

After waiting a full five, I figured maybe he'd gotten to chatting with someone and didn't realize how the time had passed. It wouldn't have been unusual for him, and though I didn't mind indulging that side of him from time to time, especially on missions when it benefited us for people to be charmed into giving information, it didn't apply now. I wanted to get back to the hotel and put this night to bed.

He wasn't at the table and the waitress already had someone new sitting there. Nearly all the tables were full, which made sense for a Saturday night. No Kurt at the bar either, and then my worry notched up again.

Maybe he'd drunk too much and was sick in the bathroom. Maybe he'd passed out. He'd only had a few beers while I was here, but sometimes he could be volatile, and he'd done this before—let me leave then called me back to get him when he'd gotten so sloppy, finding any other way home wouldn't have been an option. It'd been years since something like that had happened, but I ducked into the men's room to make sure. No dice.

Maybe he'd gotten a ride after all? I checked my phone, messaged him again, and pushed open the back door to see if he'd exited and was waiting by the truck.

The first thing I heard was a feminine voice saying, "No. *No!*"

Kurt's back was to me, but I could still make out the smaller figure pinned to the wall in front of him.

Kurt swore violently and pulled back just enough to cock his hand and slap the woman across the face—hard enough I could hear the contact as I saw it. A sharp cry came from the woman who reached for her cheek with one hand as she attempted to shove him away with the other.

My world collapsed into a pinprick of focus as all worry and tension and anything else dropped away, and I moved. She pushed him with both hands now, her head straining as far from Kurt's as she could, turning to the side as he pressed his face into her neck.

"Come on, sexy, don't worry about that, just—"

I grabbed him by the shoulder, then instantly hooked an arm around his neck and tightened, slamming a fist into Kurt's face and releasing him as he stumbled back. The woman stood alone now, curled into herself and quietly crying.

I approached her with hands up. "You okay?"

Kurt was on one knee with his head hanging, expletives and blood spewing from his face.

"I'm, um, I'm—"

"Is someone here with you?"

Her chin wobbled. "No."

"That's okay. Did you drive?"

"Yes."

"Are you okay to drive now?"

She nodded. "Yeah. I only had two beers all evening. I had dinner between. I'm good."

"Do you want to call the police? This was assault. I can be your witness."

She shook her head vehemently. "No. No. I don't want that. He didn't—I just want to leave. Can I leave?"

The pleading in her voice made my stomach pitch. "Of course. Go."

She grabbed her purse from the ground where it'd fallen and bolted around the corner of the building. I paced to Kurt and hauled him up.

He launched in. "You son of a—"

"You don't want to talk to me right now." I pulled him along by the back of his shirt and shoved him against the passenger side of the truck where he hit with a little too much force. Hopefully, he didn't dent it, but if he did I'd make sure he paid for it.

He got in, and the second his door closed I started driving, the familiar motions of flicking a blinker, turning the wheel, easing on the gas a balm to the blur of feelings threatening to break through.

By the time we reached the hotel, I'd decided. I turned off the vehicle and got out. He dragged himself out, his shirt bloodied enough it'd look alarming to the front desk clerk, but I'd let that be his problem, too.

I turned toward him and resisted the urge to smash my fist into his face again. My voice shook with barely shackled rage when I said, "You assaulted that woman."

"She flirted with me all night. When I go to kiss her, she doesn't want it? That's not assault." He turned his head and spat.

"It is the definition of assault, and if she contacts police, I'll give a statement."

He looked me dead in the eye and swore violently. "Whatever. This was nothing. Usually women give it up without a problem, and they should. They gonna get better than me? No. They should be so lucky." He wiped his bleeding face on his shirt, then whined. "Some friend. Some *brother.*"

"I'm not your brother and I'm not your friend anymore. It's been a long time since we could say that, and I think you know it. I'm a teammate, and I'm reporting this to the unit and—"

"You can't do that. That's breaking a code between—"

"There's no code that says I lie for you when you're hurting people." And he'd just admitted to cheating multiple times, so that wasn't even touching his infidelity.

He snorts. "This is about Jessie."

This jackass had no idea. "No. It's about you thinking you can take what you want, even when someone tells you not to. We do actually have rules about that, and I'm reporting it. It's up to you how you want to explain yourself."

He let loose another round of foul language and sneered at me. "You're pathetic."

All the anger rose in me then and I pulled him to me by the bloodied front of his shirt. I had six inches and probably forty pounds on him, but I didn't need my size to intimidate. He was trash, and he needed to understand what I would do. That I wouldn't let him hurt anyone again.

"Pathetic is cheating on your fiancée. Pathetic is hearing the word no and thinking it means anything else. Pathetic is thinking I don't have enough backbone to end you because you couldn't even point to North with the help of a compass. You're *done*, Spangler. Get your affairs in order."

I released him and he stumbled back, then launched a bunch of insults I didn't stick around to hear. Three days later, we were back at the unit and I reported him.

In the past, something like this might not've been a career-ending issue. There'd been a nasty history of people covering up for each other. But they'd worked on cleaning house. Leadership had agreed if they were going to give so much power and access and funding to the unit, they had to make sure the men and women who were a part of it had a moral compass. So these "little incidents" that used to get brushed under the rug as boys being boys, or whatever other bullshit, were now intolerable. By the end of the day, Kurt

Spangler had shocked everyone by announcing he'd be moving off the teams and into the school house while transitioning to retirement.

The only person not shocked? Yours truly.

The person most taken aback? Heartbreakingly, it was his fiancée.

CHAPTER SEVEN

Jess

The waiter cleared our appetizer plates as we sat in silence.

I fumed.

The waiter brought our entrees.

I fumed some more. And then nearly groaned aloud at the first bite of my steak because it was so gloriously delicious, it almost made up for having to sit across from a man I loathed.

No one could say I hadn't made a valiant effort tonight. I was absolved of any guilt when it came to this dinner or anything else. Plus, who said married couples were always happy? What if this was my caustic husband's last-ditch effort to salvage a marriage that'd been doomed from the start? Couples fought. Relationships failed. Marriages imploded.

Ask me how I know. Though at least I hadn't actually married Kurt before he'd lost it and left both the unit and me—when he'd refused to accept my help or my love for him, and he'd pushed me and everyone else we knew away.

And left me just like everyone else did.

Nope! Not a helpful thought. Not something we should whine about, and when we start thinking of ourselves in first-person plural... we can confirm working with Beast is taking its toll.

The man sitting across from me had played a prime role in all of it. I did my best not to actively remember the conversation where Kurt revealed how Beast had lit my entire life on fire, but it intruded on my thoughts now, the memory cutting through me like a slap.

I saw myself five years ago, standing there in the North Carolina heat as Kurt turned away from me.

"Why are you leaving me? This has nothing to do with our relationship. You're retiring, that's great. I'll be out in another few years and in the meantime, you can—"

"You don't get it, Jessie. I can't stay in a place where my best friend—*former* best friend—betrayed me. Where he told the command lies about me and they *believed* him."

He looked so broken. Not the confident, swaggering man who'd slowly broken down my walls and won me over.

"I'm sorry. I don't know why he'd do that, but it doesn't mean *we* can't stay together. I believe you. It's messed up, but you're not getting kicked out. You can still retire, even if it's sooner than you'd planned, and we—"

"No, dammit, Jessie. He'll stop at nothing to take every-thing away from me. He took my career because he can't bend, can't be creative, can't imagine doing something a little unconventional, and now he's gunning for you. He'll try to tell you lies about me, and my one request here is that you don't believe him. Don't let him tarnish the memory of what we had."

The *memory*.

I snapped back into the present moment, appetite lost.

Beast ate steadily, clearly no lack of interest in food like my own, and a level of manners I didn't realize he possessed. It was a wonder he could eat while I sat here, bereft of the desire, but I supposed he had to fuel his giant body somehow.

His avid dining made me senselessly furious, and I promised myself I wouldn't think about the other conversation that'd changed my life years ago—the one I'd had with a man I thought I'd known. I'd been engaged to Kurt, but Jude had been my friend. He'd been important to me. And it would never add up, never make sense, never shake out for as long as I lived.

I swallowed the bite I'd been chewing and followed it with half my glass of wine. "You know, that's a great point. Why *would* you tell me anything?"

He'd refused years ago and ever since, so he had a point, and I was playing the fool yet again. We'd put on a show long enough so I tucked my napkin to the side of my plate as I mentally apologized to the chef for wasting such a beautiful steak even though it sounded repellent to me by now. I stood, then bent to whisper in his ear.

"All appearances will look like I'm whispering sweet nothings in your ear—asking for you to come celebrate in private, to bring some champagne or dessert to the room and all that. Enjoy your dinner, Beast, and the company you're best at keeping."

I took my time walking away, a saucy little smile on my

lips like I was going to slip into something less comfortable for my husband and not like I was strategically retreating to my room where I could shower off the bone-deep chill brought on by memories of my ex, and the reality of the person I was sharing this suite with, and bury myself in a romance novel as soon as possible.

I'd recover by tomorrow. We'd finish the mission. Then, hopefully, our only contact would be clipped interactions at work when we were forced into a room by briefings.

The zero-two check-in went fine. It wasn't exactly normal to be sneaking around a hotel at two in the morning, but since we were trained operatives, stealth was firmly in our arsenal. We confirmed all staffing and security measures, walked the perimeter, and checked all the boxes. We did this in total silence, each accomplishing our list in record time.

Afterward, I entered our suite first and locked my bedroom door without looking back or saying a word because what would I say? We'd be forced into the proximity of sitting in the car together later today, so I'd reserve all my conversational fortitude for then.

Sleep came and went like a summer storm, and by the time we tucked our bags into the trunk and loaded into the vehicle, I was counting the minutes until I could get more than a few feet from him.

Halfway back to Silverton, I shifted in my seat, restlessness hounding me and too many questions—too many things I'd never said, or only said once, trying to crawl up my throat. I was worn down from the lack of sleep and probably the sheer volume of frustration pumping through my veins. Could one have a frustration-induced heart attack?

He made a sound just softer than his usual grunt, as though in response to my thoughts. Whether due to the poor sleep or the stress of being shoved into this situation with him, I snapped.

"Why are you so... frustrating? Why can't you just be a civil human being?"

He didn't respond, which only fueled my fire.

"You walk around acting like I did *you* wrong. We both know that's not true. *You* ruined *my* life. You took everything from me, and—"

"No."

"No? That's not a response. That—that doesn't even enter the conversation here. *NO?*" I crossed my arms and tucked them close, every muscle in my body tensed with fury and a wild sense that any minute now, I was going to completely lose it on this man.

"No."

His hand flexed on the steering wheel, and the sign indicating five miles to Silverton popped up. Maybe I'd time-traveled courtesy of my rampant frustration.

"No," I muttered, disbelieving this was all he had to offer. Why did I bother speaking at all when he could hardly be troubled to do me the simple respect of the same?

"I'm not the villain in your story, Pop. Never was."

I scoffed so hard, I nearly choked. The fire in me stuttered out and utter wrath froze everything but my now steady heart. He navigated through town and parked the fleet car at the back of the Saint building. I unbuckled before the tires settled.

My muscles coiled with tension and words stacked up

on the tip of my tongue, but I kept my jaw locked tight, unwilling to let loose another ounce of effort.

The driver's side door shut right as the trunk popped open. His giant form literally cast a shadow as he approached, but I kept my eyes on my bag. I reached for the handle, but his hand beat me to it, and he yanked it from the trunk.

"Listen, I—" he cut off, failing to finish the thought, his face dark.

Failing to calm the ravenous anger rearing up in me, I exhaled slowly so I wouldn't scream. He held my bag hostage at his side, and for some reason, that was the ice pick to the frosty lake of my malice.

"I won't listen to a man who refuses to accept responsibility for what he did. I asked you why and you've never told me. You've asked me to trust you, expected it, and how could I? How can I trust a man who ruined everything I had with my fiancé—who took away our future?"

His jaw flexed and his nostrils flared a touch, like he needed more air.

"You're boorish and selfish and I thought you used to have a heart, but I can see the only thing that matters to you is living in your little bat cave of solitude and doing whatever the hell you want. *Fine.* Pretend you had nothing to do with ruining my relationship. Pretend you aren't the villain. Pretend that grunting and speaking in three-word sentences is an appropriate way for an adult man to behave, especially after you were the one to ruin your best friend's career because you were petty and—and I don't even know why else. In your heart of hearts, you know the truth, but if not —" Emotion tripped me up and I cleared my throat. "If not, then that honestly sounds about right, and I have nothing more to say to you."

I yanked my bag from his hand and stormed toward my own car, satisfaction and a sick, heartbroken sensation winding through me with every step I gained away from him.

CHAPTER EIGHT

Jude

Five years ago

J ess stood at the door of my house, eyes red and jaw set with watery determination.

"Pop, come in."

I couldn't call her by name—not her real name. I'd forbidden myself from it the day she accepted Kurt's proposal—maybe even the day after I'd taken her to lunch with the grandparents. It seemed too intimate, and the same held true now.

She moved quickly inside, stopping to stand with her arms folded and tucked tight against her like a shield at the edge of my living room.

"Have a seat." I hoped she would, but when her head shook just once, I accepted the inevitability.

This wasn't a catch up. It wasn't a friendly house call.

This was it.

I sat in a chair a few feet from her, wishing she'd join me and knowing she wouldn't. I couldn't stand next to her for this—I couldn't tower over her small form without feeling worse about all of this.

Silence stretched between us, only the crackle of my fireplace providing reprieve from the roar of nothing filling the space. She needed time, and I wouldn't rush her.

Jess was petite to begin with—a tiny powerhouse of determination and brilliance and grit. She was also knee-weakeningly beautiful, but I'd long since forbidden myself to notice her dark hair or the slope of her neck or the curve of her lovely top lip.

I'd never identified so sharply as a failure until lately when I faced ruining the happiness of someone I... cared so much about while also doing the only thing I felt I could. There was no way to do this without someone getting hurt. Without *her* getting hurt.

Finally, her lips pressed thin before she spoke. "How could you do it?"

The final word in her sentence trailed off into nothing as her voice cut out, full of exhaustion and pain. My stomach clutched and a knot tied my tongue.

"I—I can't explain what happened. All I can say is I didn't lie. I didn't make anything up. I swear to you."

She swallowed hard, lashes fluttering like she might be staving off tears. *Crap.* I didn't want her to cry—couldn't take the sight of it.

"How can I believe you? Why can't you just tell me

what happened?" Her arms pressed tighter to her, a vise against her body.

But I couldn't tell her. As much as I wanted to, I couldn't tell her he'd been cheating on her—and that he'd tried to force someone, and that he'd hurt her when she refused him. He'd promised me he'd tell her, and I hated myself for agreeing not to be the one. Maybe it was selfish to avoid being the person to destroy her world, though obviously it hadn't done me any good.

"I'm sorry. I'm so sorry this happened."

Her chin jutted out. "Clearly. You're just so sorry you got my fiancé fired and now he's so devastated he's—"

Her head whipped away and she swiped at her cheeks, dashing the tears away before I could see them.

I mentally glued my feet to the floor to keep from going to her. She wouldn't want it—wouldn't want me, even if it killed me to leave her there, breaking.

I'd wrap my arms around her and just hold her. I'd tell her he was nothing and she was everything. That he never deserved her and she deserved every good thing—someone who would love her and be faithful to her and want her as much or more than she wanted them.

Hell, I'd lay myself open, get on my knees for her, if I thought she could hear me or see me. But wresting this moment for myself—for my own gain—would do nothing but hurt me and her. It would be a real betrayal of our friendship and a denial of her pain, even if it killed me that she cared enough about him to be so broken by this.

She didn't have to finish the sentence. Kurt had gone to the schoolhouse under the guise of finishing out his last six months before retirement, but he hadn't been given a choice. That he was still retiring was a generosity I wasn't sure he deserved, but the unit had at least given him that.

What loss would there be if I did tell her? Hadn't he broken his promise to tell her the truth when, instead of admitting he'd assaulted someone, and it wasn't the first time, he blamed me for ruining him and left her?

Guilt slashed through me because even now, I felt the question slither through my mind. *Are you keeping your promise to him, or are you protecting yourself so you're not the one to have to tell her the whole truth?*

"Pop, I'm sorry you're hurting. I wish I could take it from you." Damn, how I wished I could. "I don't want to hurt you anymore, and I'm worried telling you what happened will only make it worse."

She turned to me, tears in her eyes. "Worse than losing the life I thought I was going to have? Worse than being abandoned *again* by someone who said he'd love me? Worse than giving up on the home I was building, the stability and family I'd finally found? *Yeah*, sure. Try me."

The challenge in her eyes had something in me rising to the occasion, pushing past the circumspection that'd kept me from blurting out the truth about her ex-fiancé and burning everything down.

"You really want to know? He assaulted someone. A woman. And after talking with him, I know it's not the first time. He's cheated and—"

"Just stop. He might be outgoing and a little too flirty and charming, but that doesn't mean he's a bad man." She swore violently before continuing. "He said you'd do this. He said you'd blame him, and it's just bullshit." Her voice was brittle and so full of anger, it cut.

"He left you. If he was really innocent, wouldn't he stay? Wouldn't he fight for you?"

You deserve to be fought for. She deserved so much more

than he'd given her—even from the beginning. But she'd taken the scraps, and I wouldn't criticize her for it now.

"How can he fight for me when you took his purpose? When you crushed the thing he'd built his identity around?"

Her voice was shaky and she looked like any second she might bolt.

Bile climbed up my throat and my head nearly swam with disgust and anger and a raw sense of heartbreak I hadn't encountered before. How could she buy the act, even still? "Do you hear yourself? He would've retired in a few years anyway, and the fact that you take his word above the unit's judgement, and *my* word, just shows how oblivious you've chosen to be. You're a smart woman, Pop. It's hard to imagine you really don't believe what actually happened."

She reared back like I'd hit her, and my stomach rolled. I jumped to my feet and reached for her, but she did run then. She ran to the door, then out to her car.

"Wait!" *Shit.* "Wait, I'm sorry. I shouldn't have said that."

She stood with her car door between us like a shield. "I hate you for this. I'll never forgive you."

In seconds, she'd slammed the door and sped off, and I watched long after her car had disappeared from my drive. An ache had settled over my heart, caging it in like insulation, muffling any other feeling.

Except one.

Because if this woman who'd been my friend and my teammate and my—well, whom I'd cared about, if she was so determined to hate me, I couldn't keep on this way. I'd bleed out if I didn't stitch up all of this, but not before surgically removing the parts of me that belonged to her.

Then maybe I'd hate her, too—for believing the lies of a

man who'd duped her repeatedly for years. For choosing him over me time and time again, even when she didn't know that was what she was doing and especially once she did.

How much could one man give? How much could a fool hope before he surrendered? When would it finally get through to me that she refuses to see me?

Maybe now.

Reality sank in, a wave crashing over me, pulling me under to the truth.

She might hate me and never forgive me... But after this, I was fairly certain I'd feel the same way.

CHAPTER NINE

Jess

Stepping into All Booked Up was a freshly wrapped gift every time. The soft scent of new books and brewing coffee paired with the sound of my dearest friends laughing and razzing each other made the last thirty-six hours melt away.

Okay, well not exactly melt away completely, but recede enough that I could accept the glass of Prosecco Jo offered and slump down next to Elise and Dove and exhale dramatically.

"Um, okay. The floor is yours, mademoiselle." Dove pulled me into a hug that made my drink slosh over the side a little. "Whoops, sorry."

"It's fine."

Ugh, I sounded melodramatic and like I was begging for attention. *Not* my usual MO.

"Seriously, Jess. We can tell something's wrong. Are

you okay?" Nikki asked, Winnie, Catherine, and Jo agreeing with the statement by leaning toward me, while Elise gave me a kind smile and patted my leg.

I couldn't tell them everything about what happened—basically nothing about the hotel. Even though they were all trustworthy, information leak was an issue, and I couldn't break our security protocols for my own gratification. But I could explain the basics.

"I had to work closely with Beast on something yesterday and... it was awful."

Everyone reacted—Dove gasped, Elise let out a low, "Ohhh," Catherine made a face, and Nikki and Winnie exchanged glances.

"Yeah. He's just infuriating. And it's not like, cute. It's like, we have issues, and he won't even acknowledge his role in it. It's like he thinks it's all me."

Dove hooked an arm around my shoulders. "Can you tell us what happened?"

I tucked my lips between my teeth, feeling around inside myself for whether I had the explanation in me. But you know what? Yes. I needed to talk this through, and these were my closest friends—these were people who, even while I was gone for nearly half a year, didn't abandon me. As much as I hated relaying this story, maybe it was time someone else knew what happened.

"Fast version? I was engaged to his best friend back in the unit. He and I were friends, too, though less so after I got engaged. Kurt and Beast went on a TDY and when they came back, Beast claimed Kurt had assaulted a woman. Kurt was forced to retire sooner than he'd planned. When that happened, he—" I cleared my throat. I would *not* cry over that jackass—not another single tear. "He kind of lost it. Lost his way. Broke off our engagement and ended things."

Dove hugged me tighter to her and the others made sounds of shock and consolation. Elise spoke quietly when she asked, "Did he do it?"

I breathed through the flare of doubt and pain, the sickening feeling that I wasn't sure. "He said he didn't. He said Beast had always been jealous and it was his way of hurting him for things from their past. He promised me he'd never hurt anyone, never cheated, and told me that if I confronted Beast, he'd tell me otherwise."

Elise deflated and Dove released me, then laced our fingers together and kissed the back of my hand. I chuckled despite myself—this sweet little affection gremlin just couldn't help herself.

"And you believed Kurt?" Winnie asked, as much kindness in her voice as could be.

"For a long time, I thought I did. I think I still do, though I'll never stop second-guessing myself."

"And you don't believe Beast?" Catherine asked gently.

Frustration shot through me. "If he was being honest, why would he have been so cruel to me for so long? Wouldn't he be compassionate? Wouldn't he have—" Wouldn't he have warned me sooner? If we'd really been friends and he knew Kurt was a bad guy, why was he his friend anyway, and why hadn't he tried to tell me before everything fell apart?

"Oh, honey, I'm so sorry," Jo said, everyone mumbling their agreement with similar statements.

I took a deep breath and held up my glass flute. "He was particularly rude and maddening. And I finally let him have it—I finally said everything I wanted to say."

And I wished I felt better about it, but I'd decided to take it as a triumph.

Until Nikki dropped her head and Winnie's face nearly crumpled and she said, "Oh, no." Catherine sucked in a breath and held it.

"Oh, no, what?" I asked, senses sharpening.

Winnie swallowed and Nikki took a big breath like she might explain, but it was Catherine who spoke up first.

"He's going through a hard time right now."

She looked... something. Regretful? Also, why the heck did she know anything about his life? Were they friends?

It didn't shock me that Catherine would be friends with someone because she was lovely—quiet, yes, but so kind and steady. But friends with *him?* How?

"A hard time?" I managed to say while my brain ran through all the reasons it didn't make sense that she would know anything about his life.

"He's super private, you probably know. But his grandma just passed away," Nikki said, genuine empathy etched into her features.

I sucked in a breath and held it, the stabbing sensation between my ribs an ugly byproduct of the news. It'd been years since I'd thought about them, but Beast's grandparents were everything to him. *Everything.* They'd raised him. Would he have to travel back to North Carolina for the funeral? Or was that why he'd been out of work a few days last week?

"Oh, no." I studied my hands, a slew of unwieldy sensations like sorrow and regret and sadness mixing with the frustration and hurt and anger I'd been wallowing in already. He... he'd lost the closest person to a mother he'd ever had. And he loved her, I knew that much if I knew anything about the man. I could picture the soft, at-home smile he gave her the day he introduced me to her, or how he'd hug her first, then his grandpa, whenever he saw them. No hesitancy, no pretense at being too big or old or tough enough. Just... love.

And she was gone.

And I'd effectively shoved every horrible thought I'd had about him in his face while he was grieving.

My stomach pitched.

"Gram said he was devastated. He was there visiting her constantly, and now..." Nikki cleared her throat. "She said he still comes and chats with her friends."

Gram? "Wait, Gram as in your not-actual-grandmother Rosie? Who lives at Silverton Springs? How would she know that?"

How did she know anything about Beast when... *wait.*

Nikki's head tilted as she studied me. "She knew Mrs. Rawlins. Rosie didn't spend a ton of time with her lately because she hadn't been well, but they all know each other over there, even between the retirement community and the nursing home side of things. Bruce and I go see Gram and Amir, and we often saw Beast coming or going. He was extremely devoted to her."

Of course he was. He... he might've messed things up for me and I did still hate him for that, but one thing I knew down to the marrow of my bones was that Beast was a devoted grandson. More than I'd realized if he'd moved his grandmother here.

How had I missed that? How had I not realized she lived here, let alone that she'd passed? In this small community, there had to have been signs. Then again, I made it a part-time job to ignore his existence, to forget that my friends were his and my coworkers were his... I purposefully ignored any mention of him.

I was officially awful for not realizing any of this.

And so far, no mention of Mr. Rawlins, which probably meant he'd passed, too.

Oh, Jude.

Cue the flash flood of intense guilt.

Because I'd piled onto this man's grief.

Yes, he was a jerk, but wasn't he allowed to be? He just lost his grandmother and I'd... what? I'd accused him and insulted him. It didn't matter that the words I said felt true —*were* true—I shouldn't have done it. I shouldn't have dumped that on him when he was struggling. I didn't *know* it, but wasn't I a trained operator? Hadn't I built a career on being observant?

Thinking back on the last few months, he had been particularly grunty. Even less verbal. And these last few weeks... His eyes had been literally darker, not because of some new infestation of broody evil, but because he hadn't been sleeping—he'd had thick smudges under his eyes. The fact that he'd taken the out-of-town job should've tipped me off to something major in his life, shouldn't it?

All the righteous indignation I'd spewed had emptied me of the packed-full feeling I'd had around him for so long and now... there was space for nuance. Too much space to ignore how much damage I'd just done.

"I'm a horrible human being."

"No, you're not. You guys have history, and it came to a boiling point. I would guess if you'd known what was going on, you wouldn't have said any of that, even if you've wanted to for a while." Jo's words were filled with compassion.

I didn't deserve them. And I'd need to figure this out.

There was no going back to the version of me who saw him as an angry beast of a man and nothing else. I couldn't pretend my actions were justified when, clearly, I'd hurt someone who was already hurting.

Maybe I was giving too much credence to our past friendship or my hope that I was a decent human being, but I couldn't keep on like this. I'd chosen to ignore someone's pain, then I'd piled on top of it. I didn't want to be that person... I wouldn't. It didn't mean we'd be friends again, but I wouldn't pretend he was just an inhuman beast who only served himself.

He'd doted on his grandparents, and he'd lost them.

Whatever version of a heart he had, it must be broken. No one deserved to go through this.

Somehow, I needed to fix this.

CHAPTER TEN

Jude

I settled Bones into his bed on the corner of the cabin's living room couch. He kneaded the padding, then curled around himself, tail flicking, before giving me his vengeful eye.

"I know. How dare I disturb your slumber." I patted his head, which he shrank from, and I let him be despite the niggling desire to pester him just to teach him a lesson.

Sometimes, cats needed to be bothered. That was why they adopted people. That's what Omi used to say, and I'd taken it to heart.

A pang sliced through me. Familiar, and maybe slightly less jagged than they'd been since—

Since Omi passed.

A month ago.

Had it only been a month?

Had it already been a month?

I'd known it was coming. Her decline was steady and predictable. The team had done everything they could. She'd given up her fight and I couldn't fault her for it.

"I love you so much, my Jude boy. Please don't hide away. Open that big heart wide."

Gravity pulled me to sitting and I slumped forward, resting my elbows on my knees and holding my head in my hands. For all the years I'd spent in kit with body armor and gear weighing me down, nothing had ever felt heavier than grief.

First, losing the little bit of Jess I'd had when we were friends and the total destruction of my relationship with Kurt—it'd been on a ticking clock for years, but the end of it still hurt. Then losing the man who raised me, the best man I knew, and someone who'd been more father than grandfather. And now, the woman who'd been with me my whole life. The only other person who'd chosen to stay by me, even after her husband couldn't when he passed.

A soft trill of a meow made me look down. Bones butted his fluffy brown and black mottled head against my knee, then jumped up. In two swift leaps, he landed on my shoulder, his claws notching into my trap muscle with what I imagined was his version of gentleness, and then he settled into his spot. Front white-socked paws rested on one shoulder, face tucked into them, soft white-furred belly wrapping across my neck and his rear end and hind paws bunched up on the opposite shoulder.

The older he got, the more space he covered, and as a mutty cousin of a Maine Coon, he was a very large kitty. Lucky for him, he'd adopted a rather large man for his human.

And lucky for me, I'd found myself a curmudgeonly and yet surprisingly sweet little beast who had a keen sense for human emotion and seemed to need to comfort me when he felt my mood darken. Not quite the certified anxiety support dog Bear was for Stone, but I'd take this from him whenever he gave it.

Something about a cat's weight made the drag of sadness feel a little lighter. The physics might not make sense, but the easing of the tightness in my chest and throat was proof enough.

I tipped my head to one side, lightly knocking my head against the fluffy tufts of his ear. Another little meow emerged.

"Love you, too, Buddy."

The words came out rough, like so many had lately. It was why I'd come here to the cabin.

Actually, my bosses sent me here, so I wouldn't pretend I'd come of my own volition. When I'd gone inside to dump the tech and weapons Pop and I had used for the mission, Wilder, Bruce, Adam, and Tristan had all been there. Kenny came in behind me as though they needed a sweeper to make sure I complied with their ambush.

"You're going to the cabin. You need some rest," Bruce said, setting his hand on my shoulder and squeezing.

After having Pop tear into me and shred me in the parking lot, and being fully aware they'd quite possibly overheard the whole thing, I was about as raw as I had been since the day I'd lost Omi.

Words, as they so often did, failed me, so I'd made a sound of assent. I didn't have any fight in me after the last forty-eight hours. Jess's barrage of honesty—however much I might've wanted to believe she was exaggerating her anger for effect, I knew it all came from her genuine belief in what she'd said—had sideswiped me.

I'd awakened on that trip, but by the time we got back

and things split down the middle, jagged edges between us cutting up any energy I'd won from butting heads against her, I'd lost all ability to explain or defend or do anything other than take her brutal honesty.

"You and Bones head up there and find some quiet. Read, roast marshmallows, breathe in the mountain air. Get some space, *not* on a mission, and come back when you're ready," Doc encouraged, and I suspected, demanded.

Though couched in a suggestion, I could safely guess he had instigated this.

These men had comforted me while I wept for the loss of the last person who knew me my whole life. They stood with me at the funeral—served as pallbearers and helped fill the pews of the church along with the residents of Silverton Springs Retirement Community.

My jaw ached as emotion flooded in, their tenderness and care for me so at odds with how I blustered around seemingly without care for anyone else. Pop had said it, and she wasn't wrong. I'd been so focused on myself for so long —on surviving and making sure Omi was okay, and now...

Now, what?

Wilder spoke quietly but with his usual no nonsense. "Go. Rest. Grieve. Come back when you're ready."

An order, then. No hiding it.

"Well, honestly, I'm going to need you to come back before the film fest because we do not have the bodies without you, especially if anyone else gets sick like Cookie did. If that crap rolls through all of us, we're going to need you." Kenny shoved my shoulder and gave me a smile that didn't quite reach his eyes.

Sweet kid. He was trying hard to be light for me, and I loved him for it, but I could see how this month had strained him. Any confrontation with death or grief took the wind out of his breezy sails and reminded him too much of his own life. He'd been as present as he could, and every one of these men had stepped up to help me.

So now I sat in my cabin with my giant cat draped over my shoulders like a fur stole and waited. What realizations could I have in this brutal silence? What healing in the isolation I'd only just learned to step out of?

In the past, I might've tried to avoid these crashing waves of grief hitting when I least expected them. I might've seen them as weakness and pushed myself harder. I'd fallen into the trap this last week when I said I'd take the job at Snowberry with Pop. I'd thought maybe being forced to work with her would be good for me—it would help kick me out of the sadness and help me battle a more palatable foe.

I'd heard the voice whispering I was doing it for myself —not to recover, not to fill a gap Saint needed my help with, not to feel useful again after losing the person I spent the most time with—but to be near *her* in a way we couldn't avoid.

She was a piece of the past I could reach for, a way to remember who I'd been before I'd lost my grandparents and the only family I'd ever had. The only family by blood, because I did have family still, but this ache came from that cellular isolation I faced now. Everyone else was gone, and some straw-grasping instinct in me had thought being around Pop would let me escape the reality.

There was nothing left of it now, though. No part of the friendship we'd had, no part of anything good left. I knew it well enough in my head, but I'd hoped, knowing that voice might be right.

I'd heard it, and I'd ignored it.

And I'd successfully hurt us both.

Because on some level, my plan *had* worked. Being near

her was like stepping up to an open flame—not one blazing with grief, but with something else entirely. It was warm, then so much faster than I'd prepared for, too hot. *Searing.* The numbness that'd padded the walls of my mind and let me move about like a wraith the last while had been ripped away, and touching her hand, looking directly into her eyes, exchanging words with her... it'd burned me back into consciousness.

I couldn't take it, hearing her say I'd ruined her life. Did she really still see it that way?

It shouldn't have come as a surprise, but some part of me had slipped into the comfortable, lukewarm pot of believing she'd maybe not forgiven but at least moved on and simply hated me because I was an ass. And I was.

Instead, the water had turned up and up, and by the end of the ride home, I was cooked. She still boiled over with hurt and rage and I'd failed completely at making it better. I'd refused to accept the title of villain, but when I'd finally gotten the wherewithal to explain myself, it'd been too long. And she'd let loose.

She threw nothing but irritability and suspicion my way, always assuming I was trying to piss her off or get under her skin. I'd long ago surrendered to the fact that she wouldn't engage with me on any level beyond simply toler-ating me publicly and hating me privately. I'd avoided her, kept my mouth shut as much as possible, and wouldn't force myself to beg her to give me the benefit of the doubt. If she wanted to hate me, then she could go right ahead. I wasn't going to stop her.

At some point, I should probably apologize to her, but what would it gain?

She'd made clear what she thought of me. Why would I work to change that? Even if she was the only thing to make me feel alive lately, why would I submit myself to her wrath when she would never see the truth? She'd told me as much.

And I'd never apologize because what I'd done was right and had saved her from something she couldn't accept —she hadn't married Kurt, who was a predator. Who knew what else he'd done I hadn't been witness to. Who knew how many times he'd betrayed her.

I must've loosed a grumble because Bones' purr stuttered and his front claws extended, pressing into my collar bone.

"About time for a trim," I said, because if I didn't say something and get out of my own head, I'd drown.

What I didn't expect was a knock on my door—a little frantic-sounding. The cabin was basic on the outside, so I had no doorbell, though fortunately it had plumbing and all the necessities. The sun had set, and the driveway was dim enough I couldn't see any cars, and with no porch light, whoever stood outside was a mystery.

Worse, I hadn't heard the crunch of gravel or heard approaching footsteps, which meant I'd been way too far into my own head.

Never in my wildest nightmares or fantasies would I have expected to see Pop on the other side of the door when I swung it open.

I'd had more than one dream that started like this—they could go either way. But she never looked so subdued and wary. She usually showed up with eyes blazing and blades in words on her lips. In my dreams she usually came to fight or, a few times I loved and hated to remember, very much *not*.

Here in reality, her dark gaze was cagey, hair pulled back, arms already wrapped around herself and the sleeves of her dark green sweater almost completely covering her hands, shoulders hunched against the chilly fall evening. Shadows shaded her eyes and she had less color on her cheeks than usual, even in the dull light. Small snowflakes stuck to her shoulders and arms, and behind her the gravel drive and my truck were already coated in white.

My stomach dropped low.

I needed to talk to her, but not now. Not while I'd been scraped head to toe with large-grain sandpaper and was teetering on bawling my eyes out at any moment.

She didn't belong here—she couldn't be here.

I couldn't handle her on some of my best days, and I certainly couldn't right now. Grief had flayed me but I'd been working to heal, hoping maybe the work trip would aid it. Instead, it tore me open, dragging out too many longings and pains, and it'd all piled on top of me. I needed to stay buried here in solitude, to sip whiskey and talk to my cat and breathe air no one else shared. I couldn't have her here, shoving all my wrongs, all I'd lost, all I'd wanted so much it'd gutted me for a time, into my face. It would end me.

My mind tunneled back to her standing on my doorstep so many years ago, eyes bloodshot and heart practically bleeding out from the injuries she'd convinced herself I'd caused. Any attempts I'd made to repair had only torn her open—torn *me* open—further.

So, no. I couldn't do this now, not with her. Not today or any time soon.

"What are you doing here?"

Her big brown eyes shuttered and her brow pinched, gaze dropping to one side of my head, then the other—registering Bones, no doubt.

"I'm sorry to interrupt."

What was she doing here? How did she even know where *here* was? Barbie and Stone were the only two people who'd ever been to the cabin before. The others knew of it, but didn't have the address. Pop definitely didn't have the information, which meant Barbie had talked.

Impatience and the flash-flood rise of panic clipped at my heels. "Again, why are you here?"

She exhaled slowly, lips thinning and jaw tight. Clasping her hands in front of her, she leveled her gaze at me.

"I'd like to talk to you. May I come in?"

CHAPTER ELEVEN

Jess

He stood there, blocking all but the very last few inches of the door frame, a scowl on his face and a massive, ridiculously fluffy cat draped around his shoulders.

I hadn't thought too carefully about how he'd respond to my showing up here—hadn't actually considered he wouldn't at least let me say my piece.

But here he was, hulking, hand still on the knob, frowning down at me from an even greater height thanks to the two steps up into the house I hadn't yet taken.

He swallowed hard, but nodded, and stepped back. His cat chose that moment to stand and jump from his shoulder to the floor, the loud *thunk* confirming the fluffy boy or girl was a hefty fellow under all that fur.

Clear enough of a response from Beast, so I followed him in. A chilly breeze rushed behind me, sending a shiver up my back as I stepped into the warmly lit living room.

Actually, it was weirdly too hot in here, but way too cold outside. I just needed to do my thing and then get home and I could put all of this behind me.

A large worn brown leather couch lined one wall, an overstuffed chair with a footstool in the corner, and a large TV was mounted on the wall across from the couch. The walls were the wood of the log cabin on the far end and a rich, cool blue behind the couch and TV. A patterned rug with reds, blues, greens, and golds centered everything and made it feel shockingly coordinated even in its worn-in coziness.

To my right, a short hallway led to three doors—could this place possibly have more than one bedroom? It was dark enough outside I hadn't seen it in detail, but it seemed fairly compact.

Frankly, I'd expected something spare and man-caveish. Large TV, check, but something cozy and lived-in and inviting?

I stepped past the hallway after Beast and noticed a fireplace to my right, which seemed to open to both the living room and maybe around the corner to the kitchen, too. I wanted to peek around and see, but based on the way he looked strung with steel beams for bones and stress radiating from him, I wouldn't push my luck.

Plus... why did I care what his man cabin in the woods looked like?

I coughed, a little burn chasing my breath out of my lungs. The exhaustion from not sleeping on Friday and again last night while I worried over whether my treatment of him made me a horrible human being was catching up to me. I felt the pull toward his couch—a place to sit and catch my breath before I did what I came to do and then went home to sleep until the last possible moment tomorrow.

Instead of moving into the living room, he turned toward the kitchen. Reluctantly glancing at the couch, I followed, gratified to find the fireplace didn't open to the kitchen because that would just be weird.

The space looked surprisingly new—or maybe I'd made a huge assumption this place would be run down and old. Instead, a recessed farmhouse sink sat nestled to the left and some kind of gray stone countertops with dark leafy green cabinetry down low flanked it. The four-burner stove and a stunning copper hood were straight ahead, and to the left was a small butcher block-topped island. Natural wood shelves lined the top half of the walls to the side of the sink and the stove and bore neat stacks of stoneware dishes and sturdy glass drinkware. Past the island was the oven, a coffee station, the fridge, and shelves decked with non-perishable pantry goods.

It was... stunning.

"This is perfect." It slipped out, little more than a whisper.

He made no sound, but his gaze swung toward me.

"Water?"

"Oh. Um. Yeah." The offer left me weirdly discombobulated, but it shouldn't have surprised me. He'd always had amazing manners and been an excellent host.

Well. Amazing manners when he wasn't ignoring me, scowling at my general existence, or saying nasty little comments that dug right under my skin.

The dynamic between us certainly hadn't been one that would point toward his offering me anything when I arrived, though, so it did leave me a bit shaky. In fact, I must've gotten more than a little worked up on the drive here, because I felt just this side of dizzy standing here in his space, watching him move around and fill two small mason jars with water, his cat making a lap around the kitchen before coming to gingerly sniff in my direction.

Unable to resist, I crouched and held out a hand. "My goodness, you're a beautiful kitty baby."

Evidently approving of my voice and scent, the cat dipped his head into my hand, and I petted him willingly. No telling whether he was a he, and no collar indicated a name, but something told me this big fellow was a boy. He was luxuriously soft and there was no trace of matted fur or tangles... he'd been well cared for.

The cat made a sweet little sound rather at odds with his giant form and, maybe more notably, the context. A rumbly motor had revved up in his body and his purr vibrated through my hand.

"What a sweet—"

A loud *clunk* jarred me, and I glanced up to see Beast scowling down at me with disgust. He'd slammed one glass on the counter—*I guess that one's for me.* I stood, arms wrapped around myself again, sensing I'd already done more than one thing wrong.

His jaw flexed. "Drink."

My stomach clenched, his bossy tone cutting through the weird haze his lovely cabin and giant baby cat had wrapped me into. I glared at him, and he returned the look, taking a long slug of his water without breaking eye contact with me.

I wouldn't snap at him—not when I'd come here expressly to apologize for doing just that. Or at least, apologize for lashing out about our past when he was dealing with new grief in his present.

That was the tricky line here, wasn't it? I wasn't going to take back my words. I'd said things I'd often fantasized about saying to him because they were honest and true.

There'd been some catharsis in actually verbalizing them. And yet, even without knowing his circumstances, it hadn't felt solely good.

Not the triumph I'd imagined it would be.

So, I drank, especially because watching him drain his glass, his strong throat working as he swallowed, made me wildly thirsty.

His eyes didn't leave me, and I ended up chugging down every bit of the spring water in the jar before setting it a little too roughly on the counter, though still far less brusquely than he had. Being in his space was turning me into a bumbling fool and I needed to get this over with before I ended up breaking something, and then get out of here.

"Listen," I started, words and breath oddly labored. But apologies were hard, weren't they? Even if I wasn't taking anything back, knowing I'd done something wrong—that I might've made his real sadness worse—didn't sit right with me. And it did require humility.

I didn't mind that. Being a soldier taught humility. Being a woman in the military taught it even more. Working with the best of the best had trained me to admit wrongs, to admit when I didn't know something, to try my darndest to see myself in a true light. But with this person I used to know, this man I hardly recognized and couldn't stand to be around, any amount of humility felt like weakness instead of strength.

I hated this feeling even more than I hated him.

And yet, I wasn't going to let any of that stop me because once I decided to do something, I did it. Period.

Clearing my throat and bracing myself on the counter, I met his eyes. A flashbulb of nerves burst in my belly.

His impatience won out before I found the words.

"I don't know why you're here, but it's a waste of time." He paced toward the living room like he wanted to lead me back to the door.

I breathed in, searching for calm, and a wave of nausea rolled through me. I hadn't had much of an appetite for at least a day, and the mental preoccupation with getting here to face him, never mind the process of ferreting out where this place was located after grilling Kenny, had taken it out of me. I indulged in sliding a barstool out a few inches and resting my backside there to take some of the burden from my legs.

My bones were heavy in my body, like they might've started weighing more and were pulling me down. My jaw and head ached from clenching my teeth and lack of sleep, and no doubt the stress of coming to see him.

"I'm not trying to waste your time," I said, my head spinning as I squinted over at him.

He stomped back. "I'm not trying to be an asshole, but you can't just show up here and expect to—whatever. I'm not ready to apologize to you and—"

"Please, just let me—"

"No, dammit, Pop. I know you're hell bent on hating me for everything that happened back in North Carolina and maybe you've decided every other thing in your life has gone wrong because of me, too, but I call bullshit. I'm not going to take it anymore."

Take it? How had he taken anything from me? He gave me nothing but grunts and scowls, took nothing from me but my own frustration and impatience, and somehow multiplied it. The solid plan I'd walked in with had fractured into a million pieces, and I shuddered with anger.

A chill ran through me and I glanced at the fireplace, wishing he'd light it, though being as humongous as he was, he probably didn't need basic human things like heat until the ground had frozen hard and icicles hung from his nose.

Fury pulsed through me, and my head throbbed. "I can't believe this. I came here to apologize to you and now you're acting like I'm some enemy combatant. I'm just a person, *Beast*." I spat the nickname like an insult.

"Welcome to the club, *Pop*. I'm a person, too. I have a life outside of you. I don't need to encounter a snarling shrew every time I enter work or walk around or want to grab a drink with my friends. I don't need someone trying to put me in my place every damn time I do anything. I'm already *in* my place, okay? I'm in hell here, like practically on fire, and you're only fanning the flames."

His frustration—the pure number of words—I couldn't compute. All I could make sense of was his anger, and the rising ire in my chest pulsating through me so intensely I shook with it. I might be on fire, too, now that he mentioned it, because I felt swallowed by flames of rage.

Through gritted teeth, I spoke. "I. Can't. Stand. You."

He shook his head with one swift jerk and moved to the door, then flung it open and stormed out of the cabin.

CHAPTER TWELVE

Jude

S now crunched under my feet—far more than I realized had accumulated when I'd opened the door minutes ago.

Had it really only been a few minutes?

My warm skin steamed out here, the cold biting at everything so aggressively I could feel it through my clothes within seconds of exiting the cabin.

Good. Let it bite and burn—something external instead of this churning feeling in my gut, a sense that every card in a too-large house was about to fall.

I'd had no choice but to leave or I would've yelled. I wasn't that kind of man, but I couldn't stand there looking at her holding herself so tightly and judging me—hating me for something I'd done and wouldn't change.

I didn't want to spend my life raging at this woman. I hated the idea that she spent any time doing the same for me when we could have—no, didn't matter. The point was, I couldn't take her in my space, petting Bones and watching the traitorous little creature purring for her like he'd found his second home and not lose my grip on this crush of feeling.

No.

She liked to blame me for taking everything from her, for ruining her life, but here she was invading the sanctuary of my cabin, forcing her way in when I needed time. I wasn't someone who could just come up with the right words with no notice, especially not right now. Why had she come here?

I walked a circle in the driveway and as I looped back toward the cabin, her small form cast a shadow in the doorway.

"You can't just run away," she said, almost yelled because the wind was whipping through the trees and since they still held some of their fall leaves, it stirred into a dull roar around us.

"You shouldn't have come here." I paced back to her, ready to ask her to go. My emotions were already stripped bare, and I couldn't take any more of her here.

She opened her mouth to speak, then wobbled slightly and grabbed the doorframe. "I came here for a reason."

The frustration and anger and sadness pulsing through me skipped as I registered her washed out pallor and the way she leaned against the doorway—not just held on to steady herself, but now resting her head against it, like she couldn't hold it up anymore.

"What's wrong with you?" I asked.

"I think I'm—" Then she slumped and pitched forward.

I dove, catching her upper body in my arms before she hit gravel and just in time to see her eyes roll back.

"Pop," I said, sinking to my knees and situating her better so her neck was properly supported. "Pop."

I swore, but years of reacting to the unexpected had me kicking into gear. I checked her pulse, and it was slightly elevated, but steady. She felt hot, but as cold as it was out here, I couldn't really tell.

Rising to my feet, I carried her inside and set her on the couch. She roused slightly, shifting and making enough noise to reassure me she wasn't dying, at least not yet, so I jogged to shut the door. Bones blinked at me from nearby.

"She'll be okay."

Maybe I said it for my traitor cat, but maybe I said it for myself.

Back at her side, I kneeled by the couch.

"Pop—Jess." I brushed the hair that'd fallen from her bun back, my heart slowing. "Jess. Can you hear me?"

She groaned and her eyes blinked open slowly. It took her a moment to focus enough, and when she finally zeroed in on my face, her brow furrowed. "What happened?"

Her words were gummy and almost slurred, but she was already shifting on the couch, trying to ease up from the lying position.

"Hey, easy." I set a hand on her arm, not wanting to restrain her, but wanting to make sure she didn't pop up and get dizzy. "You passed out as you were coming outside."

She crushed her eyes closed. "I'm sorry." With a moan, she sat, wincing against an unseen force as though something was pulling her back down. "I'll get out of your hair."

"No."

I didn't say anything else because there was nothing else to say, but she didn't seem to register my response. If she thought I was about to let her leave here and drive home, let alone do it in a snowstorm, she was mad.

"Do you think I could use your bathroom before I go?"

Her gaze found mine, though I couldn't be sure she was fully seeing me.

"Go ahead. Right down the hall." I moved to flip on the hallway light, then snatched up Bones so he didn't trip her.

She stumbled her way into the bathroom and shut the door. I debated what to do, fearing she'd pass out again and hit her head on the tub or the corner of the vanity and have a true head injury. We'd be waiting quite a while for an ambulance.

The toilet flushed so I moved away from the hallway to avoid seeming like a creeper, hoping she'd be out soon. I refilled her water and found a first aid kit. After another minute, I'd found a thermometer and replaced the batteries.

"I'm so sorry about this." She leaned against the countertop.

"Stop apologizing." She couldn't blame herself for passing out, nor would I blame her. *Not that she knows this based on the way you've treated her lately.* "Sit down on the couch."

Her dark eyes hung on mine for a second before she moved back to where I'd put her minutes ago. The fact she didn't argue made my pulse notch higher.

Holding out the water, I ordered her to drink.

She tilted up her chin like she might defy me, but then grabbed the jar and took a small sip. While she swallowed, I slid her bangs back on her head with one hand and swiped the thermometer over her brow.

"This is weird," she said, her voice unsteady.

I swore when the display flashed. "You have a temperature of one oh three."

Her eyes grew wide, but stopped short when she winced. "What? No. I'm fine, I—"

"Stop now and tell me what's wrong. Headache? Stomach? Throat?" I demanded.

She exhaled slowly, her eyes closing as she slumped back into the couch. "Um, I'm dizzy? And hot. And freezing. And just so tired, but I haven't slept. I—I just feel bad. I'm sure it's the last few days..." She heaved another big breath. "I just need to get home."

"You're not leaving here when you can barely keep your eyes open."

Said eyes popped open again. "What? I can't stay here. I just need to get home."

I sat next to her and waited until she turned her head toward me. "I know you don't like this any more than I do, but it's not safe for you to drive right now. Take some Tylenol and let's see if we can get your fever down. Take a nap, and maybe when you feel better, you can head back to town."

Much like earlier, she didn't fight me. She took the pills I held out in a gulp, then handed me the water again, letting her head fall back and her eyes slam shut like she couldn't have kept them open a minute longer.

This was both a relief and a concern because this was not the Jess Korbel I knew—at any point in our relationship. And after the fight we'd had...

I swore internally. I'd been so focused on myself and how much I needed my little hideout, I didn't notice the signs. She'd been visibly sick upon arrival, but I'd been too flustered and upset simply having her here, in this space, I didn't see it. If I hadn't caught her...

"You'll stay here until you're better. That's final."

She didn't hear me because she was already fast asleep.

CHAPTER THIRTEEN

Jess

I woke with a start to a darkened room and the crackle of a fire. Behind me, the glow of light gave me enough so I could see the hulking form of Beast resting in the chair perpendicular to the end of the couch where I lay.

Laser beam eyes glinted next to his head. His cat was curled up on one massive shoulder, half on the chair, half on him. *Adorable.*

Wait. What?

Ow.

Everything hurt. My head. My body ached like I'd run a marathon—maybe worse than after the times I'd actually run marathons. And I was sweat-soaked, my shirt clinging to me, my hair damp behind my neck.

I hadn't felt this bad in recent memory.

"You should eat something. Then take more meds." Beast was up, leaning down to take my temperature. He showed the little screen flashing one hundred and one. "That's good. It came down a bit."

I sifted through the events—I'd arrived, we'd fought, I couldn't get out what I'd come for or what I meant to say to apologize, and then I'd... passed out. It was murky from there, but he'd made me sleep on the couch.

In a million years, I wouldn't have imagined this scenario. First, I hadn't been sick past a basic seasonal cold in a long time. Second... here? Really? Why did I have to end up here and literally pass out?

The wave of humiliation I expected didn't crash, though. Maybe because, at least from what I could recall, he had been surprisingly... calm. Insistent, yes. Bossy as all get out, of course. But kind of steadying, oddly.

"Okay. Yeah. Good idea. Then I'll leave."

He didn't say anything, which wasn't a shock, so I gingerly sat up. Good grief, a small elfin community was hammering for diamonds in my brain.

The cat brushed against my legs, then placed a paw on my knee and leaned up, extending his furry neck and sniffing. I leaned down, letting him do what he needed to before petting him.

"Bones, give her some space."

His gruff words made me look over right as he arrived with a plate and another mason jar, this time filled with an orange drink.

"You named your sweet fluffy cuteness machine *Bones*?"

His eyes narrowed and, in another life or state of consciousness, I might've thought he was concealing a smile.

"He becomes a little bag of bones when you pick him up." He settled next to me on the couch. "Eat."

On the plate was a piece of toast with what looked like butter and jam. My stomach pitched. "I don't think I can."

The corners of his mouth pulled down. "Then drink. It's just orange juice."

I couldn't think of something I wanted less except... everything... and I knew getting something in my stomach would be good. I took a sip, then another. After a few minutes of this, him patiently but unswervingly watching, he held up the plate again.

I shook my head. "I can't."

"You can."

"I really can't. I'll puke."

His expression didn't change. "Then you'll puke. But you can't keep taking medicine on an empty stomach, and you need more."

A thought wormed its way in. "Wait, what time is it?"

"Around four."

I bolted upright. "In the morning? No. No... I was just going to take a little nap."

He did the squinty thing again. "You slept for almost ten hours. I figured you needed the sleep, and I kept tabs on your temp. But it's past time to get some more meds in you, so eat up."

Without my permission, my eyes flooded and I blinked back tears. "I am so so sorry. This is—"

"Jess."

The vehemence in his voice startled me.

"Stop apologizing."

My lips firmed and I swallowed hard.

"You can't help that you're sick." He held up the plate and gave me a glare that clearly expected me to take another bite.

I took a tiny one, praying my stomach wouldn't turn.

When it didn't, I ate a bit more, and took the medicine he'd put in a little plastic cup.

"As soon as it gets light, I'll go." I coughed into my elbow, trying to minimize the spread of whatever this was. He'd hate me even more if I got him sick, too.

The hard look he gave me said he didn't agree with my plan.

"Seriously, I'll get out of your hair."

He did his usual glare thing, but somehow, it didn't come off as arrogant or infuriating. This time, I couldn't read the emotion behind his gritted teeth and slow inhale.

"What?" I finally asked when he didn't say anything.

"You are not leaving here while you're febrile and hacking and ill."

I was sick enough I didn't feel the usual magma-level rage erupt at his tone, but I wasn't dead, so... "No. That's exactly why I need to get home and leave you in peace."

I dropped my head to stare at the plate of toast balanced in my lap, begging myself to finish the slice so I'd have a little more in my system to make the drive.

Thick, cool fingers urged my chin up, up, and over toward him before releasing me when our eyes met.

"You are not leaving here. There's a foot of snow from the freak storm and you can't drive in this condition. You'll stay here until you're better."

I studied his stern face in the shadows. After a moment, he took the plate and set it on the coffee table, then stood and held out a hand.

"What?"

"You're coming to the bed. You can't keep sleeping on a leather couch with a fever."

Then, as though in a dream, I watched myself place a hand in his and rise on shaking legs, felt his arm loop around my waist and support me down the hallway, then lower me to the bed in a quaint, clean room.

"Get some more sleep. I'll be in to check on you again in a few hours."

Then he flipped off the light, pulled the door nearly shut, and I was alone.

And since none of this made sense—none of it could be parsed out or solved, and stretching out on the bed felt so good, I lay down and slept.

CHAPTER FOURTEEN

Jude

Jess spent most of the day sleeping, then she'd cough so hard she'd nearly gag and slump back against the pillows clutching her ribs. I hadn't been truly sick in years but remembered how that kind of cough could make you ache.

Doc finally called me around noon.

"Sorry, I'm just now getting back, I was in a meeting. How is she now?"

I'd texted him last night and he'd responded, advising Tylenol for the fever and monitoring, plus fluids and rest. As her cough ramped up, I'd been in touch. The snow kept coming, which wasn't entirely unusual for a fluke late October storm, but I could really go for not setting any records. It was an hour's drive back to Silverton and we were at a higher elevation here. The snow was likely worse up this way, plus the roads wouldn't be plowed. I could get us down in my truck, though I didn't have chains this early in the season... *what a mess.*

"Her fever was down when I checked an hour ago, but she seems to have chills—keeps piling on blankets whenever she wakes up. She's coughing a lot and just looks miserable."

All the raging about her showing up at my cabin had come to an abrupt halt when she'd passed out last night, but I couldn't help but feel she shouldn't be here. I shouldn't be the one to see her like this. When she was conscious and well again, she'd hate having been stuck here with me.

A pained moan followed by a round of coughing came from the bedroom and Adam must've heard it, too.

"Biggest concerns are the fever getting too high, dehydration, and adjacent complications which we don't need to worry about. I'm guessing it's flu since Cookie had it, but who knows. If that's the case, the best thing you can do is keep her hydrated, keep up with the meds, and if her fever pops up and won't come down, you've got to do a lukewarm bath to get it down."

Anxiety pulled every muscle in my body tight and I didn't respond—couldn't have found words for all the money in the world.

A bath. Give Jessica Korbel, a woman who actively hated me and thought of me as her enemy and ruiner of her happiness, a bath.

Sure, Doc! No problem! That is totally a thing I can do without losing my mind or making her feel like I've crossed every possible boundary a woman can have.

Maybe if it was someone else... Kenny? Even Catherine, if it had to be a woman. It wouldn't be *fun*, but I'd take care of a friend. But... Jess?

I swallowed hard, wondering if I was coming down with

the same thing she had. Maybe that accounted for this nausea and dread and stark feeling of *I cannot do this.*

"You can do this, okay? She's going to be okay. Snow should clear in a day or two, and I bet she's through the worst of it within the next twelve hours or so, based on what Cookie said."

I grunted, still no words at the ready, heart still galloping and breaths still short.

"Go take care of her, and do what you can to take care of yourself, okay? If you go down, too, you call me and we'll figure out how to get you both out. In the meantime, I'll keep the girls updated through Jo so they know what's going on and can rally when she's back home."

In truth, I felt fine so far, and based on the internet searches I'd done, I wouldn't be likely to get sick for another few days unless I'd already been exposed via someone else. The nervous energy stemmed from the mention of giving Jess a bath, but it wouldn't come to that. Her temp would drop and it'd be fine.

Worst case, there were ways the team could get to us—everything from bringing a truck with chains up or even a helicopter from the hospital... but it wouldn't get that bad. I wouldn't let it.

"Thanks," I mumbled, and hung up, rushing to the room when I heard another moan.

She'd stripped off her shirt and pants, her legs now splayed out on top of the bed, and her cheeks were flushed. My breath rushed out at the miles of exposed skin before I drop-kicked my brain and moved to her side.

"I feel so bad," she whispered, not even bothering to open her eyes.

I scanned her forehead—*damn.* One oh three again. "Hey, we gotta get you cooled down."

"Yeah, I know. That's why I'm nearly naked in your bed."

Words I wouldn't admit to having imagined come from her lips, but now that they had, I mentally punched the idiotic part of my mind that started giggling about it and grabbed the water. "Sit up a bit and take a drink."

"My head hurts."

I checked my watch. "You can take more medicine in an hour, but right now, you need to drink. It'll help your head, too."

She opened one eye and glared at me, then her other fluttered open. "I'm sorry."

"Hush."

Gripping her upper arm, I eased her into a sitting position and held the cup to her lips. She looked at me with brows pinched like she didn't understand, her eyes blood-shot and dry.

My heart squeezed. I slid a hand behind her head to support it. "Tip back a little, Pop. You can do it."

She eyed me as I eased her head back while tilting the drink, grateful when her lips moved and she actually swallowed the liquid.

"Good girl. Now we're going to—"

"I may be delirious with a fever, but if you ever good girl me again, Beast, we're going to have issues."

I cleared my throat, not allowing myself to laugh at her show of strength. "Apologies, Pop. I'm just glad you're cooperating. You and I both know you don't take orders well, and especially not from me."

Her eyes were barely open now, but she somehow managed to glare at me. "You don't take orders well from me either."

Might depend on the context.

I slapped the thought down and held the water to her mouth again. She complied and sighed when I rested her back against the pillow. I brought two cool washcloths and set one on her forehead, the other on her chest.

"That feels good and also awful."

I huffed a laugh. "Sorry, but Doc says you need to cool off or I have to give you a lukewarm bath."

Her eyes jumped open. "You will give me a bath over my dead body."

I bit the inside of my cheek to stay a smile. "I will do what I need to do to make sure I don't have your dead body on my hands at any point. I'm pretty sure your friends would end up in jail for murder—at least Elise and Dove would. Those two would go feral. And Winnie and Nikki would help hide my body while Jo wrote out the alternate history for the cover up. Poor Catherine would have to go into hiding so she wouldn't have to lie to anyone about what happened. So that's why we're doing wash cloths first. Bring down your temp and we'll be just fine."

A smile flickered across her face before she sighed, long and aggrieved, but then launched into a coughing fit. When she finished, she reached for the water of her own accord, then startled. "Do you know where my phone is?"

"Haven't seen it. Did you have it when you got here?" It hadn't occurred to me she might've dropped it when she fell.

"I don't know if I brought it in. Maybe it's in my car?"

"I'll get it for you. You stay here and cool down. Don't get under the blankets again. When I get back, if it's not dropping, it's bath time."

She didn't acknowledge the words, but I thought I heard something about *rude, bossy beast* as I left.

Twenty minutes later, I'd dug out her car and managed

to move it closer to the house since she'd left it at the end of my driveway like she was going to breech the property covertly instead of knock on my front door, retrieved her phone, and returned to find her asleep again. But when I checked her temp, she'd jumped another half a degree.

"Get up, Pop. Time to cool you down."

She didn't respond, so I gently shook her shoulder. When that didn't rouse her, my pulse notched up.

"Pop, wake up." Still nothing. "Pop." Again. Had she passed out instead of falling asleep? I patted her cheek. "Jess, wake up." Worry grated at me. "Jess, you gotta wake up now."

Damn, she was so hot—it felt like there might literally be fire under her skin. Her eyes opened but she looked completely out of it. I couldn't wait any more.

"I'm going to pick you up and we're going to the bathroom, okay? Don't kill me." She could, too, if she were in her right mind.

With one arm behind her shoulders and one under her knees, I lifted her nearly dead weight. She gasped and tensed as the movement set in.

"What—what are you doing?"

"You're not cooling down. I'm taking you to the bathroom."

I sat on the side of the large tub and settled her on my lap while holding her with one arm across her chest as I turned on the water, waiting until it felt right. Standing, I brought her with me gently, settling her feet next to the tub.

"Step in for me," I said, worried that if I set her in there myself, she might slip.

She gave me a look I couldn't decipher, then lifted one leg over the side while standing on the other. I held her arm as she stepped in on the other side, then slowly lowered into the barely warm water.

Everything about this was too intimate, too wrong for me to be doing with her, and yet some animal part of me was greedy to be the one who helped her. She needed help and for once, *for once*, it was me.

"This is awful. And now my underwear is wet."

She drew her knees up and hugged them, resting her head on her arms, and shut her eyes. I needed to pour some water over her shoulders and get her neck and chest and underarms wet with the cool water, but then she'd be completely soaked.

"I need to get your back wet. We could wash your hair if it'd feel good—might help."

My voice sounded weird but maybe that was due to how much I'd spoken in the last few hours. Perhaps it sounded odd because all of this was a waking dream. Touching her fevered skin, offering to wash her hair... this was the work of a lover and I...

It was the pain in my chest every time I brushed her hair from her face to check her temperature or refilled her water. It was the pressure in my head and the swoop in my stomach when she looked at me with pleading and apology, or with surrender, instead of loathing.

She stared past me now in what looked like a trance, then sat up and reached backwards without warning. I averted my eyes just in time and heard the rasp of cotton on the ground next to me.

Something... happened. Inside me. On an elemental level. And I wasn't proud of it, but my pulse hammered in my throat at the realization she'd just tossed her bra to the floor and was now sitting all but naked in my tub.

In almost any other scenario, this would be the start or end or at least part of any given fantasy. But all of those versions of the story came with a different history between us and certainly a different present reality. They didn't feature the woman in question with glazed eyes and a high fever and only here because she couldn't leave.

It wasn't just the situation, though, or her state of undress. It was this... tenderness wending through me. I didn't recognize it much less know what to do with it, so I just let it be.

"I don't think I can do my hair," she said, drawing my attention back to her.

The notches of her spine stood out as she rested her head down on her arms encircling her knees again. I could see the full, beautiful expanse of her back and sides, but everything truly private was hidden. Maybe it made me a total idiot, but I was relieved. I didn't want to see anything she didn't want to show me, and she could hardly want that right now.

She'll never want it, sucker. Damn these thoughts that'd invaded when they'd been kept under lock and key for so long.

"Be right back," I mumbled, running to get a cup to help rinse her hair. When I came back, Bones was leaning over the tub sniffing at her and she had a little smile on her face.

Lightning struck, a bolt straight from my brain to my heart. The pull at the corners of her perfect lips and the way she craned her neck to get closer to my mutant cat's furry little face... *Of course she's a cat person.*

"Tilt your chin up," I said, filling the cup with the running water.

Her instant compliance was another strike, a weird thrill that she trusted me to do as I asked, along with the more vivid knowledge that in any other circumstance, she wouldn't. Though she'd trusted me to some degree at Snowberry—she knew I'd do my part, I wouldn't break cover, and she was safe with me like I was with her—at least on a purely professional level. That was something.

But this... she was as vulnerable as someone could get. She'd likely let anyone help her, but the reality it was me —*me, dammit!*—made me want to pound my chest and maybe sob a little. Emotional whiplash was a familiar bedfellow lately, but it'd taken a dose of steroids since she'd knocked on my door hours ago.

Her mouth fell open as I worked water into her dark brown hair. I'd always liked it, and nothing had changed in that vein—it was beautiful, as was she. She likely had fancy shampoo that smelled a lot better than mine, but I used some of what I had, lightly scratching against her scalp when she sighed at the contact. With the bubbles worked from her scalp to the ends at her shoulders, I rinsed. One cup, two, the suds slid down her bare back and trickled a path along her neck, running past the ridges of her collar bone and into shadows I didn't allow myself to mine.

During rinsing, she began shuddering intensely, so I shut off the water.

"Can I get out?" Her voice emerged so small, it was criminal.

A check of my watch indicated she'd been in there six minutes. Was that really all? I'd lived a lifetime of thoughts in these fleeting moments with her at my mercy in this space. What a weird thought, because I wouldn't do anything to hurt her. The thought made me ill, despite what she might think. Still, a wild sense of satisfaction snaked through me as I felt the weight of the situation again.

When I swiped at her forehead, the temp had come

down a bit, though she was still damp and I wasn't sure whether it was at all accurate after my shoddy job washing her hair.

"It's only been a few minutes," I said, then noticed her forlorn look and hurried to add, "Let's give it another minute before you get out."

The next sixty seconds ticked by slowly, and while it did, I prepped the bathmat and got a large towel for her.

As I reached out a hand, her eyes found mine first. Her teeth chattered and she blinked fast. "Can you not look?"

It wasn't accusatory or angry, it was... pleading.

"I won't. Let's do it like this." I held out the towel in front of me to create a curtain she could wrap up in.

"I think I need your help, though. To stand up."

The last few words had a watery quality, and I internally begged her not to cry.

No. Noooo. What would I do if she cried?

I wasn't someone who cared if a woman cried, or a man did for that matter. Hell, I'd spent more time crying in the last few months as Omi deteriorated and then passed than I'd spent doing anything else. But this was Jess. And I suspected seeing her sick or naked wouldn't hold a candle to seeing her cry on the list of things she didn't want to share with me. I'd witnessed it twice before—once after a mission gone wrong and a second time when she came to me demanding to know what'd happened with Kurt.

"Grab my arm and steady yourself while you stand, and I'll get the towel around your back. Then you can wrap up in it, and I'll help you out. Just tell me when you're covered."

I tilted my head way up so my gaze was pinned on the ceiling. She steadied herself with one cool hand on my wrist, then leaned enough weight I could tell she was standing. I slipped the towel over her shoulders and felt her tugging it from my other hand.

"Okay."

Her soft word gave the all clear and I looked down to see her completely tucked into the towel, only her face and wet hair to be seen.

"Can I carry you?" I didn't want to assume, but if she was shaky enough to be worried about standing up on her own, I didn't want her to fall getting out of the tub.

"Yes." Another whispered word.

My stomach flipped.

Seconds later, I set her on the couch. "Stay here for a minute and let me change the sheets." I bolted to my bag and got out some boxers and a T-shirt. "If you want to get out of your wet stuff, toss them on the floor and I'll get them washed so you can wear them later. For now, put these on if you can."

Ten minutes later, she was nestled into the bed with my clothes on, something I wouldn't overthink, and her temp wasn't gone, but it had lowered enough to not keep me in panic mode. I'd wake her in a half hour when she could have more medicine.

I'd do anything. *Anything* to get her better. I loved and hated the way she was fully dependent on me, but it couldn't last, and I had to be able to tell her I'd done everything to get her well quickly. I'd never survive her anger when all this was over if I didn't. Maybe it'd mean another bath or maybe I'd need to hike her out of here on my back... whatever it was, I'd do it.

"I'll be back. Shout if you need anything," I said stupidly, because she could hardly summon the strength to speak let alone shout.

Just as I was at the door, I heard it.

"Thanks, Jude."

I turned, a weird tightness in my chest, and I resisted the urge to say, "No, thank *you*."

CHAPTER FIFTEEN

Jude

I spent the day checking her temperature, force-feeding her medicine and water and any little scrap she would eat, which was basically nothing, and pretending to do anything other than pace and search online for ways to help her get better.

By evening, her fever had ratcheted up, as had my anxiety. Adam reassured me she was okay based on her vitals and the fact she was still drinking, even though she seemed so out of it the last time I'd woken her. But he'd given me strict orders to get the next round of meds in before the fever went higher, so I had my task.

I sat on the bedside and nudged her a few times before she reluctantly woke.

"Jude, I'm sick."

Something burst in my chest, her use of my name never ceasing to elicit both pleasure and pain.

"I know, Pop. Take your medicine so we can get this fever down."

"I'm so sick, though," she whimpered, the smallness of her voice painting her illness across the space.

I hated this. I hated seeing her like this—so meek and miserable. I'd never take her fire for granted again, even when it was aimed like a weapon in my direction.

"Baby, please. Take your medicine. I promise it'll help."

She blinked up at me, dark eyes hardly seeing. I lifted the little plastic cup containing the two pills to her lips, then raised a glass of water and she let me guide her head back so she could swallow, the other hand cradling her and righting her head when she finished.

She shut her eyes and simply breathed, her color high and breaths pronounced. I wondered whether she was having a hard time breathing, but her cough hadn't been quite as bad the last hour or so. Maybe she'd fall asleep again for a while and after dozing, the fever would finally break.

"You called me baby?"

My stomach clenched, but I didn't answer right away, only waited for the meds to kick in. I didn't want to have to put her in a bath again, but I'd have to if this didn't work.

"It's nothing," I said, not about to explain a damn thing to her in this state.

Her eyes opened slowly, gaze unfocused as she reached for my face and brushed a hand along my cheek. I froze, not sure whether to pull away or lean into her touch.

"You know, you're almost handsome."

I couldn't hide the huff of laughter. "Am I? Just almost?"

Her glittering eyes sparkled back at me, and I knew I shouldn't listen to a damn word she was saying let alone take it to heart, but I wanted to. Somehow in the last twenty-four hours, I'd gone from eschewing anything to do with her to hanging on her smallest movement.

I wanted everything she'd tell me, especially when her guard was down. If that made me a villain, well, I was already the bad guy in her story, wasn't I?

"Thought you were dangerously hot the day I met you. And you're so big..." It came out all dreamy and almost breathless. "I thought about you too much."

I swallowed hard, the angel on my shoulder screaming at me to walk away and not take from her in this state, but the devil won out. "What'd you think about?"

She bit her full bottom lip and shut her eyes. Just this sent my pulse racing even harder, but then she said, "All kinds of things I can't tell you. What it might be like to have your big hands on me, to be under you... I'd probably suffocate, but—" She coughed, then laughed. "What a way to go, right?"

I nearly choked on air, images of exactly what she said burning into my mind in full color and vivid detail.

But then she added, "I knew you'd never hurt me."

My heart thundered in my chest as disbelief and a wanting so acute I might've asphyxiated on it hit instantly, but a painful crush of something else hit, too.

What if I'd elbowed Kurt out of the way years ago? What if I'd shed the persistent, almost superior need to be patient and let her come to me and instead let her see I wanted her? Would she have wanted me back then? Would we have had a chance to live out her fantasy, and mine, instead of spending years at odds and hurting?

As it often did, my brain locked up and I couldn't beg for more or say anything to keep her talking. She'd melted me.

She shook her head, like she was clearing it of the fog that'd settled over her, then pinned me with her glassy gaze again.

"You've got it all, Rawlins. It's just that scowl. That perma-frown you can't seem to shake." She pressed her fingers between my brows as though she could banish the lines there, then poked at the corner of my mouth to coax it into a smile. "Especially around me."

I didn't reward her, at least not with a smile like she wanted.

Her words sliced through the wondering *what if* for the past, and shoved me straight into a state of wondering *what if* for now. Because some of this felt like thoughts she had now—maybe not the more sensual ones, but this idea about my expression...

The tips of two fingers rested to the left of my mouth and I forbade myself from turning my face and letting them coast over my lips or taking them into my mouth. That was not a thing I could do, even when she was looking at me with her wide eyes practically begging for something from me.

She was delirious—consent wasn't valid in such a state. But not all of this was born of the past or fiction.

My gut told me some of this was real.

She nudged the corner of my mouth one more time, one last effort to force me to smile, and still, I didn't give in.

I wouldn't mind rewarding her with taking her mouth, claiming her in every way there was to claim another person, but I wouldn't. Not while she was sick, of course, and not when we were enemies.

Though the thought that'd sprung so freely to my mind the last few years didn't fit quite right. *Enemies?* Maybe we had been in some ways, and I'd leaned into her hatred of me in an odd kind of self-preservation. It was a bizarre version of if you can't beat 'em, join 'em, where beating her would've been convincing her she was better off without Kurt, and joining her meant letting myself play into the villain role, the grunting, muted version of myself I'd become when she shredded me repeatedly until she finally locked me out completely and then I faced loss and more loss.

This was the most she'd been able to stomach me since I'd ruined the life she had planned. I wouldn't pretend I was what she wanted when she'd told me flat out that I'd made her lose what she craved most. I'd ruined everything, even if so much of it hadn't been my choice.

As my mind ran the trails of possibility and memory and desire and regret, Jess settled back into her pillow and her hand fell away from my face. Her eyes shut firmly not long after, and she was deep asleep. The temporary fever dream and those lovely sentiments as good as a figment of my imagination.

And yet, when I settled on the couch hours later, it wasn't the years of history between us, the enmity we'd both watered like weeds on the border of a garden that had once been friendship at the very least, that replayed in my mind.

Instead, it was the soft brush of her hand on my cheek and the truth I thought I heard underneath her words I couldn't shake. Not simply the delicious reality that she'd thought about us together, or that I was almost handsome, especially if I wouldn't scowl. It was the hint she wished I'd smile for her.

She had no idea.

CHAPTER SIXTEEN

Jess

The buttery light of early morning cast the cozy bedroom in a warm glow. I surveyed my body, praying the worst was over.

Head wasn't pierced with pain. My chest was sore from coughing, but I could swear I'd coughed less overnight. I reached for the thermometer Jude had used a thousand times in the last day or so and checked—ninety-eight and change!

Jude. My heart flipped as I registered thinking his real name and then the memories crowded in.

Him washing my hair as I huddled in the freezing bath. Him wrapping me in a towel, those muscular arms holding me close as he carried me to the bed.

Him force-feeding me toast and applesauce and medicine.

Baby.

My head fell back against the pillow. That had to have been a fever-induced hallucination. Didn't it?

"How are you?" he asked, leaning against the doorframe of the room.

His room. This was his house and his room, and I'd been here for... how long *had* I been here? More than a day?

I bolted up and tried to stand, then instantly saw stars. His giant hand wrapped around my wrists and lowered me back down to the bed.

"Easy. You've hardly eaten. Move slowly."

The gruff words made me oddly homesick, though I couldn't figure out why or for what. All I knew was I'd over-stayed my welcome times a thousand, and now I needed to go.

"I am so sorry for this. Let me slip on my shoes and I'll go."

He'd resumed his post at the door, arms crossed over his chest and one foot over the other, perfectly at home. "Yeah? You'll drive home right now?"

I eyed him, because the challenge in his voice was unmistakable. "What? Why are you saying it like that?"

His eyes dropped to my shirt, then my legs, and—*oh*. I crossed my arms over my chest. *Where is my bra?* Where are my clothes?

"Your clothes are clean—I washed them. Didn't see anything I wouldn't have at a pool. I'm not holding you hostage here, but the roads are still impassible, especially in your little nonsense car."

I groaned. "Oh, you are still yourself, aren't you? My car is perfectly capable of making it back to Silverton. It may be old, but I've taken good care of it."

"I'm sure you have. But it's two-wheel drive, isn't it?"

I didn't give him a response because he was being rude

and rude people didn't get responses, especially when my energy was flagging *hard*.

He seemed to register this the minute I thought it, and he moved freakishly fast into my space and cupped a hand around the back of my head, angling my chin up so he could look in my eyes. With his other go-go-Gadget-long arm, he reached for the thermometer and swiped it across my head. When the readout showed a normal temp, his shoulders relaxed enough I could see the visible change.

"I'm not trying to be a jerk. You can't go anywhere because the roads are impassible, even for my truck. We're stuck here another while until they get plows up higher. I know that's not news you want to hear."

His face was shadowed, his beard even more unruly than when I'd arrived.

I didn't know what I wanted to hear. I'd been living in an alternate universe the last day or so and I couldn't tell which way was up.

"I'm sorry, too."

"You have nothing to apologize for."

So we sat there, me hunched over with my arms crossed now. I'd realized I wasn't wearing anything underneath his giant shirt and the boxer briefs I vaguely remembered pulling on after the horrid cold bath from hell.

"Your clothes are on the dresser." He nodded toward the pretty maple dresser on the wall in front of the bed. "Do whatever you want *slowly*, and then I can bring you some breakfast. We need to get some fuel in you, and hopefully, that'll help with the shakiness."

After an embarrassingly slow time pulling on my own clothes and wishing I'd worn sweatpants here instead of jeans, I emerged from the bedroom refusing to think about the fact he'd washed, dried, and folded my clothes.

It was so personal—intimate. Though he'd also washed my hair and changed sheets I'd soaked with sweat, so maybe clothes washing was nothing at this point.

"Think you can sit here?" He gestured to where he'd set a plate of scrambled eggs and toast at the counter.

"Think so." I slipped onto the stool and rested my forearms on the countertop. The food wasn't quite as revolting as the toast I'd been force-fed yesterday, which had to be a good sign.

"I'll be back in a minute," he said, disappearing down the hall.

Maybe that was for the best. We'd never been chatty friends. Even before we'd had our falling out, we'd been comfortable, but not chatty. I didn't imagine he was this way with anyone, though maybe Kenny could get him gabbing.

I heard the whoosh of water in the pipes and the sound of the washer lid closing. A minute later, he returned to the kitchen.

"That going down okay? I can make something else."

I shook my head as I chewed the bite. "No, this is great. Thank you."

He turned back toward the stove and presented me with his broad back draped in a worn T-shirt and pooling just a little at the waistband of his gray sweatpants. I swallowed hard and bounced my eyes away because acknowledging how completely and utterly masculine he was would not help my fever. If I'd ever had a physical type, it was his, and if he'd ever given me a clue he was interested... how different would it all have been? Maybe I wouldn't have fallen for Kurt's overt interest after resolving not to pursue someone who showed me only friendship.

Those thoughts were so far from the point right now, yet

seeing him like this, barefoot in his mountain hideaway with his fluffball cat swirling around his feet...

It broke me. Had to be thanks to the illness, but my eyes filled with tears again and I ducked my head to swipe at them before he could see. Between letting all my pent-up anger fly at him and then having him take care of me for days, there was too much space in me available for new feelings.

A niggling sensation flashed into my mind like we'd talked about something I'd regret, but I couldn't summon details. Hopefully, it'd come back to me, and more so, I hoped I hadn't said anything too honest. Had I been mean to him again?

When he settled into the seat next to me, a plate of his own filled with huge portions of what he'd made me and a steaming mug of black coffee, I turned to him.

"I never got to say what I came to say. I know you don't really want to hear anything from me"—he shook his head like my words frustrated him, but I pressed on—"but I need to."

His glare was less furious and more bracing, if such a thing could be parsed out by looking.

With a deep breath, I said, "I heard about your grandmother, and I wanted to say I'm very sorry. I know she meant a lot to you."

His jaw flexed, visible despite his even longer than yesterday beard.

No words, no surprise. *Onward.*

"I'm not going to pretend I'm sorry for the contents of what I said after the mission, but I am genuinely sorry for the timing. I—" *I thought you were just being an extra big jerk.* That didn't really work—not a great apology if it comes with a side of insults, especially after he'd taken such good care of me. "It was a lot, working together. And I didn't consider that you might be... going through something."

His eyes skipped away from mine and he took a large bite.

Okayyyy.

After a moment, he spoke to his plate. "Thanks."

I huffed, gazing around at the cozy space so at odds with this stilted interaction, unsurprised by the curt reply. A little wire basket with heads of garlic sat on the counter near the stove. A bowl of red and yellow swirled apples occupied prime placement on the island. An ornate metal bottlecap opener had been mounted under the cabinet that looked oddly worn.

Focusing on the details helped me avoid the frustration his reply ignited and how hard it was to tell if that edge to the word was sarcasm. Was it? Why would it be? And yet... hadn't most of our interactions for the last five years been something like this, minus the apology or sincerity?

"No, really, Pop. Thank you."

A glance at his face confirmed what I thought I'd heard —he was genuinely saying thank you.

So many of our encounters had been ugly and hard. His real response, one without an edge to it, softened me.

"I know she meant so much to you. I guess your grandpa passed a while back?" I hoped the words sounded gentle like I meant them and not combative like most everything else I ever said to him.

He nodded, his eyes snagging on mine. A beat passed before he said, "About five years ago."

My chest ached and my throat burned at the thought of him losing both of his people so close together. "I'm so sorry."

"Thanks," he said again, quieter this time. "How's your mom doing?"

I huffed lightly, the bizarre reality of this conversation hitting me. Talking about family, catching up almost like old friends as we sat here side by side eating eggs he'd made... it was so far from what had been our norm.

"She's good. Really happy with Guy. They moved to Tampa for his work and... yeah. She's good, thanks." My mom and I had been on our own for so long, I'd hardly known how to adjust to her meeting and falling for Guy. But by then, I was in the Army, and by the time they got married, I was engaged to Kurt.

It'd crossed my mind more than once that Mom finding her happiness had made me want to find my own place, my *person*, more urgently than I had before. We'd been a team until I'd left home for the Army and she'd supported me from afar, but I was grown, and it wasn't just the two of us against the world anymore. She had Guy, who was a better man than my father had ever been and loved her so much. He became her home.

And seeing that... I'd wanted the same for myself desperately. Both for my own happiness and future, and for her, so I could tell her I was good—that we both had what we'd always hoped for, so she could truly just relax and enjoy how her life turned out.

When my life fell apart, it was a relief that hers was still intact.

"Good. I'm glad."

He seemed to mean it, too, which warmed me. He'd met my mom when she visited. She'd been charmed by Kurt, as was typical of women who met him, but she'd been *taken* by Beast. I remembered her peppering me with questions about him and widening her eyes a few times like, *Is this guy real?*

And I remember telling her yes. He was a good friend.

A stab of sadness hit in the tender spot where I usually felt only anger with him.

Now that I'd done it... now that I'd made what little peace I could, energy was leaving me fast and my mood was dropping.

"I think I'll go rest for a while, if that's okay."

He dipped his head, eyes studying me like he might be able to sense if my fever had jumped up again. "Take your temperature before you get in bed."

Shaking my head at his unending reserves of bossiness, I waved as I walked down the hallway toward the bedroom. "Wilco."

CHAPTER SEVENTEEN

Jude

Bones and I did a puzzle and listened to music on the lowest possible volume while Jess slept.

At some point, my mind had slipped from thinking of her as Pop and had fallen into the cruel trap of Jess.

Then there was that time you called her baby, _and she wasn't so out of it she didn't notice._

She likely didn't remember it now. I couldn't say why or how the word jumped from my mouth, but I couldn't take it back.

Could it be the soul-filling tenderness you feel for her and the way she makes you want to be soft and gentle and do whatever she wants? Could that be why you called her—

Oh, well. Not a helpful line of thought, and again, she likely wouldn't remember it or might think it was all a dream. _Hopefully._

I peeked in on her to make sure she didn't seem like she

was febrile again, but she was simply sleeping. Her color looked better, and she was, overall, perking up.

She'd stepped away at just the right time earlier. Her apology and kind words about my grandparents had side-swiped me. I hadn't guessed she'd come here to apologize for what she'd said—Jess wasn't the kind of person to say something she didn't mean. But her regret over saying what she did, *when* she did, hit me in a surprisingly painful way I couldn't explain.

For a few minutes there, we'd simply talked—shared in the human connection of grief and loss over my grandparents, and joy for her mom's happiness. It'd been…

Good.

I'd needed the quiet and the mind-numbing practice of fitting pieces into place and making sense of a bunch of nothing so it turned into something. But as late afternoon approached, I started cooking. The vegetable beef stew I'd put in the crock pot earlier smelled amazing, and I just needed to turn out the dough for the no-knead bread and let it rise while the oven heated up. She'd be hungry whenever she woke, and I wanted to have dinner ready.

My appetite had reasserted itself lately, and the idea of sharing a meal with Jess made it somehow more ravenous.

Then maybe, if she wasn't too tired, we could sit together and watch a movie or… whatever. Now that she'd been here a few days, I'd gotten used to her. And now that we weren't spewing insults and frustration back and forth, it only made me want more of this gentle, if temporary, detente between us.

But the snow had stopped last night. We'd likely be able to leave tomorrow morning. Might even be able to go tonight, if she wanted, which I should really tell her. I could drive her—I could bring Kenny back with me to get her car.

Would it all crumble once she was better? Once we left here?

No doubt, the fantasy would come to an end. This waking dream I'd been stuck in since she crossed my threshold, and her words amidst delirium last night...

I was a different man than before she'd come here. I couldn't unknow what she'd said... that at some point, before everything, she'd wanted me. Wondered about how it might be between us. Maybe even wished I would smile at her.

Eyes closed, I could feel her finger press between my brows.

"Hey. Sorry I slept so long."

The sight of her standing at the edge of the kitchen with her arms wrapped around herself and a pair of my sweatpants she must've found in the drawers nearly drowning her stole my breath. I let out a *huh*, a mix of a laugh and something else unintelligible, as my gaze dropped to the excess material pooling at her ankles.

"Oh, yeah." She looked down, then curtseyed as she held out the material on either side of her thighs. "I borrowed these."

It shouldn't have been appealing. My heart should've had no response to her borrowing my clothes. After everything over the last few days, why would that make my gut tight? "Whatever you need."

She tucked her lips together, then her gaze shifted behind me. "Wait, are you making homemade bread?"

I'd just uncovered the dough. In another minute or two, I'd pull the Dutch oven from the heat and dump the dough in so it could bake covered for half an hour.

"Yes. It's a simple recipe."

Her eyes stayed glued on the dough until they shifted to meet mine. "I really don't know you, do I?"

I stepped closer, wiping my hands on a towel to give them something to do. "It's been a long time since we knew each other."

She hummed. "Maybe so."

Not wanting to drown in the memory of the past and get stuck on the landfill-sized pile of baggage between us, I pulled the Dutch oven off the heat. "Want to watch some TV until dinner's ready?"

"What do you have in mind?"

I tipped the dough into the preheated Dutch oven and slipped on the lid, a lick of satisfaction hitting at the sound of the sizzle where dough met heated cast iron.

"I have a poor selection of movies, or I have *Parks and Rec*. We can try the internet but it's never that great for streaming." I needed enough reception for calls, texts, and emergencies, but getting away from the constant scrolling and input was part of the point of being here, so I'd made no effort to improve.

"Oh, definitely *Parks and Rec*."

A half smile was already on my face when I shut the oven and turned toward her. "Excellent choice."

Two hours later, we were settled into opposite ends of the couch, her legs stretching across the cushions toward me. We'd feasted on bread still crackling from the heat of the oven—an admission that would have Dorian cringing and likely any other bread baker I knew, but oh, well—and stew. Jess had found her appetite again and I could say with certainty I'd never had more satisfaction witnessing someone eat a meal. And that was saying something, because I'd witnessed men who were literally starving take a bite of food.

Caring for Jess had taken on a life of its own. Or maybe my desire to had. In the short forty-eight hours since she'd arrived, I'd moved through so many responses and settled on one unavoidable truth—I wanted to meet her every need. And in doing so, the shroud of grief had eased a touch.

Acknowledging the thought made my gut tighten and I shifted in my seat, then decided to take a break.

"Need anything?"

She gave me those dark eyes of hers. "No, thank you." Then Andy Dwyer did something ridiculous on the screen and her face split into a wide, unfettered smile.

My stomach swooped low and I turned away, busying myself refilling my water and double-checking the stove knobs to confirm they were all off. Of course they were, but it gave me a reason to linger and take a second to calm the stupid swell of my heart.

Not this again. Not this.

Only she gave me this feeling—this skin-too-tight, heart-too-big feeling. I could feel it when I hated her for hating me, and I'd felt it... before that. I'd felt it when we were friends, before she and Kurt got serious. Before I accepted she'd never be mine because she was falling for him, so I removed myself. It'd been painful, but I'd known removing myself and locking myself down was what I had to do. It'd been clear.

Until it'd gotten murky. Until he'd screwed up so badly I couldn't give him the benefit of the doubt anymore.

Until she started hating me for ruining everything, and I

couldn't bring myself to tell her just how bad Kurt had been because it would've hurt her more.

And in truth, there had been a nasty part of me that'd been relieved. I hated myself for admitting it, but I'd been glad I finally had a reason to push him enough so he ran away with his tail between his legs. I knew he'd never confess to what he'd done, and then he was gone. But it certainly hadn't given me a chance with her.

I exhaled silently and willed away that rabbit trail. Nothing good came from digging around in those old feelings. The fact that they'd sprung up again and very much against my will... I had to hold out maybe twelve more hours. Then we'd be out of here and deal with whatever happened next.

I poured myself a highball of whiskey. I hadn't planned on getting roaring drunk and staring at the ceiling every night I was here, but it had been on the docket for at least one before Jess had showed up. While I wouldn't do that now, a drink would give me something to do—somewhere to focus the energy that kept centering in on her.

Returning to the couch, I took my same seat, but she was sitting closer to the middle and Bones had taken up residence where her spot had been. She must've shifted around long enough to let the little thief come steal her warmth.

When my thigh brushed hers, she raised a brow. "No whiskey for me?"

I scowled.

She pressed her pretty lips together, but her eyes lit in the way they did so I knew she was smiling, even if she was hiding it.

"I should know better than to think you'd give me alcohol after being so sick."

I only gave her a look.

"I don't actually want any."

"Good. You can't have any."

She chuckled and knocked into me, her shoulder bumping into mine. A cascade of sensation at the voluntary contact shimmered out from the touch point, a wave of fizzing awareness sliding down my arm and up my neck and across my chest.

She settled back into the couch, one hand occasionally testing Bones' patience by petting him as we binged the show. She laughed and grinned, commented on how much Dove reminded her of Leslie Knope, and how she imagined Wilder was actually a lot like Ron Swanson. I refilled my whiskey and teased her by bringing her two glasses of water.

But mostly, we were quiet.

After some amount of time, a soft weight pressed into my shoulder. *Her head.* She'd fallen asleep and her head now rested against me.

A sharp longing hit me. I breathed out like I would if I were queasy. She was so stubborn and beautiful and hard and soft and *everything*.

I'd never wanted anyone or anything the way I'd wanted her, and I couldn't tell if this restlessness to haul her into my arms was new and real or just a bizarre form of nostalgia.

Damn, but it would be so much better if it were nostalgia.

I should wake her and help her get to bed. Or I could carry her there, though now that she was on the mend, I didn't want her to wake and feel I'd crossed a line.

Or I could stay right here for as long as she needs me to.

So I did.

CHAPTER EIGHTEEN

Jess

The TV was dark when I woke from a nap of undetermined length and slowly stretched my arms overhead. Bones' purr activated when I moved, part greeting and part rebuke, and I leaned down to kiss his head and further terrorize him.

When I sat up, I realized just what I'd been doing—I'd been sleeping on Beast. On *Jude.* I'd had my head resting fully against him, and he'd stayed there.

Now he sat with his elbows on his knees and his glass dangling between two fingers.

Tenderness laced with embarrassment looped around my chest. I'd been *on* him, and he hadn't said a word. I hadn't worn a watch, nor had I checked the time before I passed out against him, so who knew how long he'd endured me invading his space.

I stood, wishing my sleepy mind would find the right

words, but decided to take a moment. I used the bathroom, splashed water on my face, and emerged to find him still sitting there in the dim glow of the dying fireplace and only the stove light in the kitchen.

His face tipped up as I approached, and his brows rose as I took the glass and set it down, then stepped between his legs. My heart beat fast and I was possibly out of my mind, but instead of second-guessing, I steadied myself on one of his immovable shoulders. The other hand came to his cheek, my short-trimmed nails gliding over his beard before settling against it.

"Thank you."

He shook his head, forever unwilling to acknowledge he might deserve thanks, but then leaned his head, pressed against my hand like he wanted to feel it more distinctly. I could swear his giant cat had done the same thing the day I'd met him. These two were just... precious. And what a wild feeling to experience, wasn't it?

I should've stepped away then. I should never have encroached on his personal bubble like this, or touched his face in such an intimate way, but it felt like I had the right to after he'd literally bathed me and seen me at what was very close to my worst these last few days. This dreamlike moment with gauzy, dim light and quiet between us made the barriers disintegrate, and the undeniable shift in me take hold.

The hang of his head and the shadows under his eyes were things I hadn't noticed before my time here, but I hadn't been looking.

And if I had? Would I have been glad he looked restless and sleepless? Would I have been happy he seemed to be lost?

No.

The truth echoed like a word shouted into a ravine. A place in me emptied out of the vitriol and hatred I'd let loose, now reverberating back at me. *No.* If I'd known why he was grieving, I wouldn't have been glad. And I would've laid off him.

But God forgive me, if I hadn't known... I might've reveled in it. I might've had the nasty satisfaction that came when your enemy was knocked down a peg.

This man?

Was he really my enemy?

The silence had crowded in around us, night blanketing the world and maybe because of this, I let myself ask him, "Why?"

The intensity baked into the fabric of his character didn't waver, nor did his eyes on mine. I willed him to respond—to understand what I was asking and tell me the answer I'd wanted for years.

Nothing came. He only stared into me, seeing past whatever I'd set in front of him down to my broken little heart, and then he shook his head. My chest might've been caving in, a sink hole right in the middle, eating away at more and more of me the longer he stayed quiet.

His large, warm hand covered mine where it still cupped his bearded cheek, and he pressed it more firmly against him before he pulled it away and gently guided it back to my side.

"We should be able to drive out tomorrow. I'll get you home."

Why this crushed me, I couldn't have explained for all the world. Maybe because I'd genuinely thought he'd tell me something new. I'd hoped, at least for a fleeting few seconds, he would give me *something* beyond the stonewall he'd shoved in my face for years.

I swallowed hard and nodded, then stepped away. "Right."

Before I reached the hallway, his low voice said, "You won't want to hear it."

I glanced at him over my shoulder, those coal-dark eyes burning back at me. Under another moon, maybe I would've stood my ground and pushed back on this nonsense, but I couldn't right now.

The fortitude to go toe-to-toe with Beast eluded me, and though his words were softly spoken, they had the Beast edge to them. This wasn't Jude anymore.

Jude was the man who'd taken care of me so faithfully the last few days despite how I'd barged in on his mountain sanctuary. Jude had made homemade bread and stew and watched my favorite show with me. Jude had let me touch his face.

But Beast had answered just now, harkening back to the forever rift between us that kept us from getting past anything and clinging to the hurt—or at least it did me. He had something to say, and I'd known it from Day One, but he'd refused to tell me what it was. He'd hidden it away, and I didn't understand why, especially now after so long, he wouldn't just be honest.

I slipped into bed after rushing through cleaning up in the bathroom and marveling once again at the fact he'd had a spare toothbrush and little travel toothpaste. My face would probably never forgive me for neglecting it these last few days. I needed to tell Jo she should put that in one of her books—the heroine gets stuck somewhere and instead of it being super cute and cuddly, she doesn't brush her teeth, her face breaks out because the hero doesn't have her normal skincare prod- ucts, she can't see because her contacts have dried into shriveled little husks, and she ends up looking like a foul-smelling ghoul who can barely see a foot in front of her by the end of her little stranded in a cabin adventure. *How romantic.*

But somehow, Beast had provided everything I could need, even if they weren't the same products I used. I tried not to think about how his deodorant smelled so good and I knew it smelled amazing on him rather vividly after the close contact of the last few days.

All that goodness was fading too rapidly in my mind as his words played again. *You won't want to hear it.*

What did it mean? And what kind of excuse was that?

Since when had this man considered what I wanted? If he had...

I shook that off. I was years beyond wishing for a different outcome with Kurt. I'd begged and pleaded with God and the Universe and whoever would listen to make my fiancé bold and come back to me—not to give up and hide away and become my ex.

But in the years since I'd accepted that if he'd left like that then, there was likely no magic in a marriage license that would've prevented him from leaving at some point later. I'd come to terms with the truth I'd wanted to be engaged so much. He'd done it for me, but not because he'd wanted it. And wasn't I glad I hadn't gone through a wedding and maybe even having a kid with him only to have him leave like my own father had?

I curled in on myself, the pain wrapping around me a visceral reminder of why I didn't let myself think about any of this. Kurt wasn't a part of my life anymore and I much preferred to avoid thinking about him, but how could I do that when his former best friend was constantly in my face? And even when he was standing across the conference room, a man of his size always seemed to be shoving his existence into my awareness.

Exhaling through the tears tracking down my face, I made a promise. I wouldn't be fooled by this bizarre blip in our relationship. I wouldn't let my guard down with him again, whether I woke up delirious from a high fever or actually escaped his mountain man cabin.

I'd go back to hating Jude "Beast" Rawlins, because the alternative was far too painful.

CHAPTER NINETEEN

Jude

Some people play their feelings close to the vest.

Someone could spend an hour with Tristan and never know how he actually felt about something unless he decided to reveal it. In a very different way, the same could be said for Bruce. You'd think he was casual and charming and then all of a sudden you'd face a reckoning you never saw coming.

Jess Korbel? The woman radiated her emotions.

She broadcasted them on the world wide web and to the far corners of the Earth. So when she stormed into the kitchen at zero-seven, I had no doubt my choice of words last night had come back to haunt me.

Thoroughly.

If I wanted to poke the beast, I'd probably say something like, "Morning, sunshine." But as a beast myself, I knew better.

"I'm ready."

I grabbed my keys. I would come back to the cabin after taking her home rather than try to prep everything I usually did before leaving. Plus, I needed some more food since I'd run through things a little faster than usual once she'd gotten her appetite back.

Bones sat in his triangle kitty pose and watched us for a moment. Jess moved toward the door, then turned back and said, "It was nice to meet you, Bones. You're a good guy," then flung the door open and marched out into the snow.

Bones and I shared a look before he stood and sauntered toward the living room, and I followed Jess out.

"You lead the way. I'll follow, and if you need a tow, I've got what we need." I hoped the roads wouldn't be so bad, but there were a few miles up this way that wouldn't have been plowed by the county. If we could make it out of there, we'd be fine.

Since I'd shoveled the driveway yesterday when the snow slowed, it wouldn't be as treacherous either. I'd sprinkled sand down to help traction, too.

She didn't speak, only paused for a moment before getting into her car and turning it on.

It was mercy and punishment we were in separate cars. I could feel her fuming as we descended the mountain slowly but surely. Whatever numbing agent that'd spread over me in the last few months as Omi had declined, then passed, had been washed away and I felt everything. Even her frustration through layers of metal and paint, as fictional as it sounded. Every moment between us the last few days had burned a hole through skin and sinew.

The roads were remarkably clear and only lightly wet when we reached the canyon, thankfully. We absolutely could've made the drive yesterday.

But I'm glad we didn't.

I'd spent too much time thinking about her hand on my cheek. Her warm palm against the bristles of my beard, and the intensity in her eyes could've made me crawl for her... I'd been so close to telling her exactly why. *Why.*

But what I'd said was right. She wouldn't want to hear the real reason. And yet, was this better? Was her storming around furious with me, *hating* me once again, worth it? Was there any difference between never telling her why and being the villain and finally admitting everything and her hating me anyway?

My pride.

My heart.

By the time I pulled up behind her at her little bungalow in one of the cheery Silverton neighborhoods within walking distance from downtown, I'd decided. I'd tell her everything, and she could deal with it however she wanted.

If it meant she only had more fuel to hate me, then so be it.

She slammed the car door. "You really didn't need to follow me all the way here. Obviously, I made it just fine."

Everything in me wound tight and words stuck in my mouth. "I—"

She rolled her eyes. "I appreciate everything you've done for me, okay? I can't imagine how hard it was to have me in your space all weekend. But now we're back in the real world, let's just go back to doing what we do best."

My heart thudded heavy in my chest. "What's that?"

Her shoulders rose and fell in a big exhale. "Hating each other."

She turned and carefully plodded up the short walkway

and began fiddling with her keys. She couldn't just go, could she? Not like this.

Once her door opened, panic pushed me into action.

"Wait. Jess, just wait a minute."

She turned, tucking her arms around her, and did as I asked.

Might be the last time.

"I reported Kurt because he assaulted a woman while we were TDY. What I said really happened."

I'd said as much before. She should know this. But I had to start somewhere, and just now, the embers from each moment of the weekend were stoking into something more.

Her lips thinned, and by the set of her jaw, I could tell she was clenching it. I didn't have much time.

"I told him he had to confess to you or I'd tell you. And since you knew Kurt as well as he let anyone know him, I'm guessing you can imagine how well that went over."

She shifted on her feet but didn't storm away, so I'd take that. She wasn't rejecting the very notion that my version of events was true. *Progress.*

"I never did any of it to hurt you, but I wasn't going to let him hurt anyone else, and frankly, I hated—" I swallowed, willing this next part to come out right. "I hated that he was cheating on you. And he made it clear it wasn't a new thing."

She blinked rapidly, then nodded once, but stood strong. My heart pounded in a riot of anxiety, hanging on this moment and her response.

"Why wouldn't you have said that? I know you told me you didn't lie, but he said—" She shook her head and looked to the sky. "God, he was such an unbelievable asshole."

I didn't verbalize my assent, but there was nothing I agreed with more. Distance from him and from the relationship we'd had before he'd made clear he was never really my friend had shown me he was never someone who had any but his own good at heart. Retrospect had highlighted and underlined it.

She straightened, and something about her posture made me certain she wanted to ask me something more. I wanted to tell her whatever she wanted—I needed it out there between us so I could move on.

"Go ahead. Whatever you want," I prompted.

Her gaze found mine. "If you knew he was cheating, why didn't you say anything? We were friends."

Guilt and regret sliced at me, the familiar sensation cutting deeper after the last few days. "I never had proof before that TDY. And I... I was worried about my motives."

Her brow furrowed. "What does that mean?"

Shit. Here we go.

I rocked to my toes, then planted my feet again on her wet front walk, not daring to approach her any closer. My pulse pounded in my ears and heat climbed my neck. Omi's words rang in the back of my mind—*Don't hide away. Open your heart.* I grunted through the thickness in my throat and ran a hand through my hair, then jumped off the cliff.

"Because I'd been in love with you for a long time. I didn't want you with him." I sucked in a breath. A mile-long sprint sounding like a cakewalk about now. Would she hate me even more? Or... not? I pushed on, forced out the rest. "I couldn't be sure if I was making things up—creating reasons you shouldn't be together, or whether what I'd noticed was reality. Not until I witnessed it myself."

At the word *love*, she'd bent, almost like the sounds had formed a fist and struck an uppercut straight to her ribs. She bowed over thirty degrees, and her face was utterly stricken.

My chest cinched tight with worry and I bit down on

the need to go to her—to take her by the shoulders and shake her, to make her understand me. To beg her to see I hadn't meant to hurt her or betray her, even though now, all these years later, my choices looked like anything but love.

I had to get out of here. The ticking clock had officially struck midnight.

"I'm sorry." It wasn't enough, and I'd vowed to say everything. She hadn't spoken, so what was there to lose now? Why not lay it out? Then I'd go. "I regret that I let my messed-up feelings distract me. And I'll never forgive myself for it. But in the end, I don't regret getting him removed from the unit nor do I regret that you didn't marry him because he was the biggest idiot I've ever met."

I let out a string of expletives before I could stop myself, my face and hands hot as my heart cranked with adrenaline.

"He had *you*, and that wasn't enough, and Jess..." I swore again, overcome and nearly out of words. "You have to know that you're... you're everything. And that utter trash pile of a human being squandered what you gave him, and it said nothing about you. It only proved he was worthless by choice."

She made a sound then, something like a groan or a gasp, and I *had* to go. I'd said more than I'd intended and now, I couldn't wait another second.

"I'm sorry."

And I was out. Back in the truck and on autopilot to the cabin. Forget stopping by the market or treating myself to takeout or anything else. I had to get out of here, out of Silverton, and back to the safety and solitude of my cabin and my cat and the life I'd had before she'd shown up and ruined everything.

CHAPTER TWENTY

Jess

I didn't know how long I stood on my front porch, frozen by Jude's words and—well, really, just the words.

I'd been in love with you for a long time.

I'd been in love with you for a long time.

I'd been in love with you for a long time.

They replayed on a loop, the rest of it fading into the background, until my phone buzzed in my pocket. When I finally looked, I had six messages from Dove saying she and Elise were going to bring me dinner whenever I was back, and to let them know.

Did I want them here? Didn't I need time to process this?

I huffed an odd laugh. No. I needed someone to help me make sense of it. I needed a chance to rant. And Elise and Dove would let me do that.

I replied they could come whenever they were off work

—I'd be home all day and ready for them whenever they arrived. I'd already texted the office to tell them I wouldn't be in until tomorrow. It might've felt good to go to work, but something told me I wouldn't be able to focus with Beast's—Jude's—words floating around my head.

After a long shower during which I did not miss the scent of Beast's soap, and purely appreciated the presence of shampoo made for a human woman and not something better suited to cattle hair, I slumped into bed fully intending to nap for as long as possible and forget about all of humanity for a few hours.

I'd been in love with you for a long time.

And I didn't want you with him.

You're everything.

There they came, like good little soldiers in formation. Each sentence flashing through my mind paired with the image of him, his face in absolute misery and his hand fisting, then flexing as he confessed the truth he'd held locked inside himself for years. He'd been vehement, pleading, and flushed from the neckline of his T-shirt to his hair after he'd said those words.

Sleep was a rude jerk and played keep away, so I sat there letting the disbelief grip me, then the denial. Finally, I got up and decided I'd clean everything in my place before my friends arrived just in case there were any fun germs hanging out from before I'd left—aka in another lifetime.

How was I supposed to function normally when that man just said he'd been *in love* with me? How could I possibly wrap my head around his words when he'd treated me with such glaring disdain for so long?

Could I even believe him?

Beast wasn't someone to talk for talking's sake. He didn't speak even when spoken to half the time and I didn't see what he had to gain from lying about something like that. If anything, it put him at a disadvantage. Admitting he'd loved me, even in obvious past tense, made everything so...

So...

Messy.

Confusing.

Utterly incomprehensible.

By the time Dove and Elise arrived, I was crawling out of my skin and ready to get some feedback from someone outside my own head. I'd also escalated from sadness and disbelief to... well, really, to anger.

Because how dare he.

It'd become a chant, a low-level refrain in the vein of one of his classic, barely intelligible grunts—*how dare he, how dare he, how dare he.*

It'd built and built, each passing second, each remembrance of his agonized face and that tone weaving together to create the parachute, and by the time my friends saw my face, I'd jumped fully out of the logic plane and was spiraling on gusts of confusion and untethered, irrational fury.

Dove bustled in with a large bag sporting the Guac logo splashed across it, and the sight instantly brightened my life, even through the storm of anger banging cymbals in my mind.

Nothing would help the situation like chips and guac. Since my appetite had fully returned and my stomach appeared to be behaving normally, I would drown at least some of my rage in avocado-based therapy.

Elise followed, brow furrowed and face downcast as she tapped at her phone before slipping it into her pocket and looking up right as Dove rushed me and pressed her palm to my forehead, nurse mode activated.

"Oh my gosh, you're alive. I thought for sure he would've skinned you and boiled you for stew." She squeezed me tight, then leaned back and squeezed my shoulders, then my biceps, then wrists then hands before holding my palms up, then flipping them over to inspect my unpolished nails. She raised her phone and shone a light in my eyes for a second before I flinched away. She grabbed my head and steadied me, studying my pupils before saying, "Okay, you seem okay, but are you okay? Because I would not be okay."

I laughed, grateful for her sense of drama and humor, not to mention her instant care-taking that provided the perfect momentary distraction and disarmed me for a minute.

"Seriously, it's amazing you two made it out alive," Elise added, a small grin on her stunning face.

"I'm amazed, too, though it probably helped that I was either unconscious or delirious most of the time."

And... had I? Somewhere in me, I recognized that part of who I was didn't make it out. Jude had steadily throttled the hatred out of me with his attentiveness, his gentleness, his homemade bread, and wearing his fluffy boy cat on his shoulders.

No. No. We do not think of the cat or we lose all ability to think clearly.

Dove settled the bag on my counter. "Not even lying, I knew you were in bad shape based on your texts."

Elise nodded. "Totally."

"Because they were short?"

Dove chuckled, pulling out a large bag of chips with a splotchy patchwork of grease stains on the sides. "No.

Because you were only reassuring us you were fine and not ranting about how awful he is."

I forced a laugh. "Yeah. He was…" How could I explain it? "He was actually really good to me."

Maybe that's what sent me through the loop-the-loops of anger yet again… he could be so lovely. He'd been so far from the beast he'd embodied, and yet our history… he'd loved me, and he'd let us go on like this?

Clearly, the love had died out at some point.

The silence in response to my statement had me looking up to find them both frozen, Dove holding a container of guacamole aloft, and Elise holding two glasses she must've just taken out of the open cupboard in front of her.

"What?"

"Beast was *good to you*? Should we have you evaluated for Stockholm's Syndrome?"

Elise cracked up, but Dove held steady. I rolled my eyes at her, though based on how I'd ranted about him in the past, and the many times they'd seen how tense any situation became when both of us were present, I couldn't fault her for the assumption.

"He didn't hold me hostage, for one, and two… he was great. And you know I wouldn't say that if it weren't completely true because I have nothing but contempt for the man."

Not true anymore, and you know it.

Ugh. There came the feelings to mess everything up.

"Wait, you do not sound like you have contempt. You sound… something." Elise narrowed her eyes.

Dove finished unloading the bag of takeout and gestured for us to take our meals as we moved to my small dining table.

Elise poured waters and raised her glass. "I'm sorry this

is water, but I figured after being sick, margaritas were a no go."

"Correct. Rain check on margaritas. This woman needs hydration and rest and to tell us why she's conflicted over a man she has hated for years after a few nights at his mountain cabin." Dove wiggled her brows like something salacious happened in the last few days.

How to begin? *Well, he gave me a bath and carried me to the bed and then, just before it all ended, he told me he used to be in love with me. Neat, right?*

When I didn't speak, Elise set her hand on my arm where it rested on the table. "Hey, whatever's going on, you can tell us."

The compassion in her eyes made my heart ache. These women were pure gold, and I was so deeply grateful to have them in my life.

"He really was great. It was confusing and I feel upside-down. We were almost like friends by the end, and then—" I dove a chip into the container of guac. "Then I asked him why he did what he did."

Eyes wide, Dove urged, "And?"

"And he said I wouldn't like what he had to say. So I went to bed angry and didn't sleep the whole night, and we drove back to town, and he followed me all the way home to make sure I was safe and when we got here, I told him off *again*, and he finally told me why."

"*And!?*" Elise this time.

I leaned back in the chair, the weight of these emotions and lack of sleep hitting me all at once. "And he told me Kurt really had assaulted someone. That he, Beast, always suspected he'd cheated on me. And that Kurt was an idiot for doing that."

"That steaming pile of dung," Dove said through clenched teeth.

"I'm so sorry." Elise's eyes shone with sympathy.

This bit, they already knew from what I'd said at book club. Not the Jude point-of-view, but the gist of it. Now came the hardest part.

"When I asked him why he never told me Kurt was cheating, do you know what that total jerk face had to say to me?" I said, my voice far more watery than angry, because even that heat couldn't burn through the tenderness I felt now.

They waited, rapt.

"He said he couldn't trust himself—that there was no concrete evidence, and he wasn't sure if it was just wishful thinking."

"What? Why?" Dove asked, echoing Elise's expression.

My stomach pitched but my heart flipped when I explained, "Because he was in love with me. And he didn't want me with Kurt from the beginning."

Jaws dropped. Eyes grew wide. Dove shoved up from the table and paced.

"Wait. No." She circled back to the table. "Waiiiit."

"Seriously? He said that? Just... said it?" Elise asked, as dumbfounded as I still felt.

I nodded, relieved they were as shocked as I felt, and feeling a new wave of frustration crash in me. "I mean, who does that?"

Dove nodded. "Seriously. Who does that."

Elise sat quietly, clearly still absorbing the news.

"He never once expressed interest in me. And now, he's acting like he was so in love with me he didn't trust himself to know whether his best friend was cheating? Did I enter an alternate universe?" The heat in me stoked to a flame.

"I'll admit, I'm hung up on the fact that he's saying he loved you and yet he acts like you're radioactive when you're within ten feet of each other." Elise dunked a chip in her guac. "Damn, I wish we had margaritas for this."

I laughed for a second before continuing with her thought. "I've been thinking about that a lot. Obviously, I went to his cabin before I knew I was sick when I realized I'd been so brutally honest with him while he was struggling with grieving. And I don't feel proud of that."

Elise reached for me, setting a hand on my arm. "Aw, my friend, you are amazing for doing that. As rough a time as he's having, and I don't want to discount that because it sounds like the grief is significant, I do want to acknowledge that you have been incredibly civil to him *most* of the time. After your assignment together, things boiled over, and I don't know if you can be blamed for that."

I exhaled slowly. "I don't know. I'm starting to wonder whether I'm the cause of so much of this head-butting and meanness. Like, did I create this rift between us and he just... responded in kind?"

I hated the thought, but after his kindness to me all weekend, and then his parting shot... I couldn't turn away from it. If he'd really felt that way, but I'd been so unwilling to hear him out in my own grief and disbelief over Kurt leaving... had I caused all of this?

"Mmm, no. I call BS on that. It's not like he was just gruff and avoided you. Sometimes, he was actively a jerk, right?" Elise asked as Dove sat back down.

"Yes. But I... I've lashed out at him so much. I just don't know."

We were quiet, crunching on chips and likely all wishing our water would turn into wine. Dove broke the silence first.

"Let's say it's true... what does it change? Here you are now, and you've been nothing short of enemies for the last five-plus years until approximately ninety-six hours ago. So... what? It's not like you were in love with him, too. It's not like it changes anything, other than maybe giving us insight. Unless..." Her blue eyes skewered into me. "Unless you had feelings for him, too."

I scoffed. "I was engaged to someone else. So no. I didn't."

But what I didn't say was that I had liked him almost instantly. His giant hand had swallowed mine in a shake that first day and I'd been compelled to say his name out loud because it suited him so perfectly—I didn't know how I knew that, I just did. And then he'd gotten this pleased look, almost like he'd enjoyed me saying it.

But along came Kurt, and somehow, inexplicably, he'd worn me all the way down. And he became the person on whom I pinned my hopes of finding an anchor and a solution to what I'd seen as the problem of my solitude and loneliness. And Jude never said a thing—never made a move, never even hinted.

Until now.

But that was in the past. Likely so far in the past he couldn't even recall the feeling of loving me.

And all I could feel was anger that he'd allowed me to hate him for so long without telling me the truth. And maybe more so, anger that I'd let myself be so awful for so long.

CHAPTER TWENTY-ONE

Jude

K enny cradled Bones. "You are the sweetest baby. I don't know why you live with him when I keep telling you I'll take you home and treat you right. I will love you and be the best cat dad and keep your fur untangled and—"

"Leave my cat alone, Barbie." The man was incessant with his declarations of devotion to my animal.

"It's a little much," Cookie agreed, though the smile on his stupid handsome face said he got a kick out of Kenny's ridiculousness.

"Everyone has an awesome pet. Tristan has Junie. You have Bones. Stone has Bear. I want an awesome pet." He sank down onto the worn leather couch and crossed his arms like a child.

"Three people is hardly *everyone*," Cookie rightly pointed out. "I don't, but only because I've been international so often."

"Thanks so much, *Jean-Luc*. I am not being literal. I'm just whining because I can tell Beast is beasting and we're not about to get much out of him until he warms up to the sad reality that other humans exist and he's going to have to embrace it." One dirty blond eyebrow arched at me.

Cookie cleared his throat to cover a laugh, but I heard it.

"I told you to come up here." But now they were here, I wasn't so sure I agreed with the me of six hours ago who'd been in total panic mode after confessing my past and completely no longer relevant feelings to Jess.

Kenny rose and sauntered toward me with his pretty boy smile. Cookie followed suit, rounding the kitchen island and leaning against the counter. I was now as cornered as I could get by my two so-called friends.

"Tell your Kenny-bear what's wrong, Beasty."

Cookie laughed outright. "Good grief, man, you want him to murder you."

Kenny beamed. There was that famous Barbie smile.

"He sends out the SOS and now he's mad about it. But I'm here to tell you, your instincts were good. You're never wrong to ask for help, and isn't that kind of the motto we've all agreed to? Not to go it alone?" His grin had dwindled and the sincerity in his voice couldn't be missed.

"We did. You're right." And that's why I'd texted them. Everyone else was already busy with their duties prepping for the film fest and all the madness to come with that. Plus it wasn't really fair to send out an SOS to everyone when I'd tucked myself an hour outside of town.

Cookie nodded, as on board with the agreement as any of us.

"So..." Kenny prodded.

I shook my head because he was never one to *not* push and I was never one to *not* react in kind.

"Long story short?" I asked, hoping they'd allow it.

Cookie dropped his chin to agree and Kenny shrugged like it was a letdown, but he wasn't going to fight me just yet.

"You know Jess was here the last few days. She was out of it until last night. We had a good time watching TV and just hanging out. It was... amicable."

I stopped. They did nothing to interrupt me. *Jerks.*

"Then she asked me what happened years back." They'd learned the skeleton version only recently. "I admitted part of all that was how I used to be in love with her."

A thrill chased by dread rolled from my head down to pool in my feet. I was glued to the spot, breathless and waiting for some cosmic crack of thunder in the sky now that I'd said it aloud twice.

Somehow, I'd put the panic out of my mind, but there was no hiding from it now. Every emotion I'd locked down over the years had burrowed through my defenses and here they were, bleeding out everywhere. First with Jess, and now with these two.

Kenny rolled his lips between his teeth and Cookie didn't move. His brutally handsome face—and I thought this as a man who could recognize a gorgeous human being when he saw one—just... looked at me.

But the little pressure cooker inside of Kenny exploded. "Holy crap. Yes. *Yes.* You're in love with Jess? And you told her? Are we having a wedding?" He started hopping up and down like a complete idiot.

"No."

Cookie dropped his face into his hands. "You have a death wish."

In seconds, Kenny was shaking me by the shoulders. "You love someone! This is fantastic!"

I didn't speak. He needed a moment to get it out of his system and I wasn't going to waste my breath convincing him while he was prancing around my kitchen like he'd just won the lottery. He had no idea the utter chaos pinging around in my chest—relief from sharing it, but instant awareness of the folly of the admission, too.

In another minute or so, his fervor died down and he leaned on the counter with his elbows and sobered up a bit.

"Okay, I'll shut up. But I think the question is valid."

Cookie scoffed, sounding every bit the half-Frenchman he was and then some. "The *Are we having a wedding* question?"

Kenny rolled his eyes. "No. The *Do you still love her?* question. Which I think is at the heart of all of this."

I took a slug of my beer, then realized I'd never even offered them a drink when they'd arrived. They'd hugged me, then Kenny bee-lined for Bones, and Cookie had taken in the show.

"Beer?"

They both assented, so I gave myself the minute to pull two bottles from the fridge and uncap them. They took their drinks and swallowed down some of the local brew, generously giving me another few seconds.

But now, time was up.

"I'm not sure it matters how I feel. She looked..." Her beautiful face flashed into my mind, then the way she'd bent over like she might be ill from the news. "I don't think it matters."

"Hard disagree." Kenny's vehemence filled his words.

I sat back in the seat at the counter and studied the bottle in front of me, scratching at the edge of the label. "I was in love with her for years. Then everything went to hell, and she started hating me. I lived with that unrequited nonsense for so long, in some ways it was a relief. So I let myself hate her back. Embraced it. And promised myself I'd never beg her to forgive me or admit how I felt."

After a moment of silence, Cookie prodded. "But?"

My eyes shut and I felt the weight of everything I'd said and done the last few days. "But I have never truly hated her."

When I looked up, both men were staring at me. Luc's face had a serious but maybe pleased look and—I should've seen it coming—Kenny had a maniacal grin on his.

"Oh my dear, dear friend. There's only one thing to do," he said, all twinkling blue eyes and shiny white teeth, but with a side of psycho.

"What's that?" I scraped out, bracing for whatever madness he had in mind.

He sipped his beer, creating a dramatic beat, before setting the bottle down a little harder than he needed for an exclamation. "We make a plan to get the girl."

CHAPTER TWENTY-TWO

Jess

Saint Security had enough going on that no one stopped to ask me how things had gone at Beast's cabin. Everyone inquired about my health and Doc had double-checked I was feeling up to working, but otherwise we were all going in different directions in preparation for the film fest starting next week.

Celebrities would begin flooding Silverton in a matter of days, and the staff who tended to precede them, in a matter of hours. The resort and all local lodging were packed to the gills. Reservations at restaurants and any local events were nearly sold out. It would be a fantastic weekend for the small businesses in town, and as long as everything went well, Saint Security would be counted among them.

"Pop, you good?" Bruce asked after concluding the quick stand up we'd had to kick off the event schedule.

"Yes. All good."

And by that, I meant *mostly* good because I hadn't seen Beast and couldn't totally tell how I'd feel when I did.

Did I hate the man still?

... No?

No. I didn't.

Part of the issue rested in the reality that I really didn't know how I felt other than angry. So darn angry. And yes, by now, I'd had enough interactions with the unit psychologist back at EMU, and other wise types, I knew it was my default emotion these days, but still. Talking with Dove and Elise hadn't helped me ease up on those feelings, though I had worked through some of my brain fog and developed a list of questions the man would be held to account for.

He would *not* avoid telling me the truth for another five years.

He'd let it all hang out yesterday, so to speak, and now he was going to let it hang... further out. Okay, ew, not loving the metaphor, but the point stood. Beast owed me a little bit more than "I used to be in love with you sorry, not sorry, but kind of sorry," and I probably owed him another apology.

Bruce gave me his friendly boss smile and moved on to check in with Dorian, who'd showed up for the meeting and pleasantly surprised us all. He looked strong and steady, and having Bear in the office was always a treat. Since he'd showed, he must be working at least part of the event, which meant he had to be doing even better than I'd realized. Warmth filled me as I looked at him standing tall, his beard and hair trimmed and clothes neat, and nodding softly in time with whatever Bruce and Wilder were saying.

"Hey, Pop," Kenny said, sidling up next to me.

"Barbie." The irony that his name was Kenneth and his

nickname was Barbie was... not irony. It was the root of his nickname. Everything about him said sunshine and blond and brightness. But Kenny did a lot more than "Beach" for his job and his IQ was definitely on the high end of those in this room, which was saying something since anyone who worked as an operator was screened for IQ among many other things. Basically, we were a giant pack of super capable smarties and some of us could even hold a conversation.

Me? Depended on the day.

"Have you seen my dear friend Beast?"

My head whipped toward him. "Why would you ask me?"

For all he knew, I hadn't seen him since I'd left his cabin. With this gossiping horde, there was no way every last one of us hadn't heard I'd been there during the storm, but still. He didn't need to know how Beast's name was rattling around my head along with at least twenty questions.

Kenny shrugged a shoulder. "Oh, I don't know. Seems like you've been together more often. Just asking." He held up his hands, all innocence. "Didn't mean anything by it."

I glared at him. "Good to know."

He flashed his bright grin. "Oh, look, there he is now."

As usual, Beast's bulk literally blotted out the doorway for a moment before he moved into the conference room. Our eyes snagged and my stomach flipped.

The feeling invading me was not hatred. It wasn't the usual knee-jerk repulsion and fight-or-flight response begging me to spew something mean or bolt and make for my office.

Instead it was... warm.

Soft, somehow.

Confusing.

I couldn't have been sure he actually acknowledged me, but somehow during the seconds our gazes had locked, I'd *felt* his greeting. Or, if not an actual *hello,* then a proverbial one I could almost hear.

Then he joined Stone, Bruce, and Wilder, and extended a hand to Stone and—*oh.*

I sucked in a breath at the sight of Jude's wide smile as he shook Stone's hand and pulled him into a quick hug before releasing him and saying something just quietly enough I couldn't hear it over the din of conversation buzzing in the room.

I'd thought Jude was handsome the minute I met him, but I wasn't the kind to get mushy for someone based on looks alone. Then Kurt came in and just... blocked him out. We were friendly until something shifted and... well, now I wondered if maybe it shifted when he caught feelings for me? Or, was it right around when I'd gotten engaged? I couldn't recall exactly because it had been gradual but inexorable.

And all of it led to me standing here gazing at a man I'd convinced myself I hated for the last five years with decidedly non-hatey feelings.

What a mess.

"He looks good, doesn't he?" Cookie asked, his words quiet as usual.

He was more like Tristan but not as introverted or shy. Simply less in-your-face than many of my friends, though none of them were all that bothersome. Although maybe now that I wasn't fuming over Beast all the time, they'd be more grating?

"Stone?" I asked, since we were both watching the small

circle chat and he couldn't possibly be asking me if I thought Beast looked good. *Why would he ask me that?*

"Yeah. Proud of him." And his tone and expression spoke to the sentiment. He had a soft smile on his face and a genuinely affectionate feel to his words.

"Me, too." I didn't know Dorian as well as some of the guys, including Cookie, but I'd witnessed some of his ups and more of his downs the last few years. I'd seen him struggle and work to get to a place where he could even leave his property. The fact that he was here was just freaking great.

Cookie excused himself, and when I looked up, Jude was coming toward me. His face was typically unreadable, but now, this countenance gave me more mysterious vibes than how I used to interpret it, which was something along the lines of assuming he was lightly fantasizing about murdering me.

But now... maybe he'd been fantasizing about something else entirely... something equally passionate but far less likely to end in literal death. I swallowed hard, the thought sending my heart to my throat as my pulse knocked up and I braced for the first words between us since his confession.

But none came.

He just stood there, and even crossed his arms.

What?

He was giving me that impatient stare, and it had to be thanks to my poor sleep and coming off of having the flu or whatever virus I'd hosted at his cabin, but every bit of frustration and anger I'd felt in the wake of his truth bomb exploded inside me.

"What do you want?"

His eyes narrowed.

"I don't have time to pretend I can read your mind.

Obviously, I've failed spectacularly at that for the last few years."

"'Bout a decade, I'd say."

The deadpan tone. *Funny guy.*

I gritted my teeth. "I'm sorry, but in what universe do you walk up to me with an attitude? *I* should be the one having an attitude!"

My voice had raised just a touch, but most people had filtered out of the room, apparently not interested in witnessing our face off.

His eyes blinked slowly—pointedly. "Aren't you?"

A bitter laugh escaped, and I pressed my hands to my eyes, grateful I hadn't bothered with makeup today.

"Maybe I am, Beast." Defeat dropped over my head like water from a leaking faucet. "I don't get it."

Any trace of smugness vanished on his stern face. "What don't you get?"

I exhaled, suddenly completely exhausted. "All of it. And I feel like you could explain it to me but based on whatever dynamic you've walked in with today, I don't think I have much chance."

He stared back at me, that obnoxiously big brain of his ticking away almost audibly. "Name a time and place and you can ask me whatever you want."

My brows rose in surprise, and I scrambled through my schedule until I found the only empty window I could think of. "After the opening gala. I'm off at ten. We could meet in the bar at the resort."

He nodded, gave me one last lingering look, then walked out.

I was watching him go when he turned. "Just make sure you're ready to be honest, too."

The challenge in his voice, the edge saying *I bet you*

won't dare tell the truth, had me readying my internal forces. I wasn't going to cow to this man who I thought was my enemy but was maybe never actually that. I wasn't going to let him win the honesty competition.

He could ask me anything he wanted. *I*, for one, had nothing to hide.

CHAPTER TWENTY-THREE

Jude

Each of us at Saint had a few specialty designations that came from our time on active duty, or in Eddie James-Williamson's case, service. One of mine was all things tech, so much of my time would be spent watching camera feeds and surveilling the film fest on a larger scale, though I had a few shifts of event security to help mix things up. Staring at a screen for hours could get really mind-numbing.

It was a bit more fun when the likes of world-famous Jack McKean and hilarious and beloved Jenna Halter were in their black tie attire wandering a red carpet, except you could never just watch the celebrities. Proper surveillance meant keeping an eye on the entire scene and anticipating the unseen.

Some celebrities had hired us for extra event security, but some had brought in their own. For one of the festival's big sponsoring studios debuting two movies—one feature film and one documentary—they had hired a private security firm not unlike Saint, though much bigger.

And with a far more... gray reputation.

As the lead on event security and official partners with the local sheriff's department and city, Bruce, Wilder, and Tristan were meeting with the Blackthorne Security reps this afternoon and they'd be inviting these guys and their whole team to join us for a drink at Craic.

The shakeup to our usual Friday night custom was supposed to pave the way for a positive working dynamic for the next week of the festival. The celebrities wouldn't arrive until Sunday night at the earliest, and even though some paparazzi were trickling in early, most of them would wait until the money makers showed up.

This change to the schedule was why I walked in a few minutes later than right on time instead of going to hang with Stone. I usually left this space to Jess if she was in town because it wasn't worth the hassle of showing up only for her to storm off.

But tonight, I didn't think she'd leave. We hadn't gotten to our heart to heart yet, but she wasn't running or backing down now. And she knew things had changed, even if she couldn't figure out how. I'd taken care of her and admitted to past feelings... but I had to assume she didn't quite remember everything she'd said to me when she was delirious with fever.

"What a way to go." The things admitted to—not just attraction but *wanting* me. It didn't change everything, but it did mean I didn't resist Kenny's suggestion that I attempt to "get the girl" now. While I wasn't confident, I was strangely... hopeful.

For what? I couldn't pin it down completely, only that I

wasn't dreading seeing her because of the inevitability she'd leave with a snarl the instant she saw me. She wouldn't tonight—I'd put money on it.

The bar was even more crowded than usual for a Friday night with the extra Blackthorne personnel standing around. Bruce, Wilder, Adam, and Kenny appeared to be playing host at a handful of tables, setting down pitchers of local beer and water and doing their smiley, friendly thing.

It wasn't until I saw Pop that I realized something was wrong.

As a highly trained operator, Jessica Korbel didn't cower, but one look and I could tell her whole being was broadcasting that something was very off. The rigidity in her posture, the blank mask on her face, and the way she'd glued her hands to her sides. I'd seen her upset enough to know her default would normally be wrapping her arms around herself but for whatever reason, it looked like she'd forbidden herself from doing so.

Then my gaze shifted to the person smirking at her and the blood drained from my face in the same instant I started moving. Every instinct told me to hitch her over my shoulder and haul her away from here.

Kurt didn't look all that different except for slightly longer hair and a longer goatee than he'd had when he left the unit. His body language and his "panty charmer" smile, as he'd disgustingly called it, were all too familiar.

I arrived just in time to hear him say, "Damn, Jessie. You look good." He must've seen me coming because he turned, and his grin widened. "And there's the hulking beast now."

Baser instincts said "Just deck him!" but I'd tamed those —at least for the most part—decades ago. Instead, I dipped my chin to acknowledge him, uninterested in giving him any fuel.

He'd burned everything between us long before he'd left Jess and blamed me for it. He'd lied repeatedly, and by the time I reported him, any good memories with him had turned to ash.

Now? I hardly felt anything for him. Not rage or anger or pity. But him next to Jess?

That turned my blood to lava in my veins, pumping slow, steady, but magma hot.

"Kurt."

I wouldn't give him the satisfaction of using his old unit name. None of us would. He'd become a PNG—persona non grata—and wouldn't be able to attend unit functions or reunions ever again. He'd thought he'd stay eligible, but as more truths came out after he left, he was out fully.

Jess must've missed all this, too, somehow.

"How fun to have the gang back together again," he said, and hooked an arm over Jess's shoulder. "I sure missed you, Jessie."

She hitched forward, almost like she'd dry-heaved. "Please remove your arm."

He made a face but did so.

Good to see he can listen now, at least.

"I guess you're both still bitter, huh? Silly me for imagining we'd all let water run under the bridge. But *I'm* not the one who couldn't handle losing a prize now, was I?" He raised one eyebrow at me like this would move me to respond.

It didn't.

I wasn't scared of Jess finding out he knew I'd been in love with her. He'd told her something along those lines when he'd claimed I didn't want them together. She must not've believed him based on her response to my confession, but he'd tried to place any blame fully on my shoulders. Technically, he wasn't wrong about my feelings, but it wasn't simply because I was a petty jerk who didn't want anyone to "have" her if I couldn't.

"Just do what you came to do and leave when the job's done. We'll play nice and won't even let on what a jerk you are."

Her words were completely calm, but her posture still had that stick-still quality to it.

"Aw, Jessie. Of course I'll do what I came to do. I'm with *Blackthorne*." He said it like it was something to be proud of and not where anyone with questionable ethics landed post-military. They were mercenaries at best.

"Don't say her name." It came out like a growl, completely unplanned, and I saw Jess stiffen next to me.

Kurt chuckled like my threat was empty. He had no idea how much I'd love an excuse to introduce his face to the pavement.

Jess didn't use words, but the ice in her voice and her total lack of acknowledging my statement effectively shut down any more comments I might've made.

"Good for you, Kurt. Glad you found your way."

Her eyes flicked to mine and her jaw flexed as she clenched it, then she turned on her heel and beelined for the table where her friends stood watching.

I tipped my head toward the women, whose eyes were all on me and Kurt. Dove grinned, Elise dipped her head, Nikki and Catherine offered soft smiles, and Jo and Winnie had already turned their attention to Jess as she arrived at the table.

"Pretty pathetic, man. I would've thought you'd have hit that by now."

He glanced after Jess with a leer I wouldn't have imagined possible for a man who'd supposedly loved and planned to marry the woman, but at this point, I didn't put anything past him.

I didn't bark at him or slap him across the face like I might've loved to do. Instead, I just gave him a dead-eyed look I knew he'd hate. He'd never been able to keep his mouth shut and he'd always hated how I could.

"Still pining after her. You probably followed her here, sniffing at her feet, huh? If she hasn't fallen for it yet, she's not going to. I've been out of the picture for more than five years—if she was going to move on with you, she would've done it."

A hundred thoughts raced through my mind—insults, visions of clocking him right in his stupid smile, fantasies of grabbing him by the collar and pinning him to the wall like a high school bully... instead, I just grunted and moved away.

He made some kind of dismissive noise which I ignored. In a few seconds, I'd reached Jess's table. Was she okay? Had he said anything awful before I got there? Could I do anything to make it better for her?

"Hey, do you—"

She whipped around. "I do not."

I blinked. I hadn't finished the sentence. She had no idea what I was going to say. So... I'd try again.

"I was going to say do you—"

"I. Do. Not. I don't want to talk to you. I do not want to debrief about seeing my jerk of an ex, and I do not want to talk to you after that ridiculous display in front of him." Her cheeks flushed red. "Have a good night."

I stared at the back of her head for a moment before moving away, not wanting to make her even more angry by hanging around and not in the mood to deal with any small talk her friends, well-meaning as they were, might attempt.

Why was she sending all that fire my way? Of course seeing Kurt stirred up drama, but my gut clenched at the evidence it did so between *us*. We had a lot to talk about still, but I guessed I'd fooled myself into feeling like we were allies on this front, at least.

I made for the exit, seeking the cool fall air. Kenny was chatting with someone but saw me and tipped his chin, letting me know he'd be out in a few.

Fine. He knew Kurt for a minute before he got out. He definitely knew how I felt about him.

And he knew Jess, too. Maybe he could help me make sense of why, after seeing the man who'd cheated on her and left her, she was angry with *me*.

CHAPTER TWENTY-FOUR

Jess

I waited until I was certain he was gone before glancing behind me. Relief swept in, though the rope around my chest cinching tighter by the second didn't loosen a bit.

"So that's your ex..." Jo said, breaking the relative silence of the table.

"Yep."

"He's hot. I can see why you were attracted to him initially, anyway," Elise said.

Dove shoved her. "Ew, no. He's got that 'I'm too sexy for this bar' vibe about him."

Winnie chuckled. "What is that vibe, exactly?"

Dove clucked. "Aw, you don't know because you found a perfect man who is both humble and so hot he creates his own mirage. But it's when a guy seems okay but then you realize he thinks you're lucky to be talking to him. Could be in the way he glances around for better options or might be

how he assumes you'll leave with him if he wants you...
they're all the same in the end."

I exhaled and sank onto the empty stool next to me. "I
hate myself for ever falling for it."

"Falling for him?" Catherine asked from her spot next
to me.

A dry, humorless laugh emerged. "No. *It.* The act. The
whole bill of goods he sold me for *years.* I've been pretty
good at keeping myself from drowning in those 'poor me'
thoughts for quite a while, but seeing him again is...
honestly, it's nauseating."

Nikki slid a glass of ice water to me. I thanked her with
a nod and drank up. Couldn't afford dehydration on top of
the dual-pronged breakdown I was having. First, my
horrid, abandoning, cheating ex was here, and when face to
face with him, I couldn't pretend everything that went
wrong was Beast's fault, especially after recent developments.

And second, how dare Beast tell my ex-fiancé not to say
my name? What gave him the right? Why did he even butt
his grunting, confusing self into the conversation to begin
with? What in his giant head told him he was invited to that
conversation?

Not that I was all that mad he'd interrupted, or that I
hadn't had to deal with smarmier than ever Kurt on
my own.

How had I ever liked that man well enough to let him
kiss me, let alone propose?

Sometimes, I wanted to blast back in time and shake the
me of a decade ago. I wanted to tell her to avoid the charmer
and keep her head down. Focus on work and friendships
and not fall into the trap Kurt had set.

And third, even though I just now realized there was a

third—why was I almost angrier with Beast than I was with stupid cheater-face Kurt?

"Ladies, everyone okay?" Cookie stood next to me, his handsome face the picture of calm with a side of manly concern.

"Hey, Luc. Yeah, I think we're all fine," Jo said, the other girls agreeing.

All except Elise, who just blinked at the man until his gaze met hers and seemed to intensify. Her lips parted, and I could've sworn his eyes dropped to look, then he swallowed and nodded. "Glad to hear it. Have a good night."

Cookie stepped away, and we all turned to Elise.

"What? We're talking about you," she said, fluttering her hands in my direction like she could sweep off our attention.

Dove grinned. "Oh, no, friend. I think we're talking about you and Monsieur Jean-Luc."

Her exaggerated French accent for Cookie's name had all of us snickering.

"You did just have some rather intense eye contact." Jo fanned herself. "Honestly, it's the stuff of romance novels."

Elise rolled her eyes. "Okay, seriously. I'm not available, even if there was some eye contact happening." Her cheeks bloomed with a blush.

Jo sighed. "You're single. And honestly, he's..."

"Astoundingly attractive?" Dove submitted.

"Almost problematically handsome, I'd say," Winnie said, glancing in the direction Cookie had gone.

"You know I think Bruce is about the most beautiful man I've ever seen, but I will fully admit Luc is almost unreal." Nikki widened her eyes and we all nodded, even Elise. "The symmetry..."

"Not the point. Not even in the realm of points on a line

or a plane or in a sphere or wherever else points can be. We're shifting back to Jess to remind her she should feel her feelings about her past relationship, but not guilt herself over them." Elise's eyes sparkled with a knowing compassion. "Don't let him showing up here drag you back. Move forward."

My bruised little heart grappled for her words, grasping at them and clutching them close. I wanted to move forward. I wanted to never look back.

"I don't have a lot of ex feelings, but as we all know I have a lot of *feeling* feelings and I just want to say... don't get confused about what you're actually feeling." Dove had said something like this days ago when she and Elise came to dinner, too.

We could all read what she meant, because they'd seen me snap at Beast and give him the cold shoulder. And though they didn't all know the recent revelation of his supposed love for me way back when, they knew I'd been with him over the weekend and that he'd taken care of me. And, better than I had, they seemed to know *him*. Not as the antagonistic force in my life, but as a man in their small town, a friend to their partners and even themselves.

"I'll try," I scraped out, wishing some amount of my tactical courage would rub off on the side of me that *had* to talk to Beast soon.

I had to, because if I didn't, I was going to go crazy vacillating between angry and confused and this weird, twisty, excited feeling I was currently refusing to acknowledge.

Ethan Carter, Adam's younger brother, wandered over and gave Jo a side hug. They were business partners since Jo had silently invested in Ethan's coffee shop, Joe.

"How's everyone liking the crazy crush of people in town already?" He looked around, eyes wide.

"I sold out by seven-thirty this morning. It'll be great for business, but I'm already tired." Elise slumped a little in her seat.

"That's amazing! Aren't you doing some catering at one of the events, too?" Winnie asked.

Elise winked at Ethan. "Actually, yes. We're teaming up and doing a donuts and coffee thing before a press junket on Tuesday morning. I am incredibly stressed about it, so thanks for mentioning it." She made a face.

We all chuckled, and Dove wrapped her arms around Elise in her special brand of unhinged koala hug. "You're amazing and your donuts are amazing and everything is going to go... amazingly."

Nikki raised her glass. "To the amazingness-cubed of Tuesday's event!"

We all raised glasses, and since Ethan had carried his own pint along, he joined. When we'd all taken a drink and everyone began chatting, he paused, tripping over his words.

"Um—oh. Oh. Crap. That's Jenna Halter."

We all turned to look in the direction he was staring just in time to see Cookie wrapping *the* Jenna Halter in a very cozy hug.

"Whoa. How does Luc know her?" Jo asked.

"They seem pretty comfortable together," Dove commented.

"Just a work thing. He kind of saved her life. They're not dating." I said it straight out because it was true, and also because I'd seen Elise's face fall. We'd all just witnessed the incendiary eye contact minutes ago, and I didn't want her to think he was the kind of guy running around charming everyone he met.

Not like Kurt, who was exactly that way.

"Sometimes, I forget all of you guys are actual heroes. It's weird." Dove eyed me like I might bite her.

I chuckled, glad for the reprieve from the ooze of nasty feelings coming at me from all sides tonight. "I promise we're just humans. Most of us don't even wear our spandex superhero outfits under our clothes all the time."

She laughed, and a friend pulled Ethan away. We got wrapped up in talking about which celebrities we were excited to see, and the number of times Jack McKean came up had me laughing. I couldn't tell them I'd be guarding him for at least part of the weekend, though they'd find out eventually, and I absolutely planned to troll them with a picture if the opportunity came up.

The night died down and I felt the shift in me. I couldn't focus on my friends or the frenetic energy pulsing in the bar or town. I couldn't keep my mind on the conversation here or make idle small talk with the Blackthorne team after discovering Kurt was a central part of it and feeling him haunt whatever corner of the bar I studiously kept my attention from.

So I left a little early, promising I'd see them all soon, and promising myself I'd confront Beast with full honesty after the gala. We'd planned on it, and I'd tried to keep my distance because I couldn't find the right words. For a woman who was fairly even-keeled, I couldn't find a middle ground between angry and hurt. I just ping-ponged between them and felt. Felt. *Felt.*

It was exhausting, but soon, work would get too busy to think about anything else. And the next time I had a break, I'd get answers from Beast and finally put all of this to bed.

CHAPTER TWENTY-FIVE

Jude

The gala wound down and the internal clock that'd started ticking when Jess told me we'd talk after the event grew louder.

Tick.

Tick.

Maybe I was actually losing my mind because I could've sworn I was actually hearing the sound. My blood pressure had been high, focus had been a struggle, and any time I caught a glimpse of her in her black suit, my chest tightened.

For the most part, I hadn't seen her. She'd been assigned to Jack McKean and had also done some building and event security. We were all working long hours and the fact that we both had an open window this evening felt as close to serendipitous as it possibly could be.

Tonight, we'd have it out. She was angry with me—still

snapping whenever we interacted despite the apparently fleeting peace we'd struck at the cabin.

And evidently, she didn't appreciate my admission of past feelings. Depending on what questions she asked tonight, she'd be even more unhappy.

But I'd said she could ask me anything she wanted, and I'd meant it. I didn't want this useless hatred between us anymore. I wasn't going to give it back to her if she continued to dole it out—if she needed to keep loathing me to protect herself. And there was no mistaking that part of the narrative she'd spun these last few years was exactly that —a way to protect herself.

"Hey, I'm going to sweep one time, then I'll relieve you," Kenny said, full of energy despite the late hour.

I nodded. Jess wouldn't be relieved for another twenty minutes so I was in no rush.

"Damn, she can wear a suit, can't she?"

Kurt's voice cut into the far more pleasant live jazz band playing at the far end of the ballroom, his attention pinned on Jess, who'd just walked into my sightline with McKean.

I didn't comment because yes, she could, but no, I wasn't about to talk to him about it.

"I can see you haven't learned to speak any better than you used to." He chuckled like he was funny.

When I stayed quiet long enough, he walked away. In years gone by, he would've kept talking and trying to provoke me into responding, but maybe he sensed nothing he could say would do that now, or maybe he'd actually matured.

When I saw him cast a sly smile to a very young woman, I had the confirmation that no, he had not.

"Everything's looking good. Have a good night, man. I'll see you bright and early?" Kenny patted my back.

I dipped my chin.

He lowered his voice and his eyes shifted from side to side like he was checking we didn't have an audience. "And it's happening now?"

I nodded again.

With one more pat, he sent me off. "Be brave. Be all the beast we know and love but, like, for telling her how you feel."

I cut him a scowl and made my way to the ballroom entrance. She'd likely be handing Jack off to whoever was replacing her—I couldn't recall but I thought maybe Bruce was on him since they had worked together before.

After a moment in the bathroom to give myself a few seconds of quiet, I washed my hands, then entered the stylish lounge filled with polished wood and red leather club chairs and a stage where a man strummed a guitar and a woman sang.

My heart skipped when I saw Jess at the end of the bar, already seated. She'd taken off her jacket and wore a sparkly strapless black top that showed off her toned shoulders and a rattling amount of her back.

Damn, she's gorgeous.

I'd always thought so. I'd forbidden myself from truly taking it in when she'd been sick—it'd felt wrong. But now she was well, and she was waiting for me...

If only that meant what I wanted it to mean. If only she were waiting for me to sit down and buy her a drink and talk softly to her until we couldn't stand it anymore and left to find somewhere quiet, somewhere we could explore the decade of tension that'd been building between us.

I shook out my hands and slowed my breathing as I approached.

"Wait long?"

She turned toward me, that stunning face sending my stomach to the floor. Dark lashes over darker eyes, a straight nose and full lips that made me want things. Minimal makeup I detected better now that I'd seen her bare-faced at the cabin. Soft-looking skin and despite her intensity, a kindness in the way her lips naturally tilted up and in the friendly arch of her dark, expressive brows.

"Only a minute."

She nudged the tall bar chair next to her and I slipped into it. My knee brushed hers as I settled in.

"So... you said I could ask you anything."

"No small talk then, huh?"

She shot me a look. "Why would we small talk? We've never done that before."

"Fair enough." I didn't want to talk weather with her either. But I'd regret cutting this night short with saying the wrong thing, especially if this was all I'd ever get.

She reached for the glass in front of her—a delicate flute filled with something sparkling. "Drink?"

It shouldn't have hit me like this, but it felt almost flirty. Like maybe she wanted to sit here and sip on cocktails and pretend we weren't secretly watching each other's lips when they touched the rims of our glasses.

The bartender arrived then with brows raised asking the same question.

"Whiskey neat. Your choice."

Everything they served here was good, and I knew this kid, Brandon, wasn't about to pour me one of Julian Grenier's thousand dollar a bottle pours. He recognized me from around town, and the lounge had a reputation which they wouldn't keep if their bartenders were pouring over-priced drinks.

"I tried getting into whiskey a while back but I just

couldn't. Bourbon, whiskey, gin... it's just not my thing. I can do vodka if I can't taste it and I love a good margarita, but that's about it." She raised her glass an inch. "But the bubbly?" She tipped the glass to her lips and closed her eyes as she took a drink.

"Pop." It came out a little wistful, especially as I recalled learning her nickname.

All of us garnered nicknames during our assessment and selection. It came from any number of things—sometimes something funny, sometimes a character trait, sometimes a play on the person's name. Wilder Saint's nickname? Saint, originally enough, both because of his last name and because he had this compulsive need to do the right thing on a mission.

Bruce had Jaws because he gave shark eyes when he got intense. Kenny earned Barbie because his name is Ken and he looks like a Barbie doll, plus he's plucky as all get out which fit the name. Cookie's undying love for cookies meant Jean-Luc very rarely got called by his name—though when he did it was Luc. Someone had tried to float Picard for him, but apparently that got shot down when he admitted to never having seen Star Trek.

I'd been named Beast because I am a large man with a gruff personality, and Jess? Well, she loved champagne, her last name was that of a fairly well-known champagne maker in the US (reportedly no relation), and she had energy. She had this thrumming, bubbling need to get the job done, and her peers in assessment recognized it.

Her eyes fluttered opened. "Yeah. I guess it's no secret."

Brandon delivered my drink, and I sipped it, then held it up halfway between us. "To the truth."

Her eyes hooked into mine. "To the truth."

She drank, but the placid state of things between us

slipped away and the edge returned as my sip of whiskey burned a hot, oaky trail down my throat.

"Go ahead." I might as well get it over with and deal with the fallout. See where we landed.

"When did you know?"

I swallowed hard, pulse instantly a riot, though my façade stayed calm. "Know about Kurt?"

She nodded.

"I didn't know until I caught him in the act, and I reported it immediately. But... he used to be pretty aggressive. And the day we met you, he set his eyes on you just like he had others. When it turned into a relationship instead of a one and done, I thought it meant he'd changed." Regret laced through me, followed by a familiar ache.

How often had I let my wishes draw me back to the moment I'd opted into assessing for EMU and he'd done the same? For days after they'd gotten engaged, I'd cursed the decision to encourage him to try for the unit, too, hated myself for helping him prep and train because maybe if I hadn't, he wouldn't have been there the day she walked in. Maybe he wouldn't have set his sights on her, and I would've eventually found the words to ask her out.

She shook her head and studied the bubbles in her glass, then spoke like they were listening. "I can't even remember what switched in me. How I went from finding him to be too much to finally... thinking I wanted him."

Thinking she wanted him. Interesting phrasing.

"I'm sorry he broke your heart." With an exhale, I admitted, "Or, maybe I'm sorry I did."

Damn, I hated the thought, but she'd blamed me all this time, so why did it feel new? Like a fresh wound only just beginning to heal?

She set her drained glass on the bar top in front of us so

slowly, it might've been slow motion. Without glancing at me, she tossed two twenties into the space between our drinks and turned, grabbing her suit jacket off the back of the chair.

She was leaving.

Panic hit, my gut saying that if I let her leave, I'd never have another chance to clear the air. She'd never *ever* let me. She'd close herself off to anything more than what we'd been doing these last few years, the sniping and irritation and maybe even all the way back to the hatred.

"Jess, wait—"

She spoke over her shoulder as she walked. "I take it back. I don't want any of this."

CHAPTER TWENTY-SIX

Jude

Despite having almost an entire foot on her in height, I had to work to keep up with her as she button-hooked out of the lounge and down the hallway in what had to be just shy of a jog for her.

"Jess, wait."

If she heard the desperation in my voice, so be it. I increased my pace until I reached her, daring to set a hand on her shoulder as we arrived at the end of the hallway, only a service entrance and a maintenance door interrupting the opulent wallpaper.

She whipped around and stepped back.

"I don't understand you," she said, fire in her eyes like I'd never seen. "I hate you."

Where did this come from? How had we gone from sitting there so calmly to this? "What don't you understand? I told you everything."

"You've told me nothing real and then you go and say stuff like that? 'Sorry I broke your heart.' What is that?"

I blinked. I thought maybe I should apologize for being the one to report him, though I had no doubt she agreed it was the right thing now that she believed—or I hoped she believed—he'd actually done what I'd claimed. Did she want me to apologize for loving her, too? I couldn't.

I won't.

She was so angry. I could feel it radiating from her like desert heat from the Sahara. We'd both been there at the crux of summer and this, rolling off Jess, was more intense.

"Why would you tell me that? At the very least, I thought we'd be honest with each other."

"I don't regret reporting him, but I am sorry it all blew up. I never wanted that—never felt good about you getting hurt, even though you deserved so much better than that asshat." Couldn't she see it?

She growled out a frustrated breath. "I don't even care about that. I'm over it. That's not even the point anymore."

Disbelief ripped through me, followed by a trail of fiery frustration. Everything that came between us before had been rooted in her not believing me, in her taking Kurt's word even though he lied to her and left her. And now, she was *over it?*

No attempt to soften my reaction prevailed as words punched out of me. "What? You're magically over the thing that has caused you to hate me for the last five years? Please enlighten me how that happened. I'd like to note the miracle and report it to the local authorities."

Apparently, having a conversation while she wasn't feverish and ill meant she got under my skin just like she always did.

She groaned through gritted teeth. "You said you were

in love with me, right? And that messed you up enough you felt conflicted and didn't know whether to tell me about your suspicions and as stupid as it is, I get it. As *selfish* as it is, I do get it on some level."

This woman could shoot her shot and she did not pull a punch. I ran a hand through my hair and tried to find the chill I'd promised myself I'd maintain. "Okay, great. You get it. Then what is your problem? I don't know what you want from me."

Please, Jess, just tell me what you want from me.

Through the frustration with her, I teetered on an edge. Any second now, I might slip into begging her like I'd promised myself for so long I wouldn't do.

Believe me. See me. Choose me.

I silenced the pleading voice and took a slow inhale, begging my body to calm down so I could stay in this moment, stay with her here in this hallway and not let this devolve into another version of our past mistakes.

She crossed her arms in a way that made it look like she was strapping on a shield. "I want you to tell me why the *hell* you didn't tell me you had feelings for me sooner. Why you weren't man enough to be honest. Why you couldn't tell me for the years and years and *years* after that you'd felt the way you did."

She'd inched closer to me, stretching her neck and somehow growing taller with her frustration.

This sparked real anger in me and I blew past the thrill of having her this close. "I would never have told you I had feelings for you after you were with Kurt. What would've been the point? I'm not that kind of person. You chose him —I took the note."

She let out a bitter laugh, but I continued. "And after? You wouldn't look at me, let alone talk to me. We could hardly tolerate being in the same room those first few years, and obviously, things have gone perfectly here at Saint."

She shook her head and seemed to be summoning strength from somewhere—maybe Athena was about to show up and assist her in finishing me off, if her expression was anything to go by. *Murderously beautiful* had a certain ring to it.

"So it all comes down to the fact that you're just so honorable? You're so *good* and *ethical* that you wouldn't talk to me while I was dating him, and then you couldn't force me to talk to you after? Is that it?"

This maddening woman!

"Yes. *Yes,* dammit, that *is* it. Because I'm not a jackass who's going to force you into talking to someone you've convinced yourself you hate. Especially not when I—"

Her gaze sharpened and she stepped forward, close enough we were almost touching. "When you what?"

I inhaled—fatal mistake. Her warm, fresh scent filled the space between us, and I took it in with greed. I was so rarely close enough to have this and she always smelled so good. I wanted to huff her like a drug, drag my nose along the soft skin of her neck. And maybe I'd kiss her there, just to hear the intake of breath—just to see if she'd push me away, maybe slap me, or maybe...

"Jude, what?"

There was still an edge in her voice, but it had curved into something new, and my name instead of Beast had me sucking in a breath. My eyes dropped to her lips, the perfect dip in her cupid's bow and the plush bottom one I couldn't look away from.

"Jude."

My gaze cut to hers, and whether it was the frustration or the buildup of this conversation that'd gone absolutely sideways, or the way I'd left parts of me open instead of locked down tight, I told her the truth. All of it.

"I couldn't talk to you after he left because I hated that I'd broken your heart, even if I'd done the right thing, but I hated even more that you'd broken mine."

She reared back. "How?"

"You wouldn't believe me. You believed that asshole cheater over me and I couldn't take it. I was so angry with you, but I still..." *No point in attempting to avoid it now, is there?* "I still loved you."

She shook her head. "No. You didn't."

"I did."

She loosed an incredulous laugh. "There's no way. You hated me."

"*You* hated *me*. And that does something to a man. Instead of begging you to talk to me, to see me, I decided I'd lean into all the rage and hatred you were giving me, and I'd let you have it right back. It was so much easier than the alternative."

So much easier than feeling not only the loss of her, but of her total lack of faith in me. It was twisted and messed up, I wouldn't dispute that, but I didn't have anywhere to go with the mess of feelings she stirred up in me.

The shift from confusion and disbelief happened in a matter of seconds. Her jaw firmed and her gaze sharpened and pinned me. "How dare you."

The words came out just barely louder than a whisper, and I swallowed hard. They were threaded with anger and hurt.

"I'm telling you what's true."

She inhaled. "You're telling me you were so in love with me you couldn't talk to me? That you chose to avoid me and hate me when I'm being a jerk instead of calling me on it?"

Damn, she never would pull a punch. It was always something that drew me to her, but I'd been on the wrong end of the scenario for so long, it was a wonder I could still admire it. And yet I did.

I wouldn't hold off from honesty... I hadn't, and I wouldn't start now.

"Yes."

The atmosphere around us crowded in—the sounds of the live band shrinking to some point in the distance. My chest heaved, adrenaline firing through my veins so intensely, my hands shook.

"Because you were a coward? Because you really did hate me? If you loved me, how could you do that? It's a nice story you've spun for yourself, but there's no way *that* is the truth." Her voice had gained strength and she'd gotten this wild look in her eye like she was on the verge of spinning out.

Like any second she'd leave, and no matter what I did, she wouldn't turn back.

I'd had it with her resistance to the truth. She could be shocked by my admission, but she wasn't about to call me a liar. I was anything but, and I wasn't going to stand here and let her reject the truth because it made her uncomfortable. I wasn't perfect, but neither was she, and I was done accepting the role of villain because I'd loved her and hadn't known what the hell to do with it.

I took her face in my hands and spoke slowly. "You may not like it, Jess, but I did love you. Clearly, I messed up. I've never said I'm smart, only that I had my reasons, and I—"

I didn't get out another word because she grabbed me by the collar of my jacket and pulled me in, cutting off my words with a kiss.

CHAPTER TWENTY-SEVEN

Jess

His mouth was surprisingly soft, and he'd trimmed his beard since last weekend, but he didn't respond to the kiss—I'd stunned him with the contact. His hands fell away from my face, and he pulled back.

His eyes were wild, and my breath came rapidly.

Hadn't planned on that.

Did I foresee kissing Jude Rawlins today?

No.

But had his repeated claims that he'd loved me somehow driven me so insane I was compelled to?

Evidently yes.

The confusion and fire in his eyes were torches in the dim light of the hallway. I scrambled for something to say— would *whoopsie daisy* cover it?

But then, the torch flickered and brightened, and his hands found my waist. Gaze glued to mine, he paced me backward into an even darker corner and pressed me against the wall, anchoring my hips with his giant hands.

My heart beat so fast I could hardly breathe. "I'm—"

"Sorry?"

The gravelly texture to the word and the way his hands warmed through the fabric of my clothes at my waist made me say, "No."

I wasn't sorry for kissing him. I was mostly sorry he hadn't kissed me back. But this... situation he'd placed us in certainly didn't feel like a rejection.

He waited a beat, staring at me with the intensity of an entire universe of suns before one of those deliciously large hands abandoned my waist and came to cup the back of my neck as he lowered his face to mine and took my mouth with his.

This time, there was no question he was engaged in the process—not only initiating the contact, but driving it, urging me to open for him, tasting me in a way that made me feel not just desired, but needed. Like I might be water in a desert place.

Like he'd always known I'd quench something in him, or douse a burning thing, and now he was collecting his proof.

My hands found their place at his shoulders, and I pulled him closer, urging him to glue me to the wall with his massive form. I'd never let myself think about a moment like this with him—at least not consciously. I'd had little fantasies shoot across my mind like stars when we'd first met, but since then, no.

In the last ten minutes, the cold, bruised thing known as my heart had warmed—unfurled, somehow. And hearing him insist he'd loved me... I'd had to test it. Had he really felt something for me? Was it all just talk? I'd had to push and words hadn't worked, so in the moment, a kiss had come to mind.

Now, the kiss unraveled me thread by thread, and his thumb slipping under the hem of my top to feel the soft skin of my belly stitched me back into a woman who knew exactly what she wanted.

He stepped closer, and something told me if we were truly alone, he'd hitch me up so he didn't have to bend to meet me quite so far down. He'd pin me against the wall with my legs wrapped around his hips and—I gasped as he did just that in one swift movement. His hands slipped down my hips and around to my hamstrings and we played out my vision in the most cinematic move of my life.

He groaned as he pressed me into the wall, one palm returning to cup my jaw and position my head just so. Then he utterly devoured me with kisses both generous and demanding, a give and take that nipped at my bottom lip to say *this is mine now* and followed with a soft slide saying *take whatever you want.*

I'd never felt dizzy from a kiss. I'd never had one so commanding and generous at the same time.

Because I've never kissed him.

I didn't want it to end. I'd gladly take up residence in this hallway. Julian Grenier owned some part of the resort, and he was also part investor in Saint Security—there had to be some way we could get a cooperative rental agreement so Jude and I could stay here and make out until the world burned to ash.

Far sooner than the crumbling of the planet, Jude pulled back and gave me another searing look.

We breathed together for a moment, the absolutely paradigm-shattering kiss effectively rattling us both based on the way we practically heaved in breath. He lowered me to standing, stepped back, hands settling firmly on my waist like he wasn't quite done with me.

What does one say after one's former enemy kisses one into oblivion?

I cleared my throat, searching for words, but he beat me to it.

"That should've happened a long time ago."

The low rumble made my toes curl in my shoes and I exhaled a, "Yeah. Probably so."

He released me then, those dark eyes holding me in place just as well as his hands had.

Well, no. Because there was nothing quite as delectable as Jude Rawlins' giant bear paw hands spanning my waist. I might be addicted to the feeling.

His eyes sent my stomach swooping around like a drunk eagle, and I waited for something more. He notched his head to the side and turned. "We both have the early shift."

So... that was why we'd stopped. Well, and because if we'd kept going, we might've been charged with public indecency. I couldn't argue the logic of the point or action.

The urge to slip my palm against his and lace our fingers flashed through me, but I resisted, mind racing with what would happen next as I followed him out.

But then we reached the parking lot and he stood by my car while I got in. He shut the door and waited, like he'd stand there and grow roots in the ground if I didn't start up the vehicle, so I did. Moonlight lit one side of his face and left the other in shadow as he waited.

No more words tonight, then. I guess I'd gotten all I would get during our conversation, which certainly left me more than enough to mull over.

So I eased out of the lot and left him behind, standing

there following my progress with his impenetrable mask of a face.

As the distance between us stretched, I heard his words echoing in my head. *That should've happened a long time ago.*

I'd agreed because... well, I had. Maybe if we'd kissed—if he'd told me he'd had feelings and we'd gotten through all of this nonsense, we would've gotten past the anger and hurt and gotten to... whatever this was.

But there lay the real question. What was this? What did that kiss mean?

And did his statement mean what I'd thought it did and agreed to, or did it mean...

I swallowed hard as I pulled into my driveway and stopped my car in the garage.

Did it mean it should've happened a long time ago and *not* now? That it happening now came too late?

Did it mean that our first kiss had also been our last?

CHAPTER TWENTY-EIGHT

Jude

Morning dawned with a silvery tint to the clouds, then the sun painted a cranberry sky as it rose.

So sue me if the world looked brighter. For the first time in weeks but more like months, I'd spent days thinking about something other than loss. I'd spent them thinking about Jess.

And last night?

Last night, I'd gone to bed with the taste of her on my lips and the memory of her body against mine seared into my mind. I'd had a glimpse of heaven, and it'd given me a kind of hope I'd not dared to feel in years.

I was still grieving my grandmother, but I'd been grieving. In some ways, it felt like I'd spent the last half a decade mourning losses and walking in the hazy dusk that is grief.

Until...

It sounded so stupid—like a fairytale or something—but

the assignment with Jess had woken me up. Being shoved into her space, touching her hand when we posed as a couple... it'd served as the slap across my face and forced my mind to step into the sunlight.

"You are having some serious thoughts, aren't you, big fella?" Kenny's grin could be heard from a mile away.

I turned with my coffee-filled mug and eyed him where he stood just inside the break room.

"Not gonna tell me? Fine. I'll just have to guess." He tapped his chin in a poor actor's rendering of a thinking man, then he snapped. "I know. You're thinking about kissing Pop in a dark corner of the hotel last night—"

In the split-second between when I realized he somehow knew what'd happened to the words exiting his loose lips, I'd slipped my coffee onto the nearby counter and got in his face enough that he knew not to finish the sentence.

"Do not say another word and do not repeat what you just said."

Amusement flickered across his face. "No kissing and telling then, eh? How chivalrous."

"What did he say?" Luc asked from the doorway. "Whatever it is, I'm sure it's merited, but could we ease up, gentlemen?"

I shoved Kenny away and he winked at me, evidently not at all fazed by my threats.

"It's fine. Beasty doesn't realize that we *all* saw him and Jess kiss and make up last night when we left the ballroom and spotted them in their sexy little corner."

The swallow of coffee went down hard. Kenny slapped my back as though that ever actually helped someone when they were sputtering against a bad drink.

"I would've thought you'd be happy about this, but

somehow, you seem grumpier." Kenny laughed and shared an amazed look with Luc.

Adam and Dorian filed into the room, as well. I greeted them both with nods and stepped farther away from the coffee maker so they could fuel up.

"What a nice little morning reunion," Adam said, grinning at all of us.

"Damn, man, you look like you had a nice start to your day." Kenny wiggled his brows.

I shoved the idiot, and Adam shook his head in disapproval. "None of that."

Kenny shrugged, and Adam rolled his eyes.

"We were just hoping to get details on Beast's evening." There went the damn brows again.

Interest flashed over Adam's face, but then he sent me a look while speaking to Kenny. "A story I'm sure he's just itching to share with your gossipy butt."

His expression said enough—he had something to tell me but not in front of the child. Luc ushered Kenny out of the room and Stone took a seat at the small table and sipped his coffee, wonderfully at ease.

"I saw Pop this morning. She seemed... I don't know." He and Stone exchanged glances.

"You saw her, too?" I asked Stone.

He nodded, his silence confirming Adam's statement.

"Did she say anything?" I pressed, needing to understand his concern and get a sense of what might be going on with her.

Had she not been glad we'd kissed? Did she regret it?

Had I read everything completely wrong?

Wouldn't be the first time...

"Nothing about you. She mostly talked about McKean

and their plan today. It wasn't like she was raging or anything, just seemed... subdued."

I nodded, instantly understanding why this was notable. Jess Korbel was alive and buzzing with energy and beauty and life... describing her as *subdued* was like describing someone else as sad or angry and despondent. Jess was full of life, whether it was fury at me or excitement for her friends or focus for the mission.

My heart sank at the reality of what this might mean.

"You're at the theater this morning, but after noon, you're back at the resort, right? I think she'll be at McKean's door until four. Maybe you could check in." He lifted a shoulder. "Not that it's my business. But you know. I think it's worth continuing to... bridge the gap between you."

The flicker of a smile on his face echoed on Stone's.

I grunted, acknowledging the suggestion. I wouldn't take it as an insult that he assumed I might *not* talk to her. But nothing about the way I'd treated her the last few years made sense to anyone but the two of us, and even then, it was a stretch. For both of us.

Plus, they both knew I'd been grieving and how the weight of sadness made me even less likely to share my thoughts or speak my mind. And we were sitting here with the king of hiding out, so none of us would pretend we didn't know isolating when things were hard came naturally.

The day dragged on slowly. If I was the type of person to care about celebrity, maybe it would've been a little fun. I did like what I knew of Jenna Halter, and since Cookie and Hijack had guarded her and spoke well of her, I felt reasonably sure she was a decent human. The other local celebrities were out in force—Bri Williamson, Miss Mayhem, Jamie Morris, Julian Grenier, and so many more. Plus, the town was downright flooded with tourists and film fest attendees. It was good for Silverton.

What was not good was knowing that Jess was guarding Jack McKean. Even I had a crush on McKean, and I didn't get crushes. But the man was a fantastic actor and from what I'd heard from Bruce and others who knew him, a truly good dude.

He was also the kind of Hollywood pretty none of us, save *maybe* our beloved Jean-Luc, could compete with.

And was I competing? No. Only an idiot would imagine himself in competition with Jack McKean. That man would lose a hundred times over.

But also, only an idiot would fail to notice how beautiful Jess was, and so if Jack really wasn't an idiot, he'd take notice. And, well, who could blame her for being a little taken by the millionaire, Oscar-winning dreamboat?

If it wouldn't be incredibly insulting to her professionalism, I'd be worried. But she'd never cross that line.

Unless his animal magnetism and pheromones destroy all her good sense.

I mean honestly, I wouldn't blame her. I saw *Karrigan's Muse* and that depressing Irish one he won his Oscar for.

And more than that, I could be honest about what our relationship had been for so long. I didn't know where we stood, and one messy conversation followed by a mind-bending kiss didn't exactly erase everything lying wrecked by the choices of our past.

All the logic in the world didn't keep me from internally pacing even as I stood still, alert to the potential threats and problems, communicating as needed with the team running overwatch from the office.

It didn't stop me from feeling antsy whenever I caught sight of a petite brunette only to realize it wasn't Jess.

And it definitely didn't halt my bone-deep need to track her down and address whatever this was between us. I'd spent too long assuming things and, whether she wanted to admit it or not, so had she. We weren't going forward like that, whether it meant we ended up as non-enemy coworkers or... something more.

I didn't let myself entertain what that "something more" might be as I handed off my post to Tristan and beelined for the lobby. If Jess left her spot outside McKean's door at the same time, we'd likely reach the hotel entrance around the same time. I could catch her, and we could figure this out... or start.

By the time I reached the ground floor, my heart was pounding. Anticipation and nerves, and maybe a few little visions of her sneering at me with hate in her eyes, had obliterated any confidence I had about the connection we'd made last night.

Then to top it off, I walked into the room to find her smiling up at Jack McKean, laughing as she nodded like she'd genuinely found his joke funny. It was the smile she gave her friends and people she felt safe with.

It was one she'd never given me.

When she glanced my way, her face dropped. She said a few more words to Jack, and Bruce replaced her as she broke away and squared her shoulders to me, looking like it took bravery and determination to talk to me. Far from the ease she'd just shown with Jack.

But the truth was, I couldn't blame her.

As my neck prickled with heat and my heart thudded in my chest, I could only agree. *I know how you feel, Pop.*

CHAPTER TWENTY-NINE

Jess

He approached with the neutral mask I used to interpret as arrogance or dislike. He looked a little worn down from the day, like maybe he'd worked an overnight shift, though as far as I'd seen, he hadn't been on until early this morning.

He stopped in front of me, towering over me despite my heels.

"Hey."

What a way to jump in, huh?

It wasn't like I'd been waiting to see him since the second he'd shoveled me into the car last night. It wasn't like I'd had to force my focus to Jack and the job instead of letting it wander around and play in the memory of Jude's lips and hands on me... *Not helping, brain!*

"Have a minute?"

His low, gruff voice sent a bolt of longing through me,

and my stupid lashes fluttered like he'd run his massive hands through my hair.

"Sure. Where?"

If I kept my responses minimal, maybe he wouldn't realize how embarrassed I was over my interpretation of the kiss and his *this should've happened a long time ago* thing.

Dark eyes nearly burning through me, he tipped his head to the side, toward the exit. *Okay.* Out of the very public, very busy lobby did sound like a good option. I would vote for a little more privacy than standing on the sidewalk, but maybe he just meant we should figure that out after leaving.

We walked out of the building side by side, the automatic doors sliding open and unleashing a blast of chilly fall air tinted with the scent of petrichor. It'd rained earlier, but the lows would drop to freezing overnight and it'd mean ice if the rain kept up.

He walked like he had a destination in mind, so I followed him past a dried-up fountain shut off for the season and around the side of the building. My breath caught at the sight of the little white chapel a stretch up the hill to the left, and the mountains looking vibrant with the fall colors that weren't wrecked by the early snow.

"It's so beautiful here," I said, unable to contain the thought.

When he didn't respond, I turned to see him staring at me.

"It is."

My heart flipped. "So?"

"I—how was your day?"

I couldn't hide the disbelieving laugh that escaped. "How was my day?"

He nodded.

I glanced around, feeling a little like I was on an episode of *Punk'd*. "Um, good?"

He waited, apparently expecting a more thorough report.

"Jack's great, and the fans were on their best behavior, so overall, it was an easy day. Seemed like everyone else was doing well, too. You?"

His gaze slipped up to the mountain peaks to the east of us as if drawing strength from them. "Good. And yeah, from what I've heard, no issues today."

Internally, I screamed *What are you thinking!!?* Externally, I said, "Oh, that's good."

My training as an operator had come down to this—I didn't need it to capture bad guys or find hostages or protect my assignment... I needed it to not lose my mind in the face of a man who drove me absolutely insane.

The awkward silence stretched and looped back around to stretch some more. It was the saltwater taffy of silences, bending around the bar that pulled it longer and thinner, never breaking.

He had more experience being silent than I did and proved it, because after what felt like several minutes, I broke. "So, uh, you wanted to talk?"

He nodded, eyes skating around us. I followed his gaze and realized he must've been confirming we were alone.

My pulse ticked up.

"I wanted to check in."

I waited. There had to be more. I would *make* there be more by not barging in and taking over. Because of course I wanted to check in, too, but I wasn't about to lay myself at his feet in a puddle of obviousness.

His brow furrowed. "About last night."

"About...?" I leaned against a wire bike rack cemented into the ground, casual as could be.

As unlucky in love as I'd been, I wasn't clueless and I certainly wasn't going to let him know how I felt about the kiss, let alone things between the two of us, before he gave me a hint of the same. Especially not after I'd thought I'd understood his comment and only realized later I might've been terribly, humiliatingly wrong in my interpretation.

He stepped closer. "About our conversation."

I did not let myself smile or scoff at what felt like a very euphemistic reference to the events of last night. "Our conversation."

His lips thinned. "And the kiss."

"Ah." There it was. My heart rate had continued to climb, and the word kiss coming from him was a perfect contrast—big, broody man with a butterfly of a word on his tongue.

He seemed troubled by my response, or maybe by the lack of one.

"Are you okay?"

"Yes. Of course." The words sprang from me instantly. Did he think I wasn't?

Wait, am I?

His expression darkened, like he could tell the response was rote and held no real insight into my state of being.

Well, buddy, welcome to the club. I have no idea how I am, so how can I tell you?

He heaved a breath fit for a giant, eyes following the line of the gondola up, up, up the mountain, before returning to rest on me.

"I don't know how to do this, but I'm trying. I'm asking you if you regret what we did. I need to know if you're going to go back to hating me, or if there's any other option."

The defeat etched into his words sent a pang of regret through me.

Maybe I should've been more forthcoming, but we were both so used to this posture of defensiveness. I relaxed my hands and let the physical action signal my mental way forward.

"I don't hate you. I think I never really have. And I think that's what we figured out last night." My cheeks were hot, but I wouldn't regret making it clear.

"Is it?" he asked, inching closer.

I nodded.

"Adam said you've been subdued—his word, not mine." He studied me, intensity pouring from him and wrapping around me.

"I've been a little in my head, I guess," I said, resisting the rise of the reflex begging me to push back at him instead of owning the truth.

"But not because you're upset with me?"

I opened my mouth, but he rushed in.

"I don't mean that to sound like I think I'm the most important thing going on in your life, but I'm pretty sure last night changed some things or, at least, was very new territory for us. So I thought maybe..."

Unable to resist the connection any longer, I reached out to grab one open side of his suit jacket. "I got a little confused, I guess. You didn't say anything after except the thing about how it should've happened a long time ago. And I agreed. But then... nothing else. And by the time I got home, I started second-guessing. Wondering if that meant it should've happened years ago because nothing could happen now. Maybe we have too much history, or—"

His hands came up to bracket my neck, his thumbs resting at the hinges of my jaw, and he shook his head slowly and definitively. "We have a lot behind us. There's no getting around that."

He seemed to be struggling, his throat working like he had more to say but either wouldn't, or maybe couldn't.

Could either of us sum up the seismic shift that'd happened last night? It'd been creeping in since the cabin, or maybe even since the Snowberry op, and I certainly didn't have words to make sense of everything.

"I don't know what to do now," I admitted, his warm hands a comfort and thrill at the same time.

"Do we need to know?"

His gaze didn't waver, and his presence was so steady and intense it made my mind a scattered mess. His thumbs rested at the pulse in my neck and he had to feel it singing for him.

I couldn't be the first one to declare it—to say I wanted something with him. Call it pride or call it hard-won wisdom, but I just couldn't. So I tried to walk it back a little, as though I hadn't been reliving his hands on me, his demanding, giving kiss, and what it might mean since the minute we'd parted last night. "You're grieving. And I'm..."

His lids dropped low. "Telling me how I feel now, eh? Isn't that how we started arguing in the first place?"

Mm, kind of. I'd told him he didn't love me. The memory of that brightened my blush, but I stepped closer. "I'll work on it."

A smile flickered over his face, and my whole body lit up in response. He was handsome as the broody grump, no doubt, but that rarely seen smile was absolutely devastating.

"And us?" he asked, ever pushy.

I could play coy or unsure at this point and walk away relatively unscathed. I'd just avoided admitting I might want something with him.

But *unscathed* had looked a lot less appealing as I reflected on all the choices I'd made to avoid risking anything romantically since Kurt. And even then, some odd part of what lay between me and him was a sense that I wasn't risking as much with him.

It should've waved a red flag long ago when I'd started to understand I felt more upset at the concept of my fiancé leaving me than the reality of *Kurt* leaving me. And along with that, the pain of Beast betraying me by not telling me what had been going on, if he'd known, than being cheated on.

Hindsight could be a cruel lens, and yet a helpful one.

I didn't want to get hurt again, but I was in a different place than I'd been when I'd settled for Kurt. I wasn't desperate for companionship and love. I wasn't so lonely I could feel my bones ache with longing for a family and a place I fit.

I had friends and a home and a job and even a town I loved. So choosing to try with this man... it wasn't desperation.

It was curiosity. Hope, maybe. And oddly, a sense of inevitability I hadn't been able to shake these last few days. *Not that I would ever tell him that.*

No, I couldn't let him know any of this quite so clearly as I felt it—not yet. I could be hopeful and smart, soft and guarded at the same time. That was practically my brand.

"I think before we refer to an *us* you probably need to ask me out, don't you?"

One brow rose. "Will you go out with me, Jessica Korbel?"

"Sure. I'm free—"

"Breakfast. Tomorrow before work. Diner."

I chuckled, delighted by his sense of urgency and

covertly thrilled by that pushy nature of his demanding something good and anticipatory.

But all the fun good feelings came to a screeching halt when a rude voice interrupted like a record scratch.

"Aw, isn't this a fun surprise? My former best friend and my former fiancée flirting while they're on the job. Guess some things don't change."

Sure enough, Kurt stood a few feet away with a smirk like he'd caught us in the act of something forbidden that justified his every action.

Now, I needed to rely on my training to keep from punching him in the face.

CHAPTER THIRTY

Jude

Kurt's similarities to a cockroach were growing, but primary among them were that he just wouldn't go away.

"Sorry to interrupt. Looked like you two were having a real moment. So I guess I _shouldn't_ pity you then, huh, Beast? Have you finally plowed that field? Finally got your sloppy seconds?"

Before I even thought to move, Jess was in his face.

"I don't know why you've decided to be such a jerk, but none of this is your business. Don't talk to him like that, and definitely don't talk about me that way."

She looked poised to strike—would she take my constructive feedback that a nice round house to his head would be a good starting place?

Probably not.

As reactive as she could be to me, she seemed to have

herself on lock when it came to Kurt. She must've grown a few inches, her spine perfectly straight, chin high, and a look so unimpressed I was surprised he didn't shrink on the spot. Energy coiled around her, like if he gave her any excuse, she'd not only lay him out, she'd also serve him his pinkies on a platter before he caught his breath.

Damn, she's impressive.

"Oh, don't you worry." Kurt glanced up and his attention snagged on something.

I followed his stare and sure enough, there was a group of girls giggling and chatting loudly on the way to the parking lot.

I caught Jess's eye—she'd seen where his gaze had gone, too. I felt too good about things between me and her to feel the usual anger when it came to him, but the way her face fell made me want to introduce Kurt to my fist.

"Anyway, we're all friends, right? We're all on the same team. And right now, I actually have a little side project I'm doing for the producer Anthony Pollusk, so I've got to get going. Have a good night, you two." He winked at Jess and took off toward the women.

"I guess 'side project' is his new euphemism for harassing women?" Jess rolled her eyes and turned her back to the way he'd gone in favor of the mountain view.

The man had given up having everything with Jess. How had I missed it, and how had she? I wanted to understand how she could ever stand to be with him, though right now, I wanted to forget him. Because of course, he'd interrupted us in the middle of what'd been a nice little moment, and all I wanted was to forget about him for a while.

Maybe there wasn't an us just yet, but she'd shown she was open to the possibility. Because of this, and how she'd initiated contact last time, I approached her from behind and set my hands on her shoulders. "He's a jackass."

She tucked her arms against herself and shook her head. "I know. And sometimes, it hits me the wrong way that I was ever with him."

She'd read my mind, but I didn't want to bear down on the past or dredge up any more sorrow over our previous choices. My thumb swept over the soft skin at her neck. "For what it's worth, I think he's more overtly terrible now. I think he used to use the charisma for good at least part of the time."

I'd consoled myself with the same thought more than once over the years, though of course I hadn't been around him to realize just how big of a jerk he'd become until this week.

She turned and glanced at me, a hundred unvoiced thoughts in her dark eyes.

My stomach clutched and I couldn't tell if the wanting there was for all those secrets, or for more closeness with her. More time.

More everything.

Yeah, that sounded about right. I'd always wanted more of Jess than I'd had, and I'd spent so much energy banishing that desire and embracing the distance and enmity. But now, there was a chance for more, a window opening after a firmly shut door, and I would embrace it.

"So our first date is to the diner, huh?" she said, lightening the mood and strolling toward the parking lot.

We couldn't do anything about what lay behind us, and we weren't ready to fully define what we wanted now. I'd stopped short of saying more—of saying all the ways I wanted her and just diving fully in because she'd made a point I couldn't skate past. It'd been worming its way into my head more and more—the fear that maybe we did have too much between us, too many hurts and wrongs done to one another, even with the reparations we'd begun.

But what we could do?

We could embrace now. It sounded like that's what she wanted, and so, I'd grab onto it, too.

"I'll treat you right, baby," I said, winking at her with a stupidly obvious shut of one eye.

She burst out laughing. "Oh, no. Am I discovering that instead of a broody grump, I actually have a cheeseball on my hands?"

I hid my pleased grin and stopped her, all serious. She waited, face growing concerned as I waited to speak.

"As long as I'm in your hands, I'll be whoever you need me to—"

She swatted at me, and I didn't bother holding in my laugh. Damn, it felt good, just to laugh with her.

"You are ridiculous."

"I have never claimed to be smooth."

This time, she stopped and slipped her hand into mine. "I don't want smooth, Jude. I just want you."

She flushed like maybe she'd said too much, cheeks darkening to a delicious crimson, but she didn't take it back.

On my deathbed, whenever the moment came, I'd hear those words in her voice. *I just want you.*

So, even though we hadn't had our first date or even talked about all the mess we'd left behind let alone what we might want going forward, I told her the truth. "Good. Because you're all I've ever wanted."

CHAPTER THIRTY-ONE

Jess

Jude Rawlins may have claimed not to be smooth, but he was also not a liar.

The irony there being that I'd thought of him as a liar for years and years—so many wasted years.

And now?

My skin flushed hot as I thought of the earnest way he'd said it. *You're all I've ever wanted.*

Good grief. That couldn't be true.

And yet, hadn't I been chastising myself for not taking the man at his word? Everything he'd said to me thus far had been true.

I rarely slept well these days, but going to bed with his words floating around in my head set me up for a long night. By the time I'd showered and dressed for the day and, oddly, my first date with a man I'd known for more than a decade and had long thought my nemesis, I'd over-analyzed just about everything.

The alternating sensations of genuine excitement to see Jude and sit down together for dedicated time when we weren't trying to be discreet or work out an argument paired with the total brain bust of this gear shift in our relationship had me dry-mouth-level nervous as I parked at the Saint building and walked across the street.

Beast—Jude—already sat in a booth facing the door, but I'd felt his eyes on me from the moment I stepped out of my car. Diner's mountain-facing front windows also had a perfect view into the Saint security lot.

I did not fidget. I did not lick my lips more than once or covertly sniff myself to confirm I was wearing deodorant. I was. Put it on twice for good measure because no one wants to be sweating all day and especially not in a suit. I didn't touch my hair that I normally would've worn down for a date but had twisted into a low bun since work would come swiftly on the heels of this little rendezvous, and I resisted the urge to check my teeth in my phone.

So, I was really nailing the calm, collected woman act. I probably even looked like I knew what I was doing as I entered the door and the little bell chimed to alert the entire diner.

Could there be a store that *didn't* have a little bell on the door in this town?

"Oh my gosh, hi, friend," Catherine said, beelining to me after slipping her very full tray of food onto the counter.

"Hey," I said, fully registering how busy the place was.

My eyes slid toward Jude, where he sat with a steaming mug of coffee and dark eyes shamelessly on me.

"Are you by yourself, or meeting that group?" She notched her head to the side toward the circular booth where a slightly bedraggled crew of Bruce, Kenny, Jack McKean, Eddie James, Cookie, and some other man I didn't recognize sat.

Oh. Right. So our little breakfast date was not about to be discreet thanks to the early morning crew here. I should've considered this since Diner was right across the parking lot from Saint Security and several of these people had an undying love for breakfast food.

They all looked completely cozy, if tired. And they were all already dressed for the day. If I didn't know better, I would've thought they'd been up all night, but there was no way Bruce would opt in to work overnight if he could help it, nor would Eddie want to be away from her man.

"No, I'm, um... here with Beast." My gaze flickered back to the man who had evidently not moved a muscle.

Catherine's brows rose subtly. "Oh. Great."

Her enthusiasm sat behind a tactful wall, but I could see her eyes light up. She had lovely, expressive eyes and girl wasn't fooling anyone. I hadn't told everyone we'd kissed, but they all knew something was up.

And because a month ago, me sitting down with Jude Rawlins would've been a sign of the apocalypse, I wasn't exactly keeping this a secret.

"So I'll just go sit..." I said, feeling squirmy that not only Catherine but a decent handful of my work colleagues would see me take the seat. *Cool. Nothing like a very judgy, gossipy audience to frame a first date.*

Sliding into the booth, I gave the bear of a man across from me a wide-eyed look.

His lips twitched. "Yeah. Maybe not my best call."

I stifled a smile. "Too late now."

He held up his mug right as Catherine set one down next to me, so I raised mine to meet his.

"To imperfection."

My stomach flipped. *You're just hungry. It's fine.*

"To imperfection," I echoed, my throat a little tight with an emotion I wouldn't focus on right now.

"Do you guys need menus?" Catherine held a bunch in her hands with an expectant smile.

"I'm good. You?"

I smiled up at my friend. "I can do it. I'll take the farmer's omelet with whole wheat, extra butter."

Catherine grinned and turned to Beast.

"I'll take the southwestern omelet with bacon and whole wheat, no butter. Orange juice and a silver dollar stack."

"That'll be right up." She lingered for a sec, her smile quiet but a little more obvious than the one she gave the average customers, I'd guess.

When she spun around and bustled to another table just sitting down, I took another sip of my coffee.

He did the same.

Silent, drinking coffee, and perhaps most notably, *not* arguing.

"Extra butter on your toast, huh?"

His usual cocky jerk tone made my hackles rise, though it felt a little different this time.

"Dry toast for you? That tracks."

His brows dropped low. "How so?"

"I mean it's just more evidence of your moral deficiencies."

Those same dark slashes over his eyes rose high. "Oh, yeah?"

I nodded, a regretful smirk on my lips. "Yeah. I'm pretty sure dry toast is one of the most common markers of being a serial killer."

A laugh tripped out of him, and my chest warmed.

"Is it now? So all we need to do in order to predict a person's likelihood of becoming a serial killer is check their breakfast order?"

I shrugged. "I mean, I'm not saying we *shouldn't*."

He shook his head, and I reveled in the way he pressed his lips together. I wanted to see him smile full out like I had with his friends... but I wanted it directed at me.

I'd also take his lips *on* me again. I wonder if he ever smiled in those quiet, intimate moments. If he was the kind of man who—

Whoa there. First date. Simmer down.

"I got dry toast out of habit." The smile at his eyes faded. "I used to give it to my grandma. She liked jelly only. I eat the pancakes. Guess I can just sub for pancakes now, though."

My hand shot out and grasped his large one where it rested near his mug. His *now* didn't mean because he was here with me... it meant now that she was gone, and it sent a horrible crushing ache into my chest.

"I'm sorry. I didn't mean to..." I wasn't sure how to finish the sentence. Tease him about something sensitive? Remind him of what he's lost?

"You couldn't have known. And..." He swallowed hard, his Adam's apple bobbing in a way that made my chest tight, and his hand flipped up to press our palms together. "It's just the way it goes, I'm finding. Even here, with you, on a good day, it hits without warning."

"Has Kenny ever shared his car accident analogy with you?" I asked, eyes flicking to the table where the man in question was gesticulating wildly as he told a story to the captivated table.

Hand tightening around mine a little, Jude nodded. "Yes, but I'd hear your version of it."

This pleased me more than it should've. I squeezed his hand back, then released him, because Catherine had circled back to top off our mugs.

"Food's almost out," she said, winking at us as she moved away.

I smiled after her, then focused back on the person sitting across from me who hadn't removed his attention from me.

"So as you know, Kenny likens grief to a car accident. Could be a fender bender, could be a forty-car pile-up with every car in the line totaled."

He nodded.

"I heard him talking to Cookie in the spring about when his grandma passed, and he said something like, 'this is the side swipe phase. Feels like it comes out of nowhere, but when you walk away, the car's still dented. You can't forget it, and it's changed the shape of you, and you might not bother to get it fixed right away.'" I cupped my hands around my mug, seeking the warmth saturating the ceramic and wishing it was his skin instead. "It's not a perfect metaphor, for sure, but I think putting a name to things, or giving ourselves an image like that to work with can really help."

He nodded again. "It can." He stared at the swirling black of his coffee for a moment before saying, "It wasn't a surprise, you know? In a lot of ways, I've been grieving her since we got here, but definitely since—"

His gaze met mine the instant I made the connection.

"*That's* why you couldn't leave last winter?"

His head dropped a touch. "Yeah. Believe it or not, it wasn't me trying to be an asshole just to piss you off."

I cringed and covered my face. "I'm so sorry."

I'd been so furious with him, feeling like he'd finagled the scenario where I left town for months on an overseas assignment when it should've been him. Bruce and Wilder had said things about Beast being on a no-travel agreement, but it'd never clicked until right now.

"I'm so sorry." Emotion welled up in me so suddenly, I had to clear my throat. *No crying on first dates, fun girl!*

Jude plucked my hand off the table and tugged it, demanding my attention.

"Hey. No. At some point, we're going to deal with all that more, but for now, let's just... not sink down into it. Let's not fault ourselves for things we've done when we didn't have all the information."

I scoffed. "So I'm off the hook for acting like a shrew when I could've been a compassionate human being?"

His gaze narrowed and his baseball glove of a hand wrapped around my wrist. "No, Jess. It's not a carte blanche for either of us. But it is grace for our mistakes. And it is..." His gaze flicked around the room before settling back on me. "It's something new going forward."

He leaned forward and pressed a kiss over the knuckle of my thumb before releasing my hand, and seconds later, our food arrived.

Grace.

Something new.

I liked the sound of that.

CHAPTER THIRTY-TWO

Jude

Part of me had hoped we'd get out of here before the group did, but they'd been sitting and already had their food when I'd come in.

"Well, aren't you two just *adorable*."

Kenny's all too pleased voice alerted me to the trouble, and I saw my own acceptance mirrored in Jess's dark eyes.

"How was breakfast?" she asked, completely disregarding the man-child's question.

"Delicious," Jack McKean said. "Thanks for the recommendation."

Wait. Dammit. Jack McKean was who she directed the question toward?

I shifted in my seat enough so I could see the rest of the group. Bruce and Eddie were talking in low tones to Cookie, and then here stood my idiot friend and *the* Jack McKean.

Cool.

Great.

"Couldn't let you miss it this time. But why are you up so early?" she asked, smiling up at the world-famous actor with perfect dark hair and vibrant blue eyes that gave Adam's a run for his money.

I mean sure, the guy was good-looking. He was paid to be. His livelihood rested on his ability to look good. And he was in a tax bracket a retired soldier-turned-private-security guy like me could only dream of.

Not that I was comparing myself because I wasn't an idiot.

Also, I was the one sitting across from Jess.

So. There. Take that, McKean.

Though looking at him in real life with no filters, I questioned what he did to have skin so smooth and to just look so... polished. It was like looking at a filtered photo but there he was in real life, not a blemish or errant hair to be found.

Guess when being attractive was half your job, you used the good stuff.

Jack had been saying something I missed, and Jess laughed, her wide, genuine smile bringing me back to the conversation.

"Thanks. Are you with me again today?" Jack asked.

I stoutly ignored the little geyser of envy at those words. *With me again* like they were together and that was a thing I had any business having an opinion on. Crap, my mind was scrambled with jealousy, and if I ever let on about it, Jess would probably punch me in the eye for being an idiot. Or worse, she'd think I didn't respect her because I thought she'd date someone she was contracted to guard. Or even worse, because me being jealous hinted at not believing she was a faithful person, and that simply wasn't true.

I caught Kenny's eye and he gave me a sly, irritating grin

like he knew exactly where my mind had just gone. The twerp.

"Sure am. Fueling up and I'll be with you right at eight. I was briefed to be at your room, but feel free to have the team text me and I can meet you wherever." Jess sounded friendly and professional, much as any normal person not enflamed with jealousy would expect.

"Room's good. I've got to let this settle and then get in a workout. Any chance you want to run with me?" He gave her a hopeful look.

I kept my jaw wired shut and did not look to my left where I would undoubtedly see Kenny's beady little puppy dog eyes boring a hole into the side of my head in an effort to catch a glimpse of my reaction to this exchange. I wouldn't give him the satisfaction.

"I'm up for whatever. See you soon," she said, like it really was all fine with her.

Everyone else filtered out, Cookie giving us a chin nod and Bruce and Eddie giving us a quick hello before they were all gone, leaving us to our meal.

Jess took a big bite of her omelet and waved out the window at Kenny, who was walking backwards and waving like a child leaving his parents.

She chuckled. "He's an idiot."

I grumbled. She had no idea the amount of hell I was going to pay now that he'd both seen us on our little breakfast date *and* had a front row seat to me mentally freaking out over Jack McKean talking to her.

"You'll never hear the end of this, will you?" she asked.

I shoved a giant bite of pancakes into my mouth to avoid a more detailed answer. I'd been very honest with her all along, but I didn't need to describe the torment Kenny no doubt had in store for me.

She dropped her head. "Wait, does he know about..." She cleared her throat. "Does he know we kissed?"

Her cheeks had deepened into a blush I wanted to savor for a moment, maybe explore other ways to make her blush. Jess wasn't the kind of woman who got embarrassed easily—her innate self-confidence and competence made this blush a deliciously rare sighting. I was a good man and all for taking cautious steps forward to make sure she was on the same page, but my lovesick mind didn't manage to avoid several vivid scenes flashing through my mind that might make her cheeks brighten just like this again.

That said, I also didn't want her thinking I'd been wandering around talking about kissing her like some bragging idiot. "Not because I told him—apparently, he saw us at the hotel. But I did talk to him after I left your house when I followed you home from the cabin."

Understanding dawned. "Ah."

"Yeah. So. I'll definitely never hear the end of it."

She seemed thoughtful, so I took another bite. We ate in quiet, only the steady stream of pop songs playing low over the speakers and the humming white noise coming from the kitchen and other diners our accompaniment.

Did she regret it? I wouldn't have called it fretting, but the peace I'd felt with Jess in the quiet moments at the cabin was nowhere to be found. Granted, there were plenty of times the silence had been full of me freaking out about her being so sick, but it'd felt different than this. Now, I worried she might be spooked over people knowing about this new... direction? Dimension? This new *something* between us that included brain-melting kisses and apparently jealousy thick enough to choke on.

A twinge of disheartening anticipation twisted in my

gut. I didn't want to have to talk her into this. I couldn't do that to her or me.

Her attention snagged on something outside and I followed her gaze, fully expecting to see Kenny making a scene of some sort. Instead, it was a group of Blackthorne guys standing in the Saint Security parking lot talking with Bruce and Wilder, who must've shown up in the last few minutes.

Her shoulders deflated a little as she turned back to the table. "I don't like that he's here. And then I don't like that I don't like it."

"You think it'd be normal if you liked seeing your ex?" I asked, incredulous to hear she cared. I wished she'd left him behind and never thought about him. Maybe then, we'd be different, too.

Her head tipped from one side to the other. "Kind of. I mean, not normal to not care at all, but I wish it didn't still feel like a punch in the gut to see him." Her eyes flickered up to meet mine and then quickly away.

My stomach clutched, dreading the answer before I could even form the question. "Do you still..." I couldn't say the word, though. Not after what I'd said to her, even last night, and not after everything in me waking up again thanks to her.

She raised a brow. "Love him?"

Hopefully, my wince didn't show on my face. "Yeah."

She took a huge breath. "Thankfully, no." She nudged a bite of her omelet with her fork. "I just hate that he left me. Yes, that he cheated, but then *he* left. I should've left *him*. I shouldn't have stuck around until the truth came out. It's not like it was good between us. It hadn't been for a while, but we'd both been gone and—"

The flush in her cheeks had traveled down her neck, as

though she'd just realized who she was telling and what she was saying. She never would've told me any of this before—certainly not when she was with him, but even weeks ago. We didn't talk like this.

We were different. Maybe each of us as individuals, but also our dynamic together. I could be nothing but grateful and greedy for more of this change, and I'd make sure she understood how much. I'd worked on speaking more freely, and I'd done so, and I wouldn't go back to grunting when I could find words instead, because I wanted her to know me now.

"I'll never forgive him for how he treated you." Seeing her pain, even so many years later, made me want to crush something.

How about Kurt's stupid face?

She smiled softly but shook her head. "Nah. Don't let that eat away at you. And I shouldn't let it me, either. Not anymore. I just wish... I don't know. I guess I wish I could be impervious to him."

"I get it. As much as you like to pretend you're cold as ice, I think you're actually deeply empathetic and feeling."

As my words settled between us, her face shifted from a thoughtful one to something mildly shocked. "Wait, so I seem like I'm frigid?"

I glanced from side to side. *No one to help you now, idiot!* Where was Kenny with a poorly timed interruption when I needed him? "Uh, no?"

She burst out laughing, a luscious, free sound I was instantly addicted to. "You are a terrible liar."

"I'm not lying. I've never thought of you as frigid. I knew better than that."

Our gazes held, and I wondered if she could read everything behind mine. *I was in love with you, so it didn't matter anyway*. I didn't want to fight for her to believe me right now, when we were talking about her, but she had no idea. Saying I'd thought of her as frigid would be like saying the surface of the sun was cold. She had done nothing but light me on fire from the day I'd met her. Even when I'd pushed that desire down, when I'd buried it deep, it'd still burned like the Earth's core.

I wouldn't deny the truth, but I didn't want to focus there for now. Not just yet. She had so much farther to go before she could hear all that. So I pushed on. "Point is, I get wanting to just forget about him. Move on and not let him affect your life."

She sat back in the booth, omelet nearly gone, toast in tatters, and coffee empty. "This has been such an odd first date."

"You're not wrong." Though I hoped the oddness of it didn't mean *first* would be *only*.

Catherine came to clear a few plates and soon, our first and very odd date was over.

We'd talked about grief and loss. We'd seen friends. I'd had a brief but wildly jealous interlude where I'd momentarily considered looking into better facial products. And we'd even gotten around to Kurt.

What we hadn't discussed was what came next, and so before we stood, I rushed in.

"Are you free for dinner tonight?"

Her mouth dropped open. "Um, tonight?"

I nodded. I couldn't have been clearer, and if she didn't want to see me again so soon, I wasn't going to cry about it. But I also wasn't going to pretend I didn't want to see her again—maybe with a smaller crowd around us, and maybe without our friend Catherine popping in to provide excellent service. Patience I had in spades, but I also didn't have to wait anymore, did I? And our schedules were awful during the festival, so if we both had time, we should take it.

She pressed her lips to the side, then chuckled lightly. "Okay, sure. Yes. I'm free tonight after eight."

"My place around eight-thirty?" An odd tunnel vision hit me as I said the words, the surreal feeling of inviting her to dinner at my house a moment of fantasy. And yet, my feet were on the ground, and our hands brushed as she exited while I held the door.

It was real.

Her "See you then" clinched it as we walked out into the gorgeous, chilly fall morning.

Eight-thirty. My place. Just the two of us and Bones.

I didn't bother hiding my smile as I made my way toward the office, even if I knew Kenny was lying in wait.

CHAPTER THIRTY-THREE

Jess

Jack's pace was a little faster than I preferred, but I wasn't about to tell him that. I could keep up okay and the day was too beautiful to be spent inside, so bless him for suggesting an outside activity.

I always planned on being in a suit, especially when there were all kinds of swanky events on his schedule, but the detour was welcome and exactly why I kept a bag of other outfits in my car for assignments like this. An A-lister is gonna do what an A-lister wants to do and you better be ready. All it took was one time for me to go hiking in a regular underwire with someone I was assigned to a while back, and from then on I'd learned to always be prepared with appropriate spandex and footwear.

"Do you normally run here?" Jack slowed and puffed out a breath.

"It's not my favorite form of exercise, but I do it a few

times a week." I inhaled through my nose, grateful it wasn't as cold as it had been when the day started.

He laughed. "So then, yes. You do." He huffed loudly. "I need to live in the mountains so I don't have this short-ness of breath anytime I come back and try to walk upstairs."

I chuckled. "I mean, we're doing an eight-minute mile right now..."

"I swear I get winded standing up from dinner. It's pathetic." He seemed genuinely bothered, but in a kind of self-deprecating way that made him that much more appealing.

"You realize it's science, right? Not a matter of fitness?"

He made a dismissive sound that reminded me of Beast. *Jude.* My stomach fluttered and I swallowed down the nerves.

He'd asked me out for dinner tonight like it wasn't weird —like he wasn't embarrassed to seem too interested.

I hadn't dated since Kurt had left me—simply hadn't wanted to. Maybe that was why I compared everything to my time with him. Kurt's pursuit of me had always felt extremely targeted and purposeful, like he had a goal in mind and that goal was me on his arm, in his life, in his bed.

If only I'd realized that once he'd gotten me there, locked into all the roles he'd imagined for me, he'd gotten bored. He just hadn't been man enough to admit it and cut me free.

Between Kurt's determination and my need to hurry up and nail down a secure relationship where I belonged, it wasn't a complete mystery how I let so much mediocrity between us slide. Had there ever been even a fraction of the fire between Kurt and me like there was with Jude?

No comparison. I'd never felt so distinctly desired and... sought after as I had this morning with Jude.

Our time together was water cupped in his hands and it'd seeped out through the cracks all too soon. Instead of saying, "Oh, well, let's do it again next weekend," he'd been too eager to take another scoop and hold it close, protecting the well there. He'd had no patience to wait.

His impatience had always bothered me—it was one of many qualities I'd taken as a personal failing. I'd never considered how delicious it could be when directed at me.

"You like living here? You've been here for a little over a year, right?" Jack asked, breaking through my odd thoughts.

"About eighteen months now. And yes, I love it here." We pounded the paved trail tracing the edge of the Silver Ridge Resort property for another quarter mile, and then I added, "It's the first place that has ever felt like home."

After a few minutes, he slowed so I did the same. We walked, cooling down as we neared the resort's buildings again.

"I'm not sure I've ever had a place that felt like that," he said.

I glanced at him, his chiseled, handsome face bleeding a vulnerability I wouldn't have imagined possible for someone like him before I met him this week. "Maybe it's time for a change?"

He gave me a half smile I'd seen in more than one of his films and we plodded along until I swiped a card to enter the back door, then held it for him.

There was already a buzzing sound coming from the lobby.

"We could take the service elevator and avoid it," I suggested, knowing the crowd was likely waiting for him or any number of other celebs in residence right now.

"Nah. I don't mind today." He gave me a little nod that looked exactly like a Bruce Camden gesture, and then we moved.

The instant we entered the lobby, the crush of voices and furor rose. People yelled his name, questions, proposals, everything, and fortunately the hotel had roped off the elevator access. It hadn't been this wild last year, so most of these folks were likely out of towners. Certainly, the people with giant camera lenses pointed at Jack were.

He waved and smiled, chatting amicably with a few people who had actual questions. *When will you make the next movie in* Litmus Chronicles? *Why have you been so reclusive lately? Is that your girlfriend?*

Jack took them all in stride, answering that he'd be filming in the coming year, he'd been busy working and preparing for the movie being shown at the film fest and he hoped they all loved it, and no, she was his badass bodyguard.

Love a man who wasn't scared to admit a woman was guarding him. Some people really did have a problem with it—and even if not in practice, they might struggle to admit it in a setting like this. Not Jack.

Good guy.

I ushered him into the elevator and got it moving, eying him as subtly as I could to make sure he wasn't rattled. He seemed solid.

"I'm good. Thanks."

"Good."

His phone buzzed. "Oh, it's Jenna. Do you know if Cookie's guarding her?"

My senses piqued. "Jenna Halter? I think he's assigned to her on and off. They have a history."

His smile flashed. "Oh, I know. He's good people. I'd

hoped maybe they'd do the whole 'fall in love with your bodyguard' thing, but apparently, they're just good friends now."

His level of disappointment at this was unmissable.

"Wow, that's quite romantic of you," I said, then stopped short. "Does that mean you've fallen in love with a past bodyguard? A future one? Bruce *is* incredibly charming."

He tsked. "You know Bruce only has eyes for Nikki. And no, no luck falling for any of my bodyguards. You up for it?"

His ice-blue eyes hooked into mine, and for a heartbeat, it almost felt like he was really asking. Not because of *me*, but because he wanted it—love, maybe?—that badly.

"Uh, thank you for the offer, but..."

He laughed. "I'm not hitting on you, I swear."

"I would be worried for you if you had been. And I'd also be honored, of course." What else does one say to something like this?

"It's the big guy... Brute, or something?"

I cackled. "Oh, man, I wish it was Brute! That's amazing. But it's actually *Beast,* so not far off." I glanced up at him and his pleasant smile waited for me to continue. "And yeah. It's... uh..." I scratched at my cheek for something to do. "It's him."

What *it* was remained to be seen. Did I love him? Obviously not. I'd only just realized I didn't hate him. But *could* I?

Astoundingly, there was only one clear answer here, and it was *yes*. I could. I'd always thought so. I'd always wondered... well, before everything detonated.

Jack nodded, accepting my awkwardness as proof.

The doors lurched open on the top floor and I exited first, expecting to find an empty hallway, but Kurt emerged from the left—the stairs?

"There you are," he said, and came straight toward me.

CHAPTER THIRTY-FOUR

Jess

"What are you doing here?" I asked, sounding more than a little accusatory while I held the elevator doors open and gave Jack a nod indicating he should stay put.

Was Kurt a threat? No, at least in theory.

Was he an idiot? Yes, indeed, and Jack didn't need to deal with this man.

"Hey, Jessie. I'm glad to catch you. Blackthorne was having me do a sweep—oh, Mr. McKean." Kurt's smile widened into a friendly, pleased expression that hit just the right notes of surprised but not overeager.

So he still had that ability going for him.

I sighed and waved Jack out so we could free up the elevator.

"Jack McKean, this is Kurt Spangler. He worked with

us back in North Carolina for a while and is now a part of Blackthorne."

The two men shook hands and Jack, being the congenial man he was, asked a few polite questions of Kurt. The two went back and forth a few times before Kurt brought it back around to me.

"Yeah, Jessie and I go way back. I mean, all of us do, but with her it's different." He somehow transformed his face into a puppy dog look that would fell even the least feeling among us.

"Oh, I didn't realize." Jack turned to me. "You two need a minute?"

"No, I'm—"

"Actually, could we? She can clear your room and we'll just stand right outside if that works for you, Jack." Kurt grinned.

Ugh. He still had it. I knew this because I'd seen him here and there, charming everyone he came in contact with and balancing that side with the dark, almost rough air he gave off as a member of Blackthorne. The combination was killer to certain kinds of people, and though Jack didn't seem all that enamored with him, he didn't seem bothered that this man would want to talk to me while I was working.

"No, we'll wait until after my shift," I insisted.

"Nah, Jess, really. I'm just going to get cleaned up. If you're good to talk now, that's great."

Jack McKean, everybody. World's most inconveniently accommodating client.

But instead of protesting, I nodded, my teeth clenched so hard my jaw muscle probably tripled in size. I could object and make more of a scene, draw even more attention to how much I didn't want to speak with my ex, or I could take care of Jack, shut his door, and then get real with Kurt and likely get through all this much faster.

Option B, even though everything in me pushed for Option A.

After clearing Jack's room and confirming with HQ that he was settled in and I was taking my post at the door, I turned to find Kurt leaning against the wall with arms crossed and a little smile on his face.

I used to think that smile meant something—like he was secretly admiring me and so glad I was his. Like he wanted me.

Embarrassment flashed through me at the memory of feeling *glad* I'd given in and dated him, then said yes to his proposal. How had I felt so secure?

"Even after a run, you look great," he said, his voice low and as sincere as it could be.

"What do you need, Kurt?"

His smile faded in what seemed to be genuine... something. Though *genuine* was no longer a word I associated with this man.

"I need to apologize." He stepped forward, hands behind his back and chin ducked in a way that made him appear genuinely regretful.

Dread hit, rapidly squelching the embarrassment. "I don't need anything from you."

"Then maybe I need this, okay?"

As much as I'd braced against seeing him, as much as I wasn't in love with this person and had made peace with myself for what'd happened in the past, I couldn't say no to him. And just now, I couldn't escape it even if I wanted to.

"Fine. Three minutes." Because we were not about to stand here for half an hour and hash out our relational post-mortem years and years after the fact.

"When everything happened, I was angry and hurt. I didn't do right by you, and I'm sorry." His expression sincere, his voice smooth and soft, he waited with hands pressed together as though in prayer or supplication for my forgiveness.

"You didn't." I wouldn't excuse it because you don't just ghost someone you were going to marry. You don't do that, even if your life is falling apart. "I would've been there for you."

I'd felt this so strongly—not only the regret that we were over, but the hurt that he wouldn't let me support him. Though now that I searched for the feeling in this moment, I didn't detect it.

Because wrapped up in all of this, too, had been so much anger at Beast and a staunch commitment to doubting anything he'd said. A gut-level need to believe what Kurt had said in order to avoid confronting so many things I'd known to be true about him.

And true about myself.

He'd cheated—I hadn't known it with certainty then, but as soon as Beast had hinted at it, it'd struck like an arrow to the center of its target because I'd had a few hints and suspicions Kurt had managed to talk away over the years. If I'd admitted he'd cheated, then I'd also have to admit my role in it—how I'd forced him into an engagement he didn't want. I'd made it clear I'd wanted it, but what if I'd just laid off?

He'd attempted to save himself and throw his friend under the bus—it just hadn't worked. And yet, I'd shoved all of it back in Beast's face because I was too angry and hurt...

And scared.

Standing here in this hallway a few feet from the man who'd cheated on me, lied to me, and then abandoned me...

there it was. The one emotion I hated more than anything, stemming from a truth I'd run from all my life.

I was easy to leave.

My dad had left when I was a kid, and as if to confirm my suspicions, my fiancé had left me, even when he had nowhere to go. My own mom, in a very unintentional way, had left me and stayed gone, right when I needed her most. It'd been the two of us forever, and even though I loved that she had Guy now, it meant I didn't have her, nor had I for a long time. I didn't stop needing her just because I was an adult.

Those thoughts were for another time—most definitely not when my idiot ex was standing here working up to a true confession that would no doubt just heap on more feelings I'd need to detangle.

"I know you would've. I regret not letting you be there for me. I'm sorry I hurt you, and I hope..." He trailed off, his gaze studying me like he might find the right words in my face. His shoulders slumped. "I'm just sorry. And I've been walking around here like a smug ass because I don't know how to be around you—I didn't expect it to hurt like this. And I definitely didn't expect to find you with someone who betrayed me."

My insides solidified into steel. And there, that's how he'd play it. Again. "That's enough. You can go."

"What? What the hell, Jessie. I'm trying to be honest here."

The hurt on his face felt so exaggerated, I nearly laughed. "I'm asking you to go because I can't since you've found me *at work*. But I'm not going to continue talking to you when you're still not going to own up to the truth. You cheated on me. You lied to me. Tried to blame everything on

Jude and whether you'll admit it or not, he didn't betray you by reporting you. You ruined your own career and you're lucky retiring a few years before you planned to is all that happened."

Oh, and losing me, but I wasn't going to point that out because somehow, I doubted he actually regretted it.

And though my emotions about the way things happened were complex, no part of me regretted not being with him. Not now that I knew the truth, and not for a long time.

Instead of heating or exploding in anger, his eyes did something I could only describe as deadened. The spark, the hope and pleas, they all winked out and all that remained was a sneer.

"Right." He sucked in a breath and let it out before swearing a string of expletives, then continuing with, "You always were a—"

"I'm done here, is what I am. You go your way, and I'll go mine, and you should avoid taking any assignments in Silverton again for a nice long time. Bye, Kurt." I let myself into Jack's room and shut the door.

Was it running away? No. I didn't think so. Because I didn't have to stand there and let him berate me when he was the one who'd messed up. He had hurt people—me, Jude, and who knew how many women he'd harassed or even assaulted.

I shuddered and double-checked the locks. I could hear the shower running so Jack would be out soon.

And in a few hours, I could go home and get over this. I'd tell Jude what happened and he'd probably be furious with Kurt for opening his stupid yap, but then we'd move on. We'd have our date and have a great time.

And I wouldn't let this feeling like someone tied a lead weight to my ankle drag me down and ruin the evening. I just wouldn't let it.

CHAPTER THIRTY-FIVE

Jude

Jess arrived right on time looking...
Was it disrespectful to say edible?
Probably.
So. No. She looked beautiful. And intelligent.
And unfortunately, somehow a little... off.

"I brought this wine," she said, holding out a decent-looking pinot noir before I could say anything, then stepped inside.

"Thank you. Come in," I deadpanned, since she was already more than halfway down the entry hall as I closed the door.

I watched her stop and take in the living room, then the kitchen to the right, where I'd done everything but the last few steps for our dinner. On the island countertop sat a bowl of tortilla chips and a few little dipping bowls containing salsa, guacamole, queso, and a spicy chipotle ranch.

She whipped around after a beat. "This is... how is this so perfect? Your cabin was the perfect cabin and now this?"

Her gaze swept over the food again, then rose to meet mine with what looked like accusation.

"I'm... sorry?"

She huffed out a laugh, then spotted my giant beast of a cat slinking toward her. "And the perfect kitty boy, too, huh?" she said in that voice that was just a touch sweeter than the usual smokey siren song I savored.

Though I couldn't complain about her sweettalking my cat, nor could I regret that he seemed to love her madly already.

Join the club.

Because it didn't seem particularly respectful to enjoy the view of her very fine curves in those pants as she bent to pet Bones, I moved to the kitchen and, for lack of anything else to do, washed my hands. A minute or two later, she joined me, a serious expression taking over the one of peace she'd had moments ago.

"Kurt found me during my shift and wanted to talk." She spat the last word, clearly indicating how she felt about the matter.

My gut clenched right as a fire started in my head. "Are you okay? What did he say?"

Can I punch him now? Can I beat him to a bloody pulp to teach him one of so many lessons he missed?

She eased the faucet on and pumped soap onto her hands, then scrubbed.

"He said he's sorry. He shouldn't have left me." A humorless laugh escaped as she rinsed the bubbles away. "And then he said he's been such a jerk because he didn't expect seeing me to hurt so much, and he *really* didn't expect to see me with someone who'd betrayed him."

She turned slowly, drying her hands on the towel resting next to the sink where I'd just left it. Her eyes practically burned through me when she met mine, effectively echoing the flame of anger rising higher as her words sank in.

"Betrayed him." My mouth spoke without thought, like I needed to hear it before I could fully make sense of it.

Nodding, she reached for me, her fingers gripping my shirt. "I set him straight."

She was so intense, and yet the upset and sadness I'd sensed at the door had melted into something different now. Almost like she wanted me to know she'd defended herself *and* me.

"He didn't deserve a chance to talk to you and throw his BS around like he's ever actually been sorry." My hands came to cup her face. "If he ever felt sorry, it was for himself."

"I know. I told him he should think twice before taking any jobs in Silverton again."

A smile pulled at my lips. "Left him with a threat, eh? I like your style, Korbel."

She pursed her lips, staying a grin. "It was pretty mild, but I think he got the hint I wasn't about to sign up for any more heart to hearts."

I wanted to hug her, then kiss her, then lay her down and worship her until the sun came up. But just because we'd kissed before didn't mean I was welcome to do it now, especially with the twinge of knowing telling me the resolution here wasn't this easy.

My fingers dragged along her scalp, hoping to provide a

little comfort and connection. I needed it, and it felt like maybe she did, too.

She blinked hard a few times and her eyes glazed with tears. She might as well have ripped out my heart because a front-row seat to this was more brutal than I'd ever imagined. I'd seen her furious—I'd provoked such a response from her time and time again. And I'd seen her angry and tired and fed up. I'd seen her delirious and exhausted and ill... but this was new.

A need to make this right roared through me. I'd search the world to find a solution here. I'd raze cities to stop her tears—to fix this.

She shouldn't be crying unless she was so happy it overflowed into liquid joy on her face. She shouldn't cry unless she was in a state of such ecstasy her body had to surrender something and this was one way it released an overflow of bliss.

None of that made sense, but the madness in my mind had me howling at the crescent moon, yearning to stop her sadness.

"I'm sorry." She pulled away and turned her back to me, shielding herself from my prying eyes.

With one hand soft on her shoulder, I eased her around, then pulled her into a hug.

"You don't have to apologize for anything. You've done nothing wrong." I bent and dropped a kiss to the crown of her head, desperate to soothe her.

Her arms slowly looped around my back and a trace of the gripping anxiety begging me to make everything better loosened.

"I hate that talking to him has me like this," she said into my side, her words muffled but thankfully still intelligible.

"He was your fiancé. No matter how many years and

miles between then and now, that's still something that's going to dredge up a lot of feelings, even if it had ended mutually." Did I hate that it hadn't been? Yes. But it wasn't something I would ever say aloud.

She loosened her grip on me and tilted her head up so I could see her reddened eyes.

"That's just it, though. I stopped feeling like it was one-sided not long after he'd left because even if I couldn't let myself believe that he'd cheated, he'd walked away. I realized I'd forced it—that we never should've gotten engaged and if I hadn't been so obvious about wanting that, maybe we wouldn't have been so caught up in what *should* be happening. And I never wanted to be with someone like that. I wanted to be with someone who would fight for me." Her jaw flexed against the emotion rising again and she breathed through the tears until they settled and then continued. "I hate that his leaving me felt like a confirmation."

My heart thudded a steady rhythm and I braced for what would come next. "A confirmation of what?"

Her gaze cast down and her voice softened like maybe she didn't want me to hear. "That I'm easy to leave."

My heart tripped and before I thought better of it, I crushed her to me, mind scrambling for words to refute this.

Her words dripped with conviction, like his leaving her really had been proof for this theory and not the failing of a world-class idiot.

I slipped my hands to her hips and hoisted her onto the counter, pulling back to find her face tear-tracked and staring at me with confusion.

Cupping her face, I swiped my thumbs over her cheeks. "You are not easy to leave. Kurt was an idiot for leaving you, though I can't say I'm sorry he's out of your life. And whoever else has done this to you..." I swore, the anger and hurt for her nearly choking out my words. "They were wrong to do it, and such a fool. Because you... Jess, *God*, you're everything."

How could I make her see? How could I force away the shadows in her eyes and imbue the truth that she was wonderful and worthy of love and fidelity and every good thing?

Her lips trembled and her brow furrowed, and I braced myself for what would come, summoning the ability to speak words she could hear.

Her fingers found the placket of my shirt and she focused there as one brightly polished blue fingernail toyed with a button. She was buying time, swallowing down the tears threatening again.

"I hate that I'm crying on our second date."

Her brown eyes tipped up to meet mine, a mess of emotions there I couldn't decipher. I couldn't right all the wrongs, but I could push her buttons enough to get her through them. "I told you not to apologize."

A smile flashed at the familiar bossiness in my tone before she shoved me back with no force. "Fine, then. I'm not sorry. Now feed me guacamole."

CHAPTER THIRTY-SIX

Jess

Jude had surprised me.

Ha. No. Jude had broken my brain and then knitted it back together.

I'd voiced the ugly truth that'd hounded me, that I'd been running from for years, and he'd stayed steady despite the tears and pathetic levels rising to DEFCON 1.

And then the man fed me tacos. Like, really *really* good tacos with my choice of tortilla style and two different kinds of meat and all the fixings including delicious homemade guacamole.

He was just so...

So...

He was kind of a dream, honestly. And even though I'd come to terms with this on some level more than once in the last few weeks, this new element of being in his perfectly effortless house and his gigantic, beautiful cat who'd stolen my heart the minute I met him, and then his incredibly capable handling of my feelings as I fell apart...

You're everything.

Yeah, and then that, too.

He kept saying these things that felt so bone deep. Like he really believed them. And good grief, I wanted to, too.

I wanted to take his declaration that it wasn't me who was easy to leave, but that the men who'd left were faithless twits—okay, so he didn't put it that way, but I'd added it. I wanted to hold it close and press into it, absorb it like moisture into every pore.

He didn't know it was my father who'd left, but did he need to? A small voice—likely the one of nine-year-old Jess —said yes. It did matter.

But the adult woman who'd not only endured being left again, but had worked to make something of herself and even more than that, *for* herself here in Silverton? That woman said Jude was right.

And if he was, then it meant I wasn't doomed to be left forever and that trusting someone to love me might just be possible.

I'd let in my friends, bit by bit. Jo, Catherine, Elise, Dove, Nikki, and Winnie had wormed their way into my heart. And before them, even Bruce and Wilder, Tristan, Adam, Kenny, Luc and even Stone... they'd been my friends.

But Jude... maybe we'd done too much damage to each other to have any real future. I'd failed him and he'd failed me, so how could we go forward? And yet, here we were, snuggled up on his couch playing poker after the oddest, best date I'd ever had.

Odd because I was certain I'd never sobbed into a man's shirt over my past on any other date. And best because of how he'd handled it... and how I hadn't felt bad for it. He'd never once made me feel silly for crying or even feeling the things I did. He hadn't given me a moment alone so he wouldn't be faced with the mess of my crapstorm of emotions, and he hadn't backed away when I got mad or hurt or sad.

And when he'd given me a tour of his house after dinner, each room a perfect continuation of the cozy, thoughtful home he'd built, it'd gotten better. Because he'd showed me the room where his grandma had stayed at first, and he'd explained how he'd made sure a hospital bed would fit if needed. He'd lost his words, and let me hug him —let me stay with him in another moment of sharp grief.

I couldn't help but wonder what might've happened if we'd stepped into this sooner. If, instead of pushing against each other and letting our bad feelings pile up and harden into stone, we'd humbled ourselves enough to apologize and then... be there for each other. If we'd moved toward one another instead of away.

But that line of thought hurt a little too much right now, especially when a whole other host of feelings was swirling around in my belly.

Had he always been this alarmingly handsome?

The potent combination of his emotional maturity and deft handling of hard subjects paired with the way he squinted at the cards hidden in his giant hand had my pulse thrumming.

Or maybe it was the way our knees pressed together where we sat despite the fact that he had a truly huge couch. I could've scooted down and so could he, but we'd apparently both agreed we wanted the closeness. It made no sense, sitting like this and angling our cards away like stubborn weirdos, and yet, here we were.

He lay down his card and pegged me with his stare.

I tossed a chip into the pile. "Raise."

His gaze didn't waver as he tossed a chip. "Call."

I bit my lip to hide the smile threatening. It wasn't a happy or a victorious one. It would be far too obviously melty and swoon-filled because the way this man was pinning me down with his dark eyes and an energy that felt a little like the word *mine* wrapping around us... *whew.*

I revealed my cards, a wave of triumph sliding through me because I knew I had him beat.

He tossed his down, still not looking away from me.

"I fed you guacamole and this is what you give me?"

I chuckled. "A sound loss? Absolutely." I fluttered my lashes. "Aren't you glad you invited me?"

The subtle smile tugging at the corners of his mouth disappeared and earnestness shone through his gaze. "I am. Very glad."

Kiss me. Just kiss me.

Could he read my mind? Sometimes, it felt like he could. It used to feel like he knew the perfect way to get under my skin, but that was probably due to the reality that *anything* he did made me mad. *One more thing I need to apologize for, and soon.*

His brow dipped and his eyes tracked between mine as though inspecting me like he pored over computers during a mission, sifting information and searching for the right clue or piece of intel that would break things wide open.

He'd always been so good at his job... the one area I couldn't fault him for. He might naturally be fairly taciturn, but the man knew his tech, and he knew how to handle himself in the field.

It'd always been lethally appealing, and nothing had changed on that front. The only difference now was in how he'd made his interest known, unlike so long ago, and we'd cleared the air of the things that had piled up between us.

Well, mostly.

I'd already dominated the evening with my breakdown earlier and I didn't want to ask for a DTR right this second. I just... I wanted him to kiss me. To show me this wasn't all in my head, that his words were real, and that maybe for once in the history of us, we were on the same page.

"I want you."

His tone like gravel, the words sent the air from my lungs and all thought from my mind. He'd always been direct.

"But I can't have you yet." One of his delicious big hands slipped over and cupped my knee.

"I—I mean, that's—confusing." I hadn't expected such a direct statement let alone the counter to it so instantly, especially when every cell in my body was screaming *Yes, you can!*

"I'm not trying to be. I have nowhere to go with this so I'm saying it out loud." His gaze, for the first time in a long time, slid away from mine.

I pressed my hand over his and flipped it so I could slip my fingers between his and hold his hand. Our palms sliding together felt almost as intimate as I imagined sliding into clean sheets next to him... vulnerable, charged... and safe.

The thought hit me like an uppercut to the chin and I rocked back a little. I'd always felt raw around him because he knew everything—he knew the depth of my humiliation and how I'd refused to believe him and how Kurt had cast me aside in so many ways.

But now? He had seen me in so many ugly, bare-naked

situations and he was here. I'd been vulnerable and yet I wasn't running scared, and neither was he.

Had anyone known me like this, ever?

So the question came naturally to me. "What do you need? How can I... help?"

A low, breathy laugh came out as he leaned back against the couch, and grasped my hand more firmly, bringing it closer and clasping his other hand around it.

"I've thought about having you here, to myself, even when I knew I shouldn't. Even when we hated each other."

His eyes found mine, one brow raising at my wince, then pulling my hand up to press a kiss to each of my knuckles like the gesture might soothe away the reminder of our past.

"I don't think we can act like none of that happened. And I'm not saying that's what we're doing, but along with it, we've got Kurt and..." His Adam's apple worked through his swallow. "I'm grieving."

All the fizzing expectation that'd been lingering at the edges of my mind, just out of reach of my fingers, flatlined as my heart sank. "Right. Of course."

How had I let myself forget? He'd lost the most important person in the world to him, and I'd been flouncing around like the only thing that mattered was how I'd overcome my inability to see him as a real human being?

"I see," I added, not wanting him to feel like he needed to say more, but knowing I couldn't stay here if we were just going to keep playing poker and sitting in this tension I would not be able to resist much longer.

Pulling out of his hands, I stood, only to have him tug my hand and stay my movements right as I was even with his legs. "I don't think you do."

His hands found my hips and he guided me to stand

between his legs. My pulse raced and my heart tripped around inside my chest, not sure if it was splintering or leaping or just running around like an idiot.

Holding me in place, he spoke again. "I've wanted something between us for so long, I can hardly remember a time I didn't. Even with everything these last few years..." He shook his head, stopping short of whatever he'd started to say. "The point is, I don't want to rush. I don't want anything that happens between us to be a reaction to Kurt or to be anything but a purposeful, fully cognizant choice for both of us."

"And you think if we kiss now, it'll be because of Kurt? That everything so far has been?" An edge took over as I gave voice to my suspicion.

"No. Not entirely. I guess I just don't want to sit here and make out on my couch and pretend like everything's fine when I know you're upset and sorting through huge things. I don't want to take advantage of the situation."

My heart melted a little even as I laughed a disbelieving breath. "Do I seem like I'm being taken advantage of?"

My hands had found their place on his shoulders, body happily still grasped by him. Sure, he could probably subdue me if he tried his best, but I had the advantage in several ways, one of which was that I was absolutely merciless in hand-to-hand combat.

But that wasn't what he meant, and I knew it. Still, I couldn't help but be annoyed.

"No."

"Good."

His gaze narrowed like he couldn't figure out what I meant.

"I'm not worried about kissing you being the wrong thing, Jude. I want to kiss you because..." *Because some part of me has wanted that since the minute we met, and you tried not to smile when I said your name. Because until I got my wires crossed and started believing Kurt could give me a place to belong and a real home like I'd always wanted, it was you I thought I wanted.*

I wouldn't say any of that, though. Not now. Not when I'd already spilled my guts everywhere earlier.

"Because?"

His hands squeezed me at my waist where he held me now, the physical nudge paired with an urgency in his voice I couldn't resist answering immediately.

"Because I like you. I want to keep getting to know the man you are now. And that includes the you who is grieving, just like the me who's here with you is dealing with crap I've buried for too long. But that isn't all Kurt's fault." I eyed him because he'd certainly had a hand in tossing my world upside down lately.

He waited, like he needed more from me before he could move or take a breath. My heart squeezed and my blood raced, but I womaned up and gave him more.

"I want to kiss you because you're the person I'm looking for in any room I enter and you're who I want to spend time with more than anyone else. I want to kiss you because I can't stop thinking about it, and I—"

That must've done it, because he yanked me forward, taking practically all of my weight in his capable arms, and slid me onto his lap right as our lips met.

CHAPTER THIRTY-SEVEN

Jude

If she was going to talk like that, she was going to get kissed.

We crashed together in a hurried way, but I eased off, slowing the pace to a savoring kind of lilt which eased her mouth open to taste her. Damn if she wasn't the most intoxicating thing I'd ever encountered.

And of course, she followed the rhythm, the slide and lick and press of the kiss perfectly. Like everything she did, she was excellent at this.

Jess did nothing halfway, so when she kissed it was a full body commitment. Her weight on my lap anchored me and her hands slid into the hair at my nape, nails scraping gently against my skin. She tilted her head in response to me, a pleasured sound sending my logic and all that clear thinking about how rushing things between us would be foolish into thin air.

Wait? For what?

How could I wait for anything when every good thing on this earth had collapsed into this moment with this woman and this kiss?

My hands ran along her back and down, taking liberty with her curves and relishing the way she pressed tighter into me, kissed me deeper.

She pulled back enough to tug at my shirt, then rucked it up and tossed it before I could do anything but pull her back to me. But she pushed away with a "Wait, wait," and I froze.

Her gaze tracked down to my chest.

"Sorry. Sorry. I shouldn't have done that," I scratched out, worried we'd already gone too far.

One hand slid from my sternum to the waistband of my jeans in a trail so deadly slow I could hardly breathe. My skin lit on fire in the wake of her touch and the look in her eye as she followed her own progress.

"I did that," she said, her voice kiss-roughened and low.

My heart sprinted, the glint in her eye so intoxicated, I could hardly look at her without being swallowed by the desire swirling around us.

"You did," I said, a question in the words.

That exploratory hand mapped back up my chest before she spoke again. By the time it reached my collar bone and traced along the ridge of one to the other side, I was crawling out of my skin with fast-dissipating restraint.

"I always knew you'd look like this." She swallowed and her gaze found mine. "I just don't know where we go next."

I have a few ideas.

I didn't say the words springing to mind, nor would I, but a vast majority of my body wanted to speak them and draw us into more—more heat, more connection, more moments where space collapsed between us and this tension gave way to satisfaction.

But she was halting our progress wisely. There was sense in this breath we were taking, and I wouldn't disrespect her by being flippant with my response.

I also couldn't say she was everything I'd always wanted and I would like to go to *that* next—to the place where we spent all our days waking up next to each other and soothing aches and building ecstasy.

Too much, far too soon.

Granted, I'd basically said I'd always wanted her. But we'd moved past it quickly and I suspected she didn't believe it, even though I hoped she knew I wouldn't tell her anything but the truth ever again.

So instead, I let her decide. "Where do you want to go next?"

She huffed. "You can't put that all on me. I'm sitting here in your lap—a place I never imagined I'd be—so I'm not sure I'm qualified to decide."

Her irritation with me was, frankly, adorable. People talked about how men defaulted to anger, but Jess Korbel's default setting was absolutely anger when it came to confusion or tension or... anything she didn't like. She hid it well at times, but never even attempted to with me.

I didn't hide my grin and then booped her nose.

Her mouth dropped open. "Who even are you?"

I laughed, loving her so much it sent a chill through me. What would happen if she didn't come along with me in this? What happened if old habits and heartaches proved to be too much for us?

She slid her hands up and around to ring my neck, squeezing softly.

"That bad, huh? You're going to stare into my eyes and

put me down? I guess I always knew if you killed me, you'd want to watch the light go out." Her hands stayed put, but I let mine find their way to her face. "Do what you must. At least I'll die living out a fantasy."

She made a sound of surprise and her face flashed with both horror and delight. "You fantasized about me killing you?"

Shaking my head, I traced her full bottom lip with my thumb. "No, baby. I fantasized about you on my lap."

She jolted like I'd punched her in the gut and her eyes grew wide, then she laughed out one sharp, disbelieving guffaw. "You actually just said that."

"I won't deny I've always wanted you. But that's exactly why I think we should be smart." And before all of this ran away with me, before I convinced myself I could tell her everything before she was ready, I needed some space. I shifted, taking her by the waist and lifting her off me before standing.

She stood frozen for a moment before stooping to pet Bones, who'd come to check on her now that she'd moved from on top of me.

"I should go," she said to my cat, definitely not to me.

And that, we just couldn't have.

With a hand on her arm, I turned her to me and pulled her in, wrapping her up. Her wooden posture relaxed when I ducked my head and pressed a kiss to her temple.

"We have enough history between us and patterns we've established, I'm worried that at any minute you'll go back to hating me because this all feels too good to be true." The admission emerged in a whisper against her hair.

Her arms flexed, holding me tighter, then loosening enough so she could find my eyes.

"We're not going back to that. Ever. Because I was an

idiot, and you were, too. So... no. I think I can honestly say that no matter what happens, I won't hate you again." She ducked her chin, a defeated exhale filtering out between her lips. "I'm sorry I ever let it get so bad. I hate that there's so much built up in our past."

"It wasn't just you." I tucked a lock of hair that'd fallen in her eyes back behind her ear.

She bit her lip for a moment before she nodded. "True. But I'm afraid a lot of the responsibility rests with me. I established the pattern... you just followed it." Her brow furrowed. "Sometimes, I wonder why."

"Why what?"

"Why you didn't just ignore me completely. I mean, I know I can be frustrating, and I wasn't ever *nice* to you, but I think we probably could've coexisted more peacefully without you grunting at me all the time." She raised one brow to punctuate the thought.

She really didn't get it, did she?

"If I'd just ignored you, then you would've ignored me."

She blinked, waiting for more, so I gave it to her.

"You have no idea how desperate I was. But also angry and hurt and grieving my grandfather not long after it all happened, too. So everything crashed together in this sick version of antagonism that felt awful, but so much better than silence between us."

Her chest rose sharply on an inhale. "You... you were rude to me because fighting with me was better than nothing?"

It scratched the surface. "Yes, in a way. I know it's messed up, but it's how it happened. And I'm sorry for my part in this—all of it."

She rose on her toes and pressed a searing kiss to my

lips. Before I could deepen it and let it spin out, she stepped back.

"I'm sorry, too. For all of it."

Another sweet, soft, far too quick kiss, and then she gave me a smile that made me want to beg.

Instead, I tipped my forehead against hers and said, "Just to be clear, so there's nothing between us, I should clarify I am not at all sorry for reporting Kurt." I hated saying his name, but I wouldn't bend on that.

Her lips pressed together for a minute before she loosed her smile. "I can genuinely say I'm not either."

She left not long after. I stopped myself from asking her to stay for a movie because we both had another long day coming, and we both knew we wouldn't watch a minute of anything on screen. She seemed less unsure, but I wanted that fiery confidence—in herself and in me. In us.

I had to believe it could come.

CHAPTER THIRTY-EIGHT

Jess

Guac was buzzing with energy even at two in the afternoon. Normally, an October Sunday afternoon would mean Silverton was quiet, but the festival continued and so did the crowds. People came for the celebrities, the films being shown, and even the gorgeous fall colors that'd thankfully survived the snow and would draw a trickle of tourism after the festival ended, or so all the local businesses hoped.

I didn't hate the buzzing energy in town, especially since it meant all my friends' small businesses were flourishing. During our chips, salsa, and guac course, Elise reported she'd sold out of donuts every day before nine in the morning and her maple and pumpkin spice flavors had both disappeared long before that. Jo shared similarly positive news for All Booked Up's sales, and Catherine, though she didn't own Diner, confirmed they'd been slammed.

Saint Security certainly benefited since we were all working non-stop. We'd end up with some nice bonuses at Christmas thanks to all the business this year since even guarding Jack and a few others last year yielded a sizeable check and this year we had even more clientele.

"Are you exhausted yet, though? I feel like you went from one assignment to being sick in Beast's cabin to jumping in and working twenty-four-seven. I swear I've hardly seen Adam." Jo's mournful eyes were adorable as she waited for my response.

Winnie jumped in to confirm. "I'm stealing my time with Tristan when I can get it, but I won't be sorry to see the festival end."

Nikki nodded. "Same. Bruce is wound pretty tight since they are in charge of all of the security. Seems like it's going relatively well, though."

"I'm fine. It's busy but I'm still finding moments of humanity, which is all I can ask for."

Elise jumped on that. "Please describe what you mean."

Dove gasped. "Are you blushing?" She turned her wide blue eyes to the rest of the table. "Guys, she's blushing."

"Okay so this is like *sexy* moments then?" Elise asked.

I chuckled while Jo added, "I mean, I feel like there have been developments we need to be made aware of... am I right?"

The minimal updates I'd given them were just that—basic information about how I'd made tentative peace with Beast, and then we'd had breakfast since I couldn't very well expect Catherine not to comment on it in the group text... but I hadn't mentioned last night.

Part of me had wanted to see how it went, and part of me knew how it would. Granted, there was a not small contingent of my imagination that had expected to wake up in his bed this morning, so maybe I wasn't ready to acknowledge that ahead of time.

And now that he'd hit the brakes effectively enough, I was glad I hadn't said anything to them.

"Jess? Hello? Did he hypnotize you with his nonverbal grunts and gigantic muscles?" Dove asked.

I cackled. "Wow, you have such a lovely picture of him."

Catherine tutted. "Come on. He's a sweetheart."

Everyone giggled in response.

"I'm not sure I'd call him a sweetheart, but I love that you guys are friends." Affection swelled for her and Jude.

"He's a good friend. I saw him a few times a week for a while because he and his grandma would come in for coffee and pie every afternoon. But they tapered off while she was sick and then it was just once a week. And then..." She glanced away, my soft-hearted friend swiping at a tear.

Dove wrapped an arm around Catherine's shoulders and squeezed. I gave her a moment and Winnie and Nikki chatted about something while I fended off a quick mental spiral tipped off by Catherine's memory.

Last night, he'd said he was still grieving. That had been on the list of reasons he felt we should slow down. And though I didn't completely disagree, and he'd done a pretty darn good job of convincing me it wasn't for lack of wanting, doubt niggled at me.

I was processing through years of hurt and we were so newly friends. The way he talked made it seem like he'd wanted to be friends... or more... for a long time. But how could I trust that when he'd let the dynamic between us go on for so long?

Could I believe him when he said it was his messed up way of staying connected to me? If someone else said it aloud to me, I'd laugh in their face. But this was Beast—Jude

—and he didn't say things he didn't mean. He wouldn't placate me.

And yet, could I believe him when my history shouted so loudly between us? When my past with not only Kurt but being abandoned by my father had taught me what to expect from men? Why would I expect anything else from him?

Everything in my gut told me those suspicions were wrong. He had nothing to hide. He had no reason to be nice to me or pretend he liked me let alone had other feelings for me if he really didn't.

And yet, he was moving slowly. Or maybe... *so*, he was moving slowly. And I had to figure out how to get past that, to get to the heart of both of us and see if we really had a chance, or if this was a bizarre honeymoon from what we'd been for so long.

"I don't need all the details, but I want to know what's holding you back."

Jo's fearlessness didn't end with her writing. She had this way of engaging with people that was so upfront, it was worth taking notes.

"Holding me back?" I asked, my pulse speeding up.

Nikki nodded. "Yes. Even as likely the least emotionally intuitive one here, we can *feel* you holding back."

They all corroborated this, nodding and murmuring their agreement.

I exhaled, a little caught, but not unwilling. I'd reassured myself I had their love and support so many times lately—their friendship and my belonging with them had been a kind of bastion in the storm of unsteady territory. Time to walk the walk.

"My dad left when I was a kid. You know Kurt left. And

lately, I've been realizing so much of what I've been angry about is that Kurt's leaving proves I'm easy to leave."

Expletives sounded round the table, each face twisted in varying degrees of anger or defensiveness on my behalf. Their instant rebuttal and Jude's words from last night gave me the push to keep going.

"I know. I know. But the other part of this is... I pushed. With Kurt. I made it clear I wanted marriage and a family, and I know very clearly now, that wasn't what he wanted. Even then, I kind of knew in my gut I'd forced things. And I just... I can't stomach the idea of pushing Beast. Like... he's grieving." The awful reality swirled and soured in my gut.

Elise narrowed her eyes. "We are talking about grown, adult men, yes?"

Dove nodded. "Yes. Men with free will and the ability to choose whatever the heck they want."

My brow furrowed. "Yes."

Nikki chimed in. "Kurt could've told you he didn't want marriage. He didn't have to propose. He made that choice—you couldn't have forced him."

I sighed, hearing them, but afraid they were wrong. So, so afraid.

Jo spoke and interrupted the rising tide of emotion. "And Beast can choose, too. You expressing interest or accepting what he's offering is in no way forcing anyone, unless it's something *you're* not ready for."

"Logically, I think I'm getting that. It's not me. But..." I exhaled slowly, deeply uninterested in crying but feeling the vulnerability rising. "I don't know how to believe him. After everything between us, I don't know if I have the abil-ity. And I think I want to. And I also don't even know if he wants me for more than just... now. Or a little while. I just can't force it. I don't have the heart to be with someone who won't fight for me."

As my rambling explanation ceased, Dove's warm hand slipped into mine and squeezed.

"I don't know how he feels, but I can tell you that you deserve to be loved by someone who will fight for you. That's not a misguided expectation. Because I know whoever you choose to be with, you'll fight for them." She released my hand and gave me a side hug as best she could given our seating arrangements.

"Rosie used to tell me I deserved someone who'd stick. I think for you, yes, you deserve someone who'll fight. And I can't help but wonder if there's any part of this that might show you Beast will." Nikki's voice was gentle, like she had some idea how tender all this talk made me.

I wanted him to fight for me, and I wanted to trust myself with all of this. But no one else could talk me into trusting myself. I had to do that on my own.

I thanked them and mercifully our food came. Everyone dove in, and for a few minutes, my thoughts were carried away from the angsty, uncomfortable feelings I had when thinking about Jude and hearing the echoes of a thought I couldn't quite formulate... something about how he'd always been fighting for me.

Dove groaned with pleasure as she took another bite of her dinner. "Who needs a man when I can just eat Guac? Chips, guac, and book talk." She raised her margarita.

Everyone chuckled and raised their glasses, repeating the last phrase. "Chips, guac, and book talk."

But Winnie and Nikki shared a look, and Elise pointed her fork at them. "None of those sly looks from you two. Just because you have Grade A men on the hook doesn't mean the rest of us don't need... really good Mexican food."

Jo chuckled, her smile overly blissful. She and Adam weren't married but she probably didn't *need* Guac.

"Aren't you and Callum together right now?" Jo asked Elise.

Elise's head reared back and answered for her.

"Oh, dang. I'm sorry. I thought I saw you guys hugging before you opened the shop the other day," Jo said, reaching out to squeeze Elise's arm in apology.

It took a moment, but when Elise spoke, her voice was strained. "He wants to get back together. He seems to be having a hard time accepting that we're done."

My gaze sharpened and I could tell everyone else's attention heightened, though it was Winnie who asked, "Is he being mean?"

Mean for Callum, Elise's on-again, off-again currently ex-boyfriend, meant something different than Beast's mean. Even when I thought of him as Beast, Jude was only ever impatient and rude. He wasn't physical, and he wasn't dangerous.

Callum? We never got the full story, but we knew enough that whatever had happened to break them up this last time stemmed from something nasty.

Elise exhaled. "No. He was nice. Hence the hug." She shook her head, frustration with him or herself or the whole situation brimming. "I'm just done with it. I need him to move on and just let me be."

"I'll talk to him," I said, honey in my tone.

She and everyone else seemed to think this was funny.

"What? I'm great at getting people to see my side. He'll walk away and stay gone." I shrugged a shoulder.

Dove grinned Cheshire-cat wide. "I love you, Jess, but you'd probably end up terrifying him to death."

"Would that be such a bad thing?" I asked, genuinely

wondering if I was the only one who'd gotten the sense that this man had put his hands on our friend in an uninvited way.

Elise's expression darkened and she studied her food and Dove grumbled a, "Maybe not."

Before anyone else could follow her thought, a familiar voice interrupted us.

"Hey! Aren't you Cookie's friend? And oh my gosh, hey girl."

We all glanced up to see a *very* familiar face smiling down at our table, then winking at me. I rose out of my seat and snuck around Dove's to reach Jenna Halter, Hollywood rising star and all-around amazing human being.

"Hey! You've been so busy, I feel like I haven't seen you when I could actually talk to you!" I may have squealed it a little. Jenna and I had become friends when I replaced Cookie after he came back stateside for some family issues.

She squeezed me tight, then pulled back to look at me and squinted. "We need to talk."

I flushed because I had no idea how she could know I had news about anything, but the woman had clairvoyance because it felt like she could see straight through me. Then she leaned all the way back and dragged a young woman closer to the table. "Do you all know Cara Darling? I met her on my last trip here through Calla."

Cara Darling was a high schooler, so normally I wouldn't have any interaction with her, except she was our investor's stepdaughter and a musical prodigy. She had played for some major events in town and was slated to head to Juilliard soon.

Everyone greeted Cara but Dove jumped up, her golden yellow dress twirling around her, and gave her a squeeze. "This girl is so patient with me when I stumble into Pluck."

Cara grinned. "You're literally the sweetest," she said to Dove, then leaned into Jenna's ear and mumbled, "Don't you have that meeting with the creepy producer?"

Jenna's face fell into a neutral mask. "I do." Her gaze shifted to us. "I'm so sorry, but I have to run. Can we please try to hang out before the festival's done? I head up to Snowberry Thursday, I think." She checked her phone like it might give her the answer at a glance. "Bye, ladies."

She swept away and her security team followed at a distance—I nodded to Kenny who winked at me and wiggled his brows at the others before slipping out in front of Jenna.

Dove, Elise, and Catherine were thoroughly starstruck.

"She's so nice," Dove said, staring after where she'd disappeared.

"She's so pretty," Elise said, blinking like she'd just seen an apparition of Jenna Halter and not the woman herself.

"She's so... normal," Catherine added, chuckling softly to herself.

"She's great. So is Jack. I honestly haven't had issues with any of the celebrities we contract with so far, though I know we've had a few." I glanced at Nikki whose eyes widened.

"Bruce has a few stories, which he of course hasn't told me because of NDAs." She smiled to cover the *of course he wouldn't breach an NDA to tell his wife about stupid celebrities* expression.

Jo grinned, then sobered. "I love that she's so personable. Anyone else bothered by the 'creepy producer' thing?"

We all nodded, and I raised a hand. "I'll look into it."

I might not be able to do anything, but as I sat here with

my beautiful, thoughtful, brilliant friends, I wasn't about to let the comment go unnoticed. Nor was I going to forget that Callum whatever-his-name-was had been clinging to Elise.

Jude and I had things to work out, but I wasn't someone who would prioritize my own drama and neglect something raising red flags.

First, I'd confront Jude and lay it out. We wanted to be together, so we needed to go all in with this thing, each of us sliding in everything we had, or agree to fold. I didn't want to be any more invested than I already was. I didn't have the heart for it.

I'd decided. In the last few hours, I'd nailed down what rested underneath all those fears and it was this: I trusted Jude with my life, and I wanted to trust him with my heart... if he'd only *take* it. I'd swallow my pride and offer it up and see what happened... and if it was meant to be, we'd move forward.

If not?

I'd accept a different path. I'd trust myself to know that, to accept it, and to move forward with hope. We wouldn't revert to enemies. We'd be friends, or if not that, then at least acquaintances. And we'd both be fine. Maybe a little hurt, a little raw, but fine.

And then?

We'd get back to work.

So... time to play capture the flag.

CHAPTER THIRTY-NINE

Jude

Kenny's stupid grin widened so far, he practically became a disembodied Cheshire Cat head.

"So you need me..." he said, dragging every word out like my request was some kind of salacious secret and not just that—a simple request.

"Yes."

"And you're asking me to start a double shift a half hour early because..."

I glared at his sparkly eyes and grunted.

"Let's use our words," he tutted.

"Because I need to get off an hour early."

"Because..."

Because I haven't seen Jess in two days, and I feel like I can't breathe.

"Because I do."

He crossed his arms, but the wild smile went nowhere.

"Now here I was thinking you'd learned to use your words a little better lately."

I glared.

Impossibly, he smiled even wider.

"I'm just saying I'll do just about anything for you, even take your boring shift at the desk in HQ, and I think you know that, but..." He let it hang between us.

"But?" I prompted, an irritated edge making itself known loud and clear.

"But you have to tell me why you need the time."

Speaking of, I had zero time left on the brief break I'd taken, so I gave him what he wanted. He clearly knew anyway, or he wouldn't have made such a big deal of it.

"I want to catch Pop before she goes on shift. I think things are going well but we've been on opposite schedules, and I want to check in." Hopefully, he wouldn't notice the flush of my cheeks.

He pushed off the door frame "Yes. *Yes.*" He kept coming and rammed into me, wrapping his arms around my shoulders and squeezing me. "That's what I'm talking about."

I laughed at his dramatics but accepted his praise. "Thanks."

He pulled back and swallowed, his throat working like it took effort. *Aw, hell. Here we go.*

"I know you're gonna roll your eyes at me, but I'm gonna take a minute and then I'll do what you asked without mentioning it again, okay?" His words were watery, right along with his eyes.

I cleared my throat, in no mood to start down an emotional rollercoaster with him. No one could make me cry faster than this kid. "Fine."

His gaze shifted into something so soft and affectionate,

another version of myself would've died at the proximity to it. But getting closer with Kenny the last few years, I'd learned a lot.

"I'm so proud of you. You're still grieving Omi but you're out here fighting for Pop like you've always wanted to. And from the sounds of things, it's going pretty darn well. So"—he slapped my back—"way to go, brother."

I exhaled as though impatient, but really I needed to breathe past the knot in my throat that never failed to rise when he called me brother because I knew he meant it like Adam meant it for Ethan or Wilder meant it for Warrick and Wyatt, even though we didn't share blood.

Then I hooked an arm around his neck to draw him into a quick hug. "Thank you. And thanks..." I cleared my damn throat again. "For being here. And for the twenty minutes."

Kenny pulled back and swiped at his eyes quickly before wiggling his brows, gear shifted instantly back to teasing and annoying. "I can probably do an hour if you need more time."

Like any good brotherly relationship required at such a time, I palmed his face and shoved him away.

He laughed, then waved me off as I left him in the break room. I had two hours and forty minutes until he'd start his shift early and swap out with me. Jess and I had never once texted so I felt weird about doing so now, but I also didn't want to miss seeing her. We were all moving in different directions and coordinating with our CP here at the home-base, but since she was man-on with Jack again tonight, she very well might not show up here at all.

Swallowing the nerves that hounded me as I tapped out the words—then deleted them, then made another attempt —I exhaled sharply and sent the message.

"Everything okay?" Bruce asked, Tristan and Luc at his side.

I shoved a hand into my hair. "Yeah. All good with you?"

Bruce's brow was furrowed, and he glanced toward the other two. "I'm... I don't know. I've got a feeling something's off."

"With what?" I asked, certain that if Bruce suspected something was iffy, he was unlikely to be wrong.

"Julian mentioned something to me the other day that hit me weird. You know Cara, his stepdaughter, has been hanging out with Jenna Halter?" he asked.

"Had heard something like that and saw them at the event two nights ago," I confirmed.

Bruce nodded. "Yeah, she's sort of assisting her, but it's mostly because they've become friends in a roundabout way and Jenna loves Cara and wants to introduce her to some music people here or something. Anyway, Julian casually dropped that Cara had an odd interaction with someone from Blackthorne."

I already knew. "Kurt."

Bruce, Tristan, and Luc all confirmed with simultaneous nods.

"What kind of odd?" I asked, dread sliding through me. Kurt was a jackass, but he'd never been after underage girls... at least not that I'd been aware of. If he was hitting on a teenager...

Bruce scowled. "Unclear. I guess she just seemed a little put off by him. Cookie's asking Jenna about it to see what she knows." He searched my face. "Any concerns on your end?"

And this was where I'd never found the right note to strike because I no longer believed I had an ability to separate out my feelings about Kurt and what I knew he used to be like with what I knew about him now. I hadn't seen anything particularly damning, though he certainly seemed to be focused on women. But that wasn't necessarily a crime. That he was rude to Jess made me want to ask his face some questions with my fist, but it still wasn't a professional failing.

"He'll always raise a flag for me. We know Blackthorne has had its issues. I'd say we keep an eye out just in case."

"Agreed. And I'll see if Jenna can elaborate on what Julian got from Cara." Luc ducked his chin and then he was gone, likely off to do just that.

"Sounds good," I agreed, and hoped the sick feeling would ease up before I went to see Jess. I didn't want to be thinking about Kurt The Idiot when I stole a few minutes with her... assuming she'd be able to arrive early.

Bruce and Tristan continued down the hallway, and I found my way back to the CP. Adam was nestled in and watching all the surveillance feeds, all of which were completely bereft of anything to see. Video monitoring was minimal, and this afternoon, everyone was static—most celebrities we were guarding were getting ready for the evening, so our personnel were at their doors. All quiet.

My phone buzzed right when I sat down. I braced for disappointment, but instead had to work to hide my smile.

"Looking forward to it."

Whatever insecurities might still exist, we'd figure them out if we'd keep showing up for each other.

CHAPTER FORTY

Jess

I slipped into the giant truck at exactly nineteen minutes until my shift. I'd hoped to be even earlier, but my alarm hadn't woken me from my nap quite as early as I'd planned and well, here we were.

Vanity should've had no part in my life at this point, but I couldn't stand the thought of skipping the basic makeup and hair prep I'd planned on, even if Jude had seen me at my worst. I wanted him to like me, or *keep* liking me, and showing up looking like these long days with endless variables for pretty celebrities were dragging me through mud wasn't high on my list.

"Hey," I said, stomach flipping as I pulled the door closed and got hit with the fresh scent of his laundry paired with the leather seats of his truck.

His gaze traveled over me like he was checking for injuries and then hooked into mine. His expression was so severe, a sensation akin to panic flashed though me. Had I misread his text? I'd read it as fun and flirty and kind of like he was desperate to see me.

Maybe he'd been worried. Or about to tell me that all of this between us was just too much of a mess to keep bothering with.

"How are you? Are you… good?"

The soft hope lingering on his face and in the pinch of his brow shifted something enough that it clicked, a key turning in a lock. He wasn't done, but he'd started to worry *I* was.

"I'm great. I'm glad to see you, and—"

Breath rushed from him, and he grabbed my head on either side and drew me into him, melting me with a demanding kiss, all in about two seconds.

My eyes, wide open from the surprise of his movement, slowly fluttered closed as the heat of his mouth on mine, ravenous and just as needy for me as I felt for him, took over all my senses.

He groaned as I opened for him and he took what he wanted, kissing me deeper and mesmerizing me. I couldn't stand the center console between us or the way I had to lean, so I broke the kiss for a second and scrambled over, seating myself in his lap, and took his face in my hands this time.

No words passed between us, but the heat in his eyes sent fire low in my belly, and I dove back in. I'd never been so happy about his propensity for *sounds*, not words, because he was showing me just how much he enjoyed this with his nonverbal cues. Funny how I'd never thought about how much I could like this about him.

We only came up for air when my alarm sounded, loud and cruel, shocking me into breaking the drowning kisses between us with a gasp. I dove for my purse, jammed my finger against the screen to stop the racket, and then looked back at Jude to find him wide-eyed and bracing me at my hips so I wouldn't tumble off him.

I started to giggle—yes, giggle, because he looked so genuinely confused about what was happening and he had bee-stung lips and ragged breaths—and soon, he joined me. His low chuckle rumbled between us, and in another few seconds we were both laughing hysterically. I laughed so hard I could hardly breathe and rested my forehead on his shoulder while I worked to regain composure.

His large hands smoothed up and down my back in a motion so deliciously comforting, my laughter soon melted away and I reluctantly sat up.

"I didn't plan to spend the time that way," he said, reaching up to tuck some hair behind my ear.

My stomach flipped again—it had taken up part-time acrobatics whenever he came close. "Me neither. But I'm not mad about it."

His gorgeous lips twitched into the tiniest hint of an upward tilt, almost like he felt he'd overshared his smile during our laughing fit.

"No? Good." The humor tapered off into another one of our eye-locking stares, and my heart rate ramped up again.

"I really have to go," I said, glancing at my stupid watch and seeing I was right—I really, *really* had to go. "When can we..." Do this again? Do more? Sit and talk? Snuggle on your couch with your beast-sized cat? "Hang out again?"

One big hand slipped up my neck and his thumb and index finger pinched my chin and guided my face to his. He pressed a long, slow, delectable kiss to my lips. "I'll talk Kenny into switching so we both have tomorrow night off?"

My answering grin could not be contained. "I like your style, Beast."

He gave me a smug little look that sent heat to my toes.

"I like your everything, Pop."

I floated on the nineteen stolen minutes with Jude for the next day and a half. Our schedules were as opposite as ever, but his text confirming Kenny had agreed to take his assignment tomorrow night sent me soaring.

Why did I suddenly have such trouble thinking about anything but him? I mean, I was standing in a room with Oscar winners and famous producers and geniuses of show business and all I wanted was to jump my taciturn ex-soldier's bones.

Okay, wow. The kissing had left me feeling... well, hot. But it was that parting shot, his, "I like your everything," that kept swirling around in my head.

Could it be true? Funny enough, I could say the same thing about him, so I didn't necessarily disbelieve him. It just seemed... too perfect. Too much like something I'd always longed for.

That comment, and the way his hands felt so good wherever they touched, lingered in my mind. The way he knew when to challenge me, when to chase me, when to tease me... so good.

If I'd ever had doubts about his interest in something *now*, they were non-existent. The trick was feeling like maybe that's all this was, that maybe we were running off of his past feelings, my growing current ones, and if we kept going I'd end up head over heels while he felt free to walk away.

But there it was—the specter that haunted any relationship I even considered. With Kurt, I'd thought I'd found a home and a partnership. I'd decided he was it and maybe I'd even forced myself into believing it. Forced him, too, maybe. He was charming and easy and made me feel like I was his whole world and I'd let it happen because it fit the narrative I wanted. It had been a lovely little fantasy I didn't mind wrapping up in right up until I realized it was just that—a total fantasy. I was the emperor standing naked, finally realizing his new clothes were nothing but the stuff of imagination and deception.

But things with Jude were different. First, I had no doubt he was a deeply faithful person in every aspect of his life, even to the point of being maddening. He'd refused to tell me what happened all those years ago in explicit detail because he'd believed it was wrong. This wasn't the kind of man who cheated.

He would never cheat. And he had a life here with more than just me—he hadn't built me up to be some kind of "everything" that set me up to fail. He had friends and a support system so robust I hadn't even realized he was grieving his sole remaining family member.

But if he lost interest or never regained the depth of feeling he'd had for me, or worse, realized that what he thought he'd felt before he got to know me as he had lately was nothing substantial, he'd walk.

He was faithful, honorable, and ruthless. In work, and in life, he wouldn't waste breath on something he didn't care about. And I could only imagine how painful it would be to face an ending with Jude when he was ready to dispose of me.

So along with my cheery thoughts about hot kisses and warm, rough hands, I also had a plague of doubts and questions swirling around making me itch to see him for more than a few minutes so I could verbalize some of this.

By the next afternoon when I finally came off duty, only a few minutes from running home and getting showered up so I could go to Jude's after turning my gear in, Luc and Bruce were talking in the entryway.

"Everything okay?"

Bruce wasn't easily disgruntled, and as far as I was tracking, things had been going well with the event for us on the security end and the town overall.

Luc responded first. "I spoke with Jenn about a concern. Her response didn't alleviate that concern."

The beautiful man's wrinkled brow went nowhere, and I could almost see his mind racing through what he'd learned. The comment sparked my memory of Cara's odd statement a few days ago.

"Does it have anything to do with Anthony Pollusk, the producer?" I'd heard the name whispered and had gathered this must've been who Cara meant.

Both Bruce and Luc turned to me, eyes keen.

"Yes. What do you know?" Bruce asked.

"Not much. Only that when I saw Cara and Jenna the other day for a minute at Guac, Cara said something about going to her meeting with the 'creepy producer.' Jenna visibly deflated and they left almost immediately." I'd made a point to track down information on the situation, but I'd utterly failed... so now was my chance.

Luc's jaw ticked. "She's been off for a few days. It has to be thanks to him."

Bruce put a hand on Luc's shoulder. "We don't know

that for sure, but I think it's wise to dig deeper. I'll call Julian and see if we can meet with Cara."

"What can I do?" I asked, eager to help.

Bruce smiled. "You can go to dinner at Beast's and take a night off. We'll update you tomorrow."

I sputtered, not expecting him to know about the plan or say anything if he did, but since he and Luc both chuckled, they clearly *both* knew.

"Don't be so surprised. Your man had to ask Kenny to cover his shift. Didn't take long to break Kenny wide open about why he traded, and from there..."

I rolled my eyes. "From there, you pack of gossipy old ladies disguised as ex-soldiers spread it around. Got it. Did Barbie even officially pass SERE?" Frustration and something closer to... happiness, sifted through me.

"Hey, I'm happy for you," Bruce said, a genuine Bruce Camden special sparkling back at me.

"Thanks, Jaws. Cookie... see you both tomorrow."

With that, I left, eager to get home, anxious to see Beast, and reeling from the idea that Bruce had called Jude *my man* and the realization that I very much wanted it to be an accurate title for Jude Rawlins... as long as he wanted it just as much.

CHAPTER FORTY-ONE

Jude

Jess stood outside my door at a few minutes after eight.

Air rushed from her lips, the heat from her body freezing into a white cloud in the chilly autumn air. Temps had dropped and I wouldn't have been surprised to see snow in the forecast again, though tonight was crystal clear with glittering stars winking behind her.

"What are you doing without a coat? Come in." I pulled her into the house and Bones immediately dismounted his post on the couch and sped toward her, only stopping when he'd headbutted her calf and rubbed himself along the leg of her jeans.

"The temperature dropped like crazy since I went home. I didn't realize."

She shivered, and I pulled her into a hug.

All the wild, rampaging pieces of me settled as she wrapped her arms around me and rested her head on my chest. She breathed long and slow breaths, and I did the same, relieved to have her here in my space again.

The stolen moment yesterday had left me longing for her, but when I woke today, it hadn't been with lust in mind. I'd had this aching hollow in my chest that begged me to find her, be close to her, *love her.*

Nothing in me was surprised, and yet I didn't want to push her.

So this quiet moment brought necessary soothing to so much of my heart.

Bones' desperate little meow broke the spell, and she pulled back with a soft smile, then dropped to a knee to pick up my boy.

"You are just a little beggar, aren't you? But I love you so much." She buried her face in his neck, and he closed his eyes as though just her nearness was bliss.

As usual, my cat and I were on the same level.

"Lucky guy," I said, chuckling at the semi-truck level rumble coming from the little purr machine.

Jess carted him back to his bed on the back of the couch and he kneaded it into submission before circling up and tucking his face into his hind legs for another nap.

"All that hard work wore you out, huh? Sleep well, sweet boy." Jess gently petted his head, then joined me in the kitchen.

"I love your cat." She pumped soap onto her hands.

There was that word again. *Love.* I couldn't be sure I'd heard her use it ever before, and so soon after I'd thought it in my head.

"He seems to return the sentiment." I stirred the sauce on the stove.

"Whatever you're making smells amazing," she said,

sliding one hand up my spine in a way that made me feel instantly ravenous.

"Roasted red pepper sauce. We'll put it over tortellini if that's okay, and I have some burrata—"

Her hand firm on my neck, she guided my head toward her and took my mouth in a kiss that notched up the hunger levels to never before experienced. When she released me, I took in the kiss-ravaged lips and glittering eyes.

"You like pasta that much?" I asked, desperate to know which part of the meal had prompted the kiss and planning to provide it for her whenever possible.

She laughed softly. "I like *you* that much. And I am very excited for more of your cooking because everything I've had has been amazing."

"Omi taught me. She insisted I learn more than the basics—for myself and for whoever I ended up with." I didn't glance at her meaningfully and betray just how much I wanted that to be her. *Too soon.*

I'd never forget when Omi sat me down around fourteen and leveled with me. *"You've got the looks, honey, and you're going to have the size. You've got the manners. Now we need to get you the skills."* She'd taught me the basics of cooking but from then on, she got serious about homemade sauces and from-scratch pie crust and biscuits... so many recipes I'd carved into my heart.

I continued to stir, the moment braided with grief and love and nostalgia.

"She was wise. I'm sorry to say I don't have much in the way of cooking skills beyond grilled chicken and really basic stuff on the stove. I can keep myself fed decent food, but it was never an art or an act of love like it seems to be for you."

Her gaze flicked up to meet mine and my gut clenched. *There's that word again.*

"Why are you sorry?" I asked, instead of pushing on the words that came after, forcing her to confront how she'd let those four letters cross her lips so many times tonight.

Her eyes followed her fingers as they traced a pattern in the granite of my countertop.

"I guess I've always felt the need to apologize for what I don't bring to a relationship, especially if it's stuff that traditionally a woman does." Then her head snapped up and her eyes were wide. "I mean, not that we're in a relationship, or that we—"

"Are we not?"

She swallowed and breathed through the panic shining in her eyes. "Um, I mean, are we? We have this history..."

Cheeks blazing, she wouldn't look at me anymore.

"I think it's obvious we are."

She nearly singed my eyebrows off with the fiery glare she sent my way, but no words issued from her lips. Apparently, my statement had stunned her—or possibly infuriated her.

This required full attention and not splitting between avoiding burning dinner and her. I turned the burner off and grabbed her hand, guiding her to the living room and taking a seat, which she did, as well.

A hundred things shot through my mind—reasons she had to know we were dating and not just hanging out or some such nonsense, the way I felt about her, the things I wanted.... And all of it felt too soon and too little and not enough.

And then, taking her hand in mine and cradling it like the precious part of her it was, I stopped hedging and protecting myself. I stopped hiding behind my pride and the fear of rejection it masked. I stopped hiding behind bitterness at not being chosen over Kurt the first time or not being believed when her world crashed down around her.

I stopped everything but honesty.

"For me, this has never been small or temporary. I have wanted more from you since the moment I met you."

She reared back and I rushed to continue. "Yes, we have a past, but we've apologized. And it doesn't make it go away, but I believe we can change—that we already have."

She swallowed hard.

After a moment, her mouth dropped open and she blanched, but no words emerged—not the response I wanted. Where had I lost her? She seemed stunned. I'd never witnessed a deer in headlights until now. But now that I'd started telling her how I felt, it was welling up in me, spilling over, and I couldn't stop myself.

"I have loved you since the minute you said my name and I'll die with your name on my lips. Jess, I can't pretend you weren't the person who means the most to me. If you want it, then yes, we're in a relationship. If you say so, then yes—yes to anything you want."

Her eyes glazed with tears. "How could you keep this from me if you really felt that way?"

Panic struck. No, this wasn't how this would go. She wasn't still questioning me, was she? "I didn't keep it from you. I've told you from the beginning how I felt—"

"How you *felt*. Past tense. Before we started fighting and hating each other." She stood and paced away. "And it's not about what I want, Jude. It's—"

I followed close behind, though stopped shy of hauling her into my arms. "I'm sorry for that. I felt like I couldn't fight my way through the weeds between us, and even if I had—"

She turned, jaw clenched, and waited, but when I didn't speak, she prompted me. "Even if you had…"

My chest caved in, sand funneling to the lowest point of gravity and collapsing the structure of my heart. "You deserved more."

Instead of appeasing, this only seemed to inflame her frustration with me.

She glanced at her phone, which had started ringing, then shoved it in her pocket and put a hand in the middle of my chest. "Don't you dare act like you had self-esteem issues. I know you. I know your grandparents loved you, and your friends, all except my idiot ex, would die for you. Don't you pretend you thought I was too good for you or that you'd put me on a pedestal."

I was shaking my head, ignoring the phone in my pocket that'd started buzzing. "It wasn't that. It was how I'd bungled everything else. How I'd treated you even though I felt the way I did—"

A knock on the front door, then the doorbell itself, cut me off. Our gazes connected and we moved in tandem. I opened it and we found Cookie standing in full kit with black tactical gear, a radio in hand.

"Got 'em. They're both here. Over."

A garbled response came through, but Cookie jumped in.

"We've got a lead. It's a strong one. Clock's ticking. We need you."

And that was all it took to interrupt the most important conversation of my life. In seconds, we were out the door and on the move.

CHAPTER FORTY-TWO

Jess

Minutes later, Jude and I were pounding up the stairs to the Saint Security building, ready for a full briefing. Cookie's rushed explanation—that they had reason to believe the producer Jenna mentioned was preying on the young women of Silverton under the guise of casting a new movie and something bad was going down tonight—hadn't connected many of the dots other than we needed to move asap.

I let myself get swept up in the moment because my mind needed the distraction from... everything. *Everything* Jude had just laid at my feet.

In effect, he'd laid himself out and said, "I wanted you to take me," and here I was, focusing on work because my bone-marrow-deep fear was that I couldn't do it. I wanted to, I'd talked myself into it, almost, before I'd gotten there, but then he'd said so many beautiful, heartfelt, *real* things, and I'd...

I kept hearing the past tense. He'd said, "*I felt, I felt, I felt...*" and though he'd said those insane things about my name on his lips when he died, it was all enclosed in a past tense parenthesis. A bone deep fear had hit when he'd said we'd changed. We *had* changed... but what if he'd changed *for* me? What if he didn't want this, not really, and I was doing it again? What if it was happening again and I was forcing an idea of the future on someone new? He'd said he wanted what I wanted, that it was a yes to everything *I* wanted. And I couldn't have this. Not again.

So I'd gone back to what I always did. I got mad at him for... what? For not telling me he was in love with me? Like he could've done that without me thinking he was a liar or rejecting him? What could I possibly have expected, and yet I hadn't said it back. I couldn't have summoned those words in that moment, even though my heart felt like it was bleeding love for him even now, as scared as I was.

And then Cookie had interrupted, and for now... for now, that had to be it. Because this was one place I didn't doubt myself, and I needed my feet on this solid ground. I needed to clear my head, and I knew of nothing better than a boots-on-the-ground work crisis to bring me the clarity my mind so very much lacked and craved.

We didn't know details yet, and we needed them. Had they alerted the local PD? Sometimes, we got information we could act on and then nudge their way, but sometimes we dove in headfirst and dealt with the fallout. Since Bruce schmoozed with the Chief as often as he could and we'd only ever helped with cases they had, they tended to appreciate us.

In my gut, I knew Kurt was involved. He'd been on the

producer's security team, so he had to know something was up. But... how much? And was he a part of it, or only on the periphery?

In the briefing room, Tristan was stone-faced, and Kenny was pacing.

"Finally! Damn, were y'all naked or something?" Kenny said, no real heat in his voice.

"Glad you made it," Tristan said, completely ignoring Kenny's nonsense and diving right in. "Cara Darling is in the conference room and she's with Wilder and her stepdad. Between her statements and what Jenna has mentioned to Cookie, we're fairly certain we need to intervene tonight. Can't wait on the locals."

So they wouldn't wait for the police. Good in some ways, bad in others.

Just then, Julian Grenier ushered his stepdaughter into the room. Her eyes were red-rimmed, and her oversized sweatshirt was pulled down over her hands like it could shield her from the outside world.

Wilder nodded at me and Jude, then said in the gentlest voice he possessed, "Can you tell the team what you told me?"

Cara nodded and tucked her long hair behind her ears. "I was with some friends who wanted to go to a party at a house up the canyon. There was a rumor Jack McKean and some other celebrities were going to go, so everyone was freaking out." She rolled her eyes, then shook her head like she hated the memory. "But then we got there, and it was actually some kind of audition or something? And we got in the house and I saw some people I recognized."

Her eyes flicked up to mine, then over to Jude's, then down to her hands. "I saw someone come out of a room and she looked so upset, so I went to check on her and she just freaked out. Wouldn't talk to me, and just kept saying, 'he said he'll make it worth it,' or something." Her gaze found Julian's. "That's when I called you. I just had this sick feeling, and then I saw the same security guard that'd been with the producer and—" She crushed her lips together, eyes glassy.

Julian pulled her into his arms and hugged her. She clung to him as he said, "You did the right thing. I'm sorry this happened." Then his silvery eyes rose to find Wilder's, and with a voice hard as steel, he said, "We'll take care of it."

"I'm so sorry."

The whispered words came from the doorway where Jenna Halter now stood, a hand pressed over her mouth and eyes full of pain. Cookie moved to her, and she let him tuck an arm around her and usher her inside. But Jenna's eyes didn't waver from Cara, who turned to face her.

"I'm so sorry. I should've spoken up sooner. I should've told someone." Jenna reached for Cara's hand. "I'm so sorry."

Cara launched herself at Jenna and hugged her, talking rapidly as she squeezed her. "I'm sorry you ever had to deal with him. I hate him."

They separated and Jenna turned to the rest of us. "Anthony Pollusk is most likely sexually harassing these girls, or setting up opportunities to do so. I know this because he harassed me a few years ago right before I got my break and he said he'd ruin me if I told anyone. At the time, I believed him, but obviously, the fear of anything happening has stuck around—even to the point where I have still interacted with him." She exhaled and looked ill, like the memory of her interactions brought on nausea.

"You're speaking up now, and this gives us more than

enough to know we need to get there," Wilder said, then turned to Luc. "Let's get there."

In a matter of minutes, Jude and I were driving in a Saint Security truck outfitted with all kinds of gear our personal vehicles didn't have. We'd spoken only in clipped, professional phrases, both sensing we wouldn't have a chance to return to the major subject of our conversation at his house until after this op. Maybe by then—whenever it was—I'd know how to figure out where we both stood in this relationship, how much of ourselves was in there and how much was compromise we thought the other wanted or even needed.

The goal tonight? Stop this Hollywood producer jerk from hurting anyone else, and clear the girls out of there.

"How deep in do you think Kurt is?" I asked, giving voice to the dread that'd been building steadily since we'd opened the door to Cookie.

"I don't know, but I have a bad feeling maybe all the way." His jaw flexed and his eyes stayed forward.

"We can handle it," he said, right as I said, "Of course we can handle it. We'll just—" I stopped, huffed and smiled at the way we'd both said it.

"We will," he confirmed. No lightness in his eyes, but maybe something there—not regret for what he'd said, and not even anger with me from how I'd reacted.

I exhaled, banishing the nerves and the sick feeling that seeped into my gut and nodded. "We will. That jerk's not going to hurt anyone else, and neither is Kurt."

We weren't certain what we'd find, but from what Cara filled in for us, it sounded like the party was under the guise of casting extras and some main parts for an upcoming project. By the time she left, the crowd was thinning and it sounded like maybe the situation was becoming even more concerning.

We'd alerted the police after Jenna confirmed her experience with the man, and they were on the way. They'd be on hand to take statements if anyone wanted to press charges, assuming our fears were legitimate, and the awful realities we'd seen in our years in the military meant that even the shine of Hollywood and the glamour of this film fest couldn't make us believe they weren't.

Cookie and Wilder pulled over on the road at the base of a long driveway. Most homes in Silverton were within the city limits, but there were a few larger places on the outskirts, and this was one. It was isolated, and frankly, the perfect place to take advantage of someone if you could get them there.

We moved up the driveway with purpose, swift-footed and eyes wide, spotting the security guard loitering at the front door instantly.

"We're here as part of the cooperative agreement between Saint Security and Blackthorne. Let us in quietly." Wilder's tone brooked no arguments, and since he and Bruce had spoken to the whole Blackthorne crew before the film fest kicked off, the man likely recognized him.

"Oh, sure. Is this some kind of op we weren't briefed on?" the guy asked, though we moved inside without responding, first Wilder, then Cookie, then me, and Jude brought up the rear.

Inside and down an oddly dark entryway, we came to a recessed living room where several girls lay on low, off-white modern couches over matching carpet and were clearly under the influence of a substance based on their glazed eyes and the heavy way their heads hung. Cookie moved to the one nearest him right away, Wilder to another.

"Hey, can you talk to me? What's your name?" Cookie said, his voice gentle and filled with concern.

The girl reached a hand out and nearly swatted his face. "Oh my crap, you're so hot like a model or like a hot guy or something. Are you in the movie, too?"

He spoke to her again while Wilder radioed to our HQ telling them to dispatch an ambulance.

The large living room had four possible hallways leading away from it. I turned to Jude, about to debate it, when he notched his chin toward the one to his left, the only one with a light on.

We moved together, leaving Wilder and Cookie to deal with the girls. Maybe they were the only ones left, but knowing more than likely there were more people in the house who might need help, the urgency pressed in on us.

Several rooms stood open—an office with floor to ceiling bookcases, a piano room with a baby grand, and then the hallway turned and led to an open area with a small love seat and a man seated there with his eyes on his phone until he heard the quiet shuffle of our feet over carpet and looked up.

Kurt.

He stood instantly, a smirk on his smug face.

"Well, look who it is. How can I help you this fine evening?" He tucked his phone away and hooked a thumb into one of the gromets on his flack vest.

My body had leveled into what we called war calm. Adrenaline cranked through you but with the right training, you could funnel it into a steady hand rather than a shaky one, a practiced posture instead of noodle knees. "We're here to check on someone. Step aside and we'll have a look and be gone."

One cocky brow raised. "Yeah? Bummer. I can't let you do that."

"Yeah, you can," I said, not surprised he wasn't going to let us by, but also supremely annoyed that in theory this guy was supposed to be a good person. Not that I had any illusion he was anymore, but at least he shouldn't be engaged in protecting an actual criminal.

Jude stood to my left and a step back. I could practically feel the fury rolling off him. Evidently, he hadn't locked down all those pesky feelings like I had.

"Nah. Don't think I will," Kurt said, then shrugged a shoulder like he thought all of this was cute.

Jude's voice came low and as close to a growl as could be and still be intelligible. "Move."

The smug expression melted from Kurt's face, and for maybe the first time, I saw every bit of ugliness he'd hidden from me when his lip turned up in a sneer.

"You want to get past me, *Beast*, you're gonna have to make me."

I wouldn't have believed it years ago, but now that I'd accepted the truth about this man, it didn't shock me when he pulled his gun and aimed it at Jude.

In seconds, too many things flashed through my mind as Jude took a giant step in front of me and raised his hands. *No, you idiot!* He was protecting me, even when he was already the target. Maybe Kurt really would shoot us both, but now this big, lovely, beautiful man was literally shielding me with his giant body and I loved him for it.

No, I loved him, full stop.

He'd told me time and again how he felt, but today, he'd laid it out plainly. My fear of rejection and being left had twisted such a beautiful moment into something to be questioned, but here he was, loving me with his actions like he had so many other times before, even when I didn't realize it.

And Jude telling me yes to whatever I wanted? It wasn't him changing for me or humoring me. It was him giving me space. Space to come to him. Space to find my own footing in whatever I wanted *us* to be because he had already committed to this *us*, all the way.

The pressure and adrenaline of seeing his life threatened distilled every frantic emotion into a clarity like I've never known, and even more, a certainty.

I loved Jude Rawlins. I believed him. And I wasn't about to let a damn thing happen to him on my watch.

The certitude I was good at what I did infusing in me when I left the Saint office? It flowed through me now, highlighting another part of me that knew it loved this man, that I needed to take the chance on him because he'd already shown me he'd fight for me. That's what he'd been doing ever since we reconnected in his cabin.

When Kurt's weapon stayed trained on Jude despite my shouts to put it down, that's when I got mad. And for once, my anger, my rage, it wasn't directed at Beast. It would find its rightful target now.

CHAPTER FORTY-THREE

Jude

Kurt being a murderous dickhead didn't strike me as a real turn of events since he'd always struck me as a sociopath. But had I expected him to pull a gun on me in the name of some random Hollywood jerk who was hurting young women?

Somehow, I hadn't.

In a combat situation, I'd draw, and he'd be dead in seconds. But we weren't in combat, I wasn't about to kill this idiot, and I didn't want to give him any reason to shoot me or, far more importantly, Jess. My body would likely cover her and we were both wearing Kevlar, but still. Not worth the risk.

In the seconds these thoughts slipped through my mind, Jess evidently had other ideas. Before I could so much as tell Kurt to back down or assure him I wasn't going to go for my weapon, she'd crossed the space and held her Glock to his temple.

"Shoot him and I shoot you. That easy."

The utter steel in her voice spoke just as loudly as the muzzle of her gun at his head, but Kurt didn't relent as easily as I might've expected.

"Jessie, come on. You're not going to hurt me. And I'm not going to—"

I dove behind the love seat right as I saw her move—she hammered both arms down on the one he held out and his gun fell. Thankfully, he hadn't had a chance to squeeze the trigger, but I didn't regret not waiting around to see if he would.

I popped up to the sound of scuffling and just in time to see Jess knee him hard in the groin, then shove him to the ground and wrench an arm behind his back, his face buried in the carpet, her booted foot pressing hard on the back of his neck, keeping him immobilized. She held it until I came to take it from her, and she nodded, then eased the bedroom door open.

A man's agitated shout rang out and she was talking, but Kurt was babbling at me.

"My goodness, she just did all that to save you? So you really got what you wanted after all this? I'm surprised you both didn't just take me out, get rid of the evidence."

I nudged his arm further back, causing him to arch to avoid separating his shoulder. "Evidence of what? That you've chosen to be human garbage? That you've thrown away any semblance of moral judgement or personal values?"

He laughed. "Oh, please, like you're some paragon of morality when you're sleeping with my ex-fiancée."

I didn't dignify this because Jess emerged, her arm

around the back of a girl who looked far too young to be there and absolutely terrified. At the same time, footsteps in the other direction drew near and we heard, "Weapons down, hands up."

Ah, Silverton police had arrived. I tossed my gun away from Kurt, and Jess moved slowly to set hers on a side table near the couch, both of us raising our hands to show we didn't possess any weapons.

"Go on to them, Brittany. You're okay," she urged, and the girl bolted down the hallway into the arms of one of the female officers who instantly ushered her away.

"This is ridiculous," Kurt said from where he still lay, my foot on his neck to ensure he didn't get any bright ideas.

"You being complicit in some pretty nasty business? Yeah. It's pathetic," I spat, more than done with this clown.

"We're security. We shouldn't be treated like this. I was just doing my job. Plus the fact that you're finally boning—"

"Stop talking." Jess's voice cut through and must've finally pressed Kurt's off button as the police moved toward us.

Or maybe that was the little love tap I gave his kidney when my fist slipped. *Whoopsies.*

Hours later, we'd given our statements to the police, helped find the girls' parents or emergency contacts before they were taken to the hospital to get checked out, and very happily watched both Kurt and Anthony Pollusk get escorted out of the house and into police custody.

It was all so dark, but we'd gotten there in time to stop at least one person from being harmed any more than simply being there at all would do. And watching Kurt be carted away... honestly, it didn't bring me any kind of satisfaction.

At one point in my life, I'd cared about him. I'd thought of him as a brother. Even though time and distance had helped me see he'd never treated me well, nor had he been a good man, I hated how he hadn't grown into someone better.

After we'd turned in our gear, I found Jess waiting for me on the front steps of the Saint building. The night had stayed clear and pitch black save the twinkling stars and moonlight. Fall scented the air—dead leaves, smoking chimneys, and the changing season somehow smelling comforting and soft. She stood and reached out her hand, which I gladly accepted. We walked a ways into the lot and stopped by our cars.

"Do you want to meet tomorrow before we start?" I asked, hoping we'd circle back to the very important conversation before we both dove into the last few days of this festival that wouldn't end.

"No. I can't wait. I want to talk now." She squeezed my hand and released it, then tucked her arms close.

My heart began racing, trying to read her body language, the tone in her words, her expression in the moonlight.

"Okay. Yeah." I swallowed hard, more nervous now than I had been all day, save for the moment I'd confessed my undying love for her.

She shifted on her feet, then dropped her hands, shook out her arms, and exhaled sharply. "You said you loved me... a lot."

A gust of air escaped me, no words to make sense of it. "Yeah."

She shook her head. "But I don't know whether I've done too much damage... whether my stubbornness has ruined everything."

Her eyes found mine and the pleading there nearly undid me.

"I could say the same. I never told you the whole truth. I was too hung up on doing what I thought was best and I never allowed you to decide—I should've. I'm sorry for that."

I truly was. How much of the hurt we'd caused each other could we have avoided if I'd only been braver?

"Maybe all of this comes down to trusting each other to know what we need instead of assuming we know what's best for the other person," she said, her gaze searching mine in the darkness.

I dipped my head. "Tell me, then, and I'll trust your answer. Could I ever, in some version of this story, be what you need?"

She reached up, pressing a hand over my thundering heart.

"There is nothing in this world that could make me forgive myself for failing to see you and hear you and insist I believed you back then. And nothing in this life or the next could compel me to turn away from you now."

I swallowed hard against the hope rising so rapidly I could hardly breathe. "I do forgive you, though, and I want you to forgive yourself. As for the rest... you'll have to translate it. Tell me what you mean."

Her smile flashed. "I mean I'm sorry. I believe you when you say you always cared for me." She sobered and stepped closer, clutching at my shirt. "Always loved me, even if you didn't know how to show it. That you were fighting for me all along in some messed up way. And now I say... I need you and want you. *You,* Jude Rawlins, and no one else."

The sun rose in my chest, pulling back shadows and splaying light into every recess of my bruised and broken heart. She needed *me.* She wanted *me.*

There was no chance of holding out another second. I'd already told her and I'd tell her again—every day, if she'd let me.

"I love you, Jess. I love you so much it physically hurts sometimes, and if you don't feel the—"

"I literally just told you I need and want you," she said, a baffled look on her face, a laugh sneaking out. "Don't you get it? I love you. I love you so much, it's stupid."

It took her no time to react to the way I pulled her in, sifted my hand into her hair, and guided her mouth to mine. In a matter of seconds, she'd hopped, and I'd lifted her, her legs circling my hips, and backed her into my truck, pinning her there as we savored each other. This was no frantic kiss, but it was all-consuming.

She loved me.

Jessica Korbel loved *me.*

I hadn't let myself sink down into the fear she might not return my feelings—I'd lived with the unrequited reality of my love for her for nearly a decade, so I could handle that. Anything shy of the hate she seemed to feel for so long.

Now, we had repaired something broken between us. We had hammered through the walls we'd built and miraculously let each other in. We were stronger now, on this side of the rebuild.

"Now that's what I like to see!" Kenny's voice invaded the moment.

I briefly plotted murder as Jess pulled away and chuckled, her dark eyes shining back at mine.

"Go away, Barbie." He would be able to hear the displeasure in my voice, though whether that would do anything, I couldn't say.

"Nah. Don't think I will," the little twerp said with no small amount of joy in his tone.

Jess bit her lip like she might laugh, and a flood of wanting and love washed through me.

"Damn, you're beautiful," I said, because now, finally, I could.

Her grin lit the space between us, and she reached up, sliding a hand along the beard at my jaw. "You are, too."

Even if Kenny was still watching, I dropped my head to steal another kiss. I had a feeling that if she let me, I wouldn't ever stop telling her she was beautiful, that I loved her, or taking this liberty.

CHAPTER FORTY-FOUR

Jess

I slept better than I had in months at least and probably more like years and woke feeling... well, freaking *amazing*.

Watching Kurt threaten Jude shifted something fundamental inside me. Or, more like, it cemented a realization I'd been slowly but surely moving toward.

Kurt hadn't left me because I was leavable. Kurt had left me because he was a garbage human and couldn't handle being honest. And while I believed in the innate value and dignity of every human, I also believed that when a person persists in choosing to harm others, they lose the right to the benefit of the doubt.

So when Kurt held out his weapon and pointed it at Jude, a man he used to call his best friend, it clicked. I no longer had to give him the benefit of the doubt like I'd been trying to do since seeing him again. Even though he'd pissed me off and been rude to me, some hopeful little voice in my head said I needed to admit he might've changed, at least to some degree, in the last few years. I certainly had, so who was I to say he was excluded from the possibility?

If he had, it was only for the worse. Because if he was now the kind of man who would stand by while young women were being harassed and assaulted, then he'd gotten worse... or he'd hidden just how awful he'd always been.

As I moved through the day with Jack, the antsy *need* to see Jude gave me a shot of energy. Or maybe that was the sound, delicious sleep I'd had knowing Kurt was getting what he'd chosen after all this time.

Boy, bye.

"I'm going to miss Silverton," Jack said, straightening his jacket as we descended in the elevator on the way to the cocktail hour of the final festival event.

"I think it'll miss you," I said, meaning it. He seemed to fit in here, and he had so many friends already settled in our small town. "Have you ever considered living here? At least part of the year?"

"Julian's been trying to get me to move here since he first did. I keep taking shoots at far-flung locations and I guess..." His gaze went distant, like he'd gone somewhere else entirely in his mind... "I guess when I move here, I want to feel like I can be settled for a while."

Interesting.

Get ready, ladies of Silverton! Hollywood's heartthrob is thinking about settling down in our beloved little town.

"Makes sense." I held out a hand, a little sad to be saying goodbye. He was a good guy. "It's been a pleasure."

He grasped my hand and shook firmly, then released. "Likewise. Thanks for being low key. And best of luck with... everything. I hope you find great love and happiness."

See? This guy. Sincere, kind, easy on the eyes... a good egg. "Thank you. I hope the same for you."

We entered the ballroom then, the room already buzzing with conversation and energy. The festival had gotten incredible press, several of the movies that premiered receiving rave reviews, and the town had flourished. The drama from last night and Anthony Pollusk's arrest had already been splashed across the news, but as more and more actresses came out and spoke about their experiences, the stories hadn't been focused on it happening here in Silverton, but that it'd gone on so long and so many had been affected.

Bruce gave me a nod and ushered Jack away, officially relieving me of my duties for the night, and for the festival.

I suspected we'd have a skeleton crew at the office for the next few weeks while everyone recovered. I couldn't wait to sleep in and have a real weekend soon... hopefully spent with Jude.

Nikki, Winnie, Dove, Jo, Elise, and Catherine approached.

"Are you off? Can we hang out now?" Dove asked, hands clasped in front of her.

I laughed. "Yes. Thank goodness. It's been a really long week."

"Lots has happened," Winnie said, her eyes darting over my shoulder.

My stomach flipped as I turned to see Jude talking to Adam. Goodness, he was handsome in that severe way of his. But I'd coaxed smiles out of him. And now, I knew he loved me.

Not just a little. But like... a whole lot. *I'll die with your name on my lips.*

Yeah. Not gonna lie, that had played on repeat in my mind. So had last night, after the drama had ended, and I'd finally been bold enough to tell him how I felt. Terrifying, overwhelming, and so... possible. No longer something I felt I couldn't have access to, I reached out and took what he offered, and I trusted him. And in a way I never had before, I trusted myself.

"He looks at you like you're the best thing he's ever seen," Dove sighed out.

I chuckled. "Not to be cheesy, but I think *he* might be the best thing *I've* ever seen."

They all let out resounding *awwwws* and then we laughed until Dove nearly snorted her sip of champagne and it ended up coming out her nose.

"I kind of love this, though. I mean, you used to hate him and now you're in love. It's just so perfect." Jo beamed at Jude, and Adam must've sensed her attention because he turned and sent her a wink.

"I don't know that I ever actually hated him. Looking back, I mostly hate how I acted, how I made him the default target for all my frustrations and shortcomings. But I do love him, and there's something pretty beautiful about the fact that he's seen me at my worst in basically every sense."

Jude followed Adam's look and found me. He sent no wink, nor did he smile. He just *looked* at me, into me, and it felt like a promise.

"Whew. Yeah. You guys are fire." Dove fanned herself with her free hand and the others giggled, clearly loving her comment and, I suspected, the reality of me and Jude.

I couldn't blame them.

Jude and Adam joined us, and Adam's hand slipped

around Jo's waist before he leaned in and whispered something in her ear. A blush rose to her cheek, and she shook her head but wouldn't look at him.

Jude simply came to stand next to me, close enough that my shoulder brushed against his arm. I sent him a smile and he gave me more smoldery eyes.

My stomach did a somersault.

"So what's next for you two?" Winnie asked.

I glanced up at Jude. "Next? Well, I guess scheduling gets easier at work."

He huffed a reluctant laugh. "True."

"Oh, Bruce will be happy about that," Nikki added.

"Anything else? Big plans? Dates? Engagements? Weddings and babies?" Dove pushed.

Elise shook her head, quieter than usual but not so quiet that she didn't say, "Way too much too soon, crazy face."

I laughed, though my insides were dancing the conga at the mention of all those future things Jude and I hadn't gotten anywhere near talking about. I wanted it all, but I genuinely didn't know where he stood.

But then, he leaned down and dropped a kiss to my cheek. "Sure. Put us down for all of that, as long as it's okay with Jess."

His dark gaze found mine and my mouth dropped open. I laughed once, a disbelieving, overjoyed sound, and said, "Yeah. All of that."

EPILOGUE

Jude

Because I'd always known Jess didn't return my feelings, I'd forbidden myself to fantasize about being with her in any way. Nothing physical, and no weddings or houses or kids together, though occasionally, they snuck into my subconscious. Even then, it just hurt too much to feel how desperately I wanted those things in the midst of our dark time.

Waking up with her next to me in bed wearing just shy of nothing except a wedding ring on her finger?

I didn't need to dream up a fantasy because I was living it.

She stretched and rolled over, the gorgeous expanse of her back bare and calling to me. I shouldn't wake her. We'd traveled for a full day to get here and now, in our little bungalow on the sea, we had a full ten days to just be together.

Married and together.

"Are you already awake?" she mumbled.

It didn't surprise me she wasn't a morning person, but her level of disdain for waking early when she didn't have to cracked me up. For as proactive and energetic as she was, the woman loved to sleep in.

"Just admiring my naked wife." I caved to the impulse and trailed my fingers from the curve of her hip and up her spine, savoring the warm, smooth skin.

Sleepy eyes blinked open and my gut clenched. I would never *ever* tire of her looking at me like that—like her hunger for me matched what I felt for her.

"And do you have plans for me, now that you've taken me to this remote location and have me all to yourself?" she asked, slowly pushing up on an elbow and rolling with the sheet so she wore it like a backless gown.

Shame. Why did they have sheets here anyway? Who even wanted them?

It had been a matter of hours and yet, here it was, this need gripping both of us, demanding. But now, the longing and the borderline angst of the wanting could be sated.

I drew close and nipped at her earlobe. "I have so many plans, wife."

Her smile stretched wide and she bit her lip, sitting up and letting the sheet fall away. "Then show me, husband."

Jess

The island breeze cooled us and rustled through my hair as we sat in the warmth of the morning sun and ate fresh fruits and pastries for breakfast.

Jude's face held a softness, a relaxed stasis I wouldn't have imagined existed before the last few months. But day by day, the closer we'd gotten to our elopement and this trip, the more ease he seemed to embody. Maybe it was the passage of time and the settling of some of the sharpest moments of grief, too.

"Have I mentioned I love you?" he asked, linking his pinky around mine as he sipped his coffee and gazed out at the ocean.

The thrill of his beautiful lips forming those words for me would never get old. We'd spent too long without honesty between us, and too long missing out on a version of our relationship that could be so good.

It was why we'd spent two months dating and were already married. Rushed to some, sure, but what else did we need to wait for? We were adults who knew our own minds. The challenges of combining households and adjusting to factoring in another person were just that—challenges we'd handle together. And because we both had friends and a community—some of which overlapped and some that were independent of each other—we weren't putting pressure on each other to be *everything* to one another.

We were partners. Lovers. Friends. And all of those words felt feeble compared to what it *felt* like to be with Jude after so long.

We'd created patterns of how we treated each other when we were fighting and foolish. Breaking those defaults of mistrust and suspicion hadn't been automatic, but since we'd both committed to it, even in the space of a few months, we'd formed new ways of handling frustration, doubt, and upset.

There was still so much work to be done, but we'd do it together. And the reality that Jude knew me better than anyone ever had—that he'd seen me for how petty and vengeful and mean and ruled by anger and stubborn I could be and he loved me still? It freed me to be better. To own my faults and keep going, moving toward him even when everything wasn't perfect. And he could do the same.

I'd stayed quiet too long, so I moved to seat myself in his lap. I cupped his handsome, beard-roughened cheeks in mine and tipped my forehead to touch his, so full of gratitude and love and hope, I could burst.

"And I love you."

He grinned, the action rivaling the sun beaming behind me, and then he sealed the moment, the next in a line of a lifetime, with a kiss.

I hope Jude and Jess's story brought you as much joy while reading as it did me while I wrote it. Don't miss the bonus epilogue starring... well, read on to find out, and get your copy of his book, Known By You!

BONUS EPILOGUE

Kenny

I made no attempt to hide my gigantic grin. Why should I? It reflected the rainbows exploding out of my chest.

Basically, this situation was causing a Care Bear Stare of Joy to unleash from my body.

Tristan gave me a look, just the smallest lift of his left brow that said *simmer down*.

I would not.

Adam held his hands out and pressed them down like, *chill, man*.

Bruce, ever one of our collective dads these days, hooked an arm around my neck. "You cannot attack them when they come in. We're not supposed to know."

"Impossible. Literally impossible."

Cookie chuckled, Wilder suppressed a smile, and my boy Stone gave his head a slight shake. Eddie walked in, eyes wide, and nodded at Bruce, but before I could do anything to calm the explosion of excitement, Beast walked through the door and my legs catapulted me to him.

He took the hit to his body with far more acceptance than I would've imagined, one arm patting my back even as he kept moving through the doorway, sliding me back along with him.

When I pulled back to smile at him, one of the founding members of the Saint Security too-cool-to-smile club, he was beaming.

"Guess you all know, huh?" he asked.

"Legit, though? It's true?" I asked, hope tinging my voice.

Jess was laughing and grinning. "Yes. It's true. I'm pregnant."

The room exploded then—party poppers bursting with confetti, a cheer rising from everyone, and hugs of congratulations all around. Damn if I didn't love good news more than anything else in the whole world, save the people who were sharing it.

"I don't think I've ever been happier about anything in my whole life," I said, a little twinge plucking in my chest.

Jess hugged me, still laughing, then patted my cheek. "I love you for saying that."

Her eyes seemed to say something else, but I couldn't tell what. Maybe she was just so radiantly happy, she was shooting meaningful laser beams out to all of us.

"Alright, let's circle up, everyone," Bruce said, corralling us all to the conference table where we each found a place. "Again, congratulations to you both, Pop, Beast. We're thrilled to be adding another little member to the team."

Beast slid a hand up his new wife's back and gently squeezed her neck.

I'd only gotten to see them like this for a few months because they'd only given us a few months before they'd up and married and flown off on a two-week honeymoon. Since coming back, we'd all been busy with assignments and I'd hardly had a chance to catch up with them. I'd heard the rumor she was pregnant and now here they were, being all cute and affectionate in front of all of us.

"Pop, you want to say anything before we, uh..." Bruce notched his chin down a touch in a gesture that instantly sent me on alert.

Something was happening... something that required explanation.

She nodded and gave us all another smile. "Thanks for the very dramatic congratulations. We are very happy. But... my body is *not* super thrilled thus far. I'm going to be dropping my hours significantly, if not, uh, taking a little break." Her gaze found Beast's and they shared a moment. "I've been diagnosed with hyperemesis gravidarum, and I'm not sure when it'll get better. I spent a few days in the hospital and—"

"What!? How did you not tell us this?" The words jumped from my mouth before I could stop them, so I slapped a hand over my stupid face. This wasn't about me, even if I had to wonder why Beast hadn't called me.

Beast grunted and gave me a glare like he'd talk to me later, and Jess gave me a soft look.

"My friends were helping, and there wasn't much anyone could do. Point is, I just wanted to see you guys today, but I'm going to need a lot of rest. This, it's like morning sickness on steroids and kicking in twenty-four-seven." She sighed. "And I'm probably going to go insane, but after the last few days, my denial has decreased."

The group murmured their sympathies and exchanged glances, all of us clearly aware that something else was coming up with that t-up from Bruce and Jess.

"With this change in mind, we will bring on a new team member," Wilder explained, and all focus shifted to him.

"Nice. Who's coming on board? Anyone we know?" I asked, always happy to add more to the fam.

"Some of you do, from what I hear," Wilder said, his eyes on me.

Me? Huh. Maybe Rob Waverly was finally out. It'd been six months since I'd checked on the guy. Or possibly Shane Easton? He was getting to retirement age. You never knew with EMU guys. Some liked to hang on as long as they could before transitioning to being a regular old person.

"So? Who is it?" I prodded again. How was no one else asking this question?

Every eye in the building shifted to the space where the door was, so I followed suit.

And my heart stopped.

My stomach dropped.

My eyes ate up the sight of her standing in the doorway of the Saint Security conference room like every dream and nightmare I'd had for the last few years.

Elizabeth Malcom.

And then she answered the question like it was something simple and not the most life-altering phrase I'd ever heard.

"It's me."

Don't miss Kenny and Elizabeth's black cat and golden retriever romance!

ALSO BY CLAIRE CAIN

Veterans of Silver Ridge Series

Small Town Veteran Romance

Love Undercover

Romantic Suspense Light

Back to Silver Ridge Series

Small Town Romance

Exceptional Mission Unit: The Cardinals

Military Romantic Suspense

The Silver Ridge Resort Series

Small Town Romance

Soldiers Overseas Romances

Sweet Military Romance

The Rambler Battalion Series

Sweet Military Romance

Married to the Military Series

Military Marriage of Convenience Romcoms

AUTHOR'S NOTE AND ACKNOWLEDGMENTS

Thank you for reading Fighting For You! I really love this couple. Ever since they popped up in book one, I've been eager to dive into their story.

Remember when Jack McKean guesses at Beast's name and calls him Brute? That's a nod to what I'd originally nicknamed Jude. My wise editor said it might be a bit much to have a Bruce *and* a Brute... and I saw the point. But will I someday name a character Brute? Probably.

Thank you, as always, to my family. Thanks especially to my son for being so excited to spot the entrance to Weber Canyon on a visit to Utah and for exclaiming, "let's get a picture of Silver Ridge!"

Thank you to Genny Carrick for rooting for Jess and Beast with incredible enthusiasm, even if there was more conflict than you wanted ;) Thanks to BR Goodwin for being amazing and letting our kids play in your living room at least half the time so I could get edits completed.

Thank you to Jess Mastorakos for the gorgeous cover. When I saw Beast, I swooned, and now may or may not have a crush on my fictional character's hand drawn image. (Totally normal, right? Ha.)

Thank you to Zee Monodee for continually catching my vision for this series and helping me bring it out through each couple. Thanks, also, for encouraging me to let Kenny take the reins... I think we were good to allow it.

Thank you to Jamie McGillen for helping me polish the

book, and for being an integral part of my writing and personal life.

Thank you to my amazing beta readers Amanda and Genny. I'm always delighted to read your feedback, and I deeply appreciate you blazing through this book and sharing your thoughts.

A huge thank you to my ARC team, who reads early and shares and reviews to help the book find more readers (and who also, whether they know it or not, provide me with so much joy and encouragement). Thanks especially to Carol Ann, Judith, Suzan, and the many other ARC team members. To Darla, Elise, Aubrey Ann, Joanna, Rebecca, Jordan, Hannah, Kayleigh, Abby, Rachel, and so many other wonderful bookstagrammers who do so much to help share and spread the word about my books, thank you for your generosity. I am perpetually amazed you choose to spend your time with my books and I'm genuinely honored you enjoy them enough to share them with your own followers. Thank you.

And then you, dear reader. You come here so, if you skipped the middle, you get the TL;DR: Thank *you*. I couldn't do this without you and I don't ever take the true joy of writing romance novels for granted. I think almost daily how grateful I am that this is my actual job, and I thank you for making that possible.

Now, about Barbie...

ABOUT THE AUTHOR

Claire Cain lives to eat and drink her way around the globe with her traveling soldier and three kids, but is perhaps even happier hunkered down at home in a pair of sweatpants and slippers using any free moment she has to read and cook. Or talk—she really likes to talk. She has become an expert at packing too many dishes in too few cabinets and making houses into homes from Utah to Germany and many places in between. She's a proud Army wife and is frankly just really happy to be here.

You can also join Claire's facebook reader group for exclusive content and fun: https://www.facebook.com/groups/clairecain/

Website: http://www.clairecainwriter.com

E-mail: Claire@ClaireCainWriter.com

Newsletter sign-up for new releases, exclusives, and freebies, including a free book:

http://www.clairecainwriter.com/newsletter

amazon.com/author/clairecain

bookbub.com/authors/claire-cain

instagram.com/clairecainwriter

facebook.com/clairecainwriter

goodreads.com/clairecainwriter

pinterest.com/clairecainwriter

www.ingramcontent.com/pod-product-compliance
Lightning Source LLC
Chambersburg PA
CBHW061634190726

48289CB00006B/1604